AIR AND ASH

TIDES BOOK I

By Alex Lidell

DANGER BEARING PRESS

ALSO BY ALEX LIDELL

TIDES

FIRST COMMAND (TIDES NOVELLA)
AIR AND ASH (TIDES BOOK I)
WAR AND WIND (TIDES BOOK II)

TILDOR

THE CADET OF TILDOR

Reviews are an author's lifeblood. Please consider saying a few words about this book on Amazon.

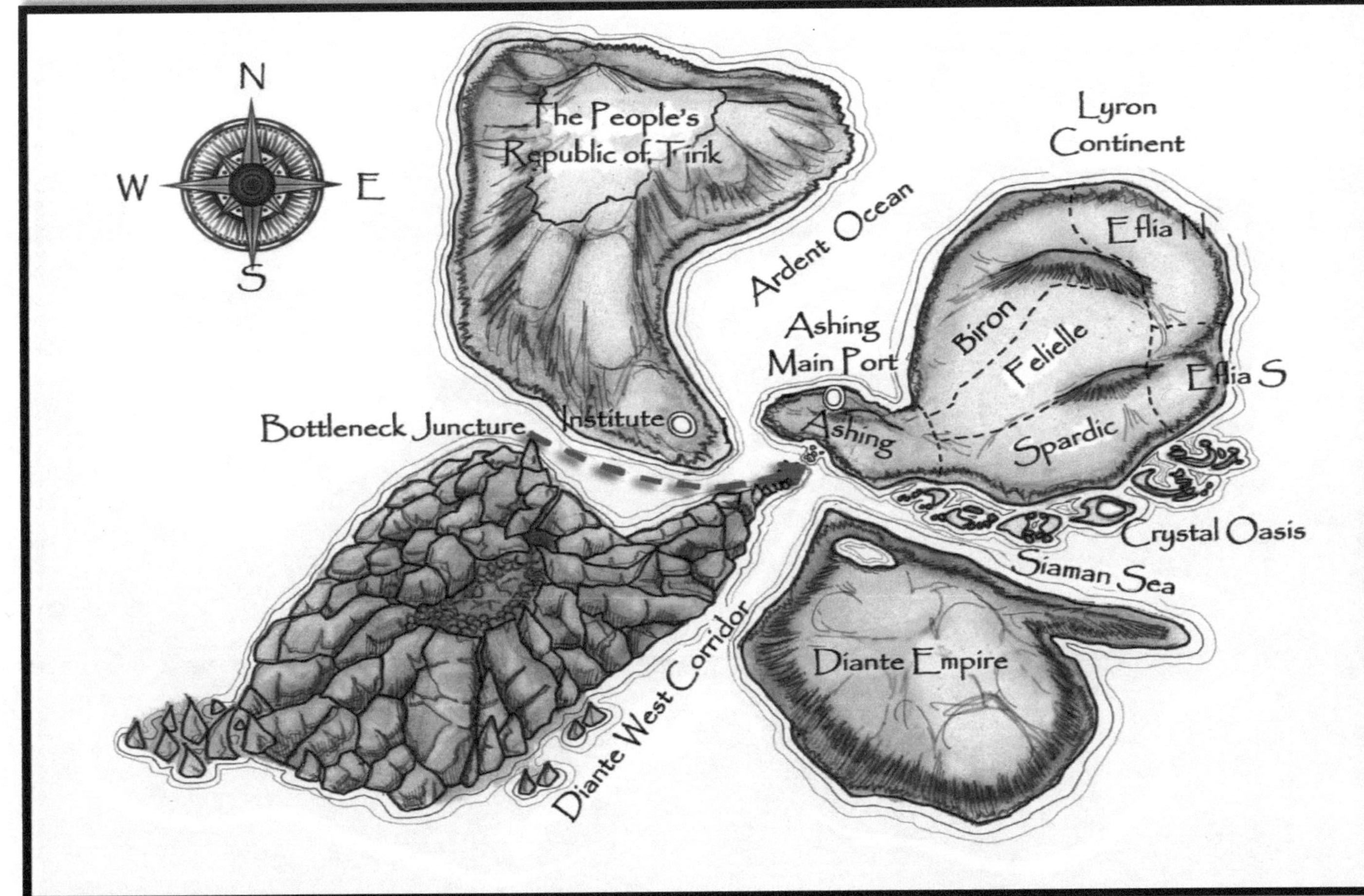

N
W
E
S
The People's Republic of Tirik
Lyron Continent
Ardent Ocean
Eflia N
Ashing Main Port
Biron
Felielle
Eflia S
Bottleneck Juncture
Institute
Ashing
Spardic
Crystal Oasis
Siaman Sea
Diante West Corridor
Diante Empire

1

I fall to my knees as His Ashing Majesty's Ship *Faithful*'s mainmast breaks in two and crashes to the deck. The fallen sails drag through the waves, and smoke from the great guns fills the air with a blinding fog. I cough and wave the thick metallic air away from my face.

Captain Fey gives me a tight smile. Of average height and a solid, slightly pudgy build, the captain stands tall on the quarterdeck, his hands on his hips. His dark, intelligent eyes, speckled with a bit of silver like his hair, take in the carnage around us with preternatural calm. "I believe we have one last broadside for the Tirik Republic in us. Don't you agree, Ms. Greysik?"

One last broadside. The words hit me in the gut as surely as enemy shot. In the nine years I've served under Fey, from the eight-year-old girl in a midshipman's uniform who'd walked wide-eyed onto his deck to the lieutenant I am today, I've never heard him utter such a thing. An admission of the coming end.

"Ms. Greysik." The stern note in the captain's voice jerks

me free of my thoughts. The officers, those of us trained from childhood to command, must always keep a straight back and high head. I cling to Captain Fey's confidence like a lifeline and climb to my feet. Ashing, my kingdom, is a land of seamen. Of fighters.

"Reload and run out your guns!" I call to my starboard battery. Crews fall to their tasks with a will, from middle-aged, experienced seamen to small powder monkey girls scampering over the dead to carry gunpowder. On the far side of the deck, twelve-year-old midshipman Jax echoes my commands to the outlying crews. The curious synergy between the officers trained to know which orders to give and the common seamen trained to execute those tasks is a naval machine of greatest power. One that roars throughout each inch of the *Faithful*'s deck. If I must die, I would be honored to lie beside the *Faithful*'s crew.

But we can't die. The *Faithful* carries a code book stolen from our enemy, the People's Republic of Tirik. A code book that will turn the course of this decade-long war.

My gun captains raise their fists into the air, signaling that their great beasts are aimed and ready.

I watch the sea, waiting for the ship to roll up with a wave. Midshipman Jax, one of the young officers in training, watches me intently.

"Fire!" I call as we crest a wave. Jax echoes my order, and the satisfying report of two dozen guns booms over the sea.

Then it's the Republic's turn and their ship carries twice the weight of our broadside. The barrels of fifty guns spark with flame, and deadly shot explodes from their iron throats. Half the heavy balls land harmlessly in the sea, spraying great salt fountains around the *Faithful*'s hull. Another handful hit the rigging, leaving round holes in battered sails. The shot that finds hull and flesh is the deadly one.

Three sailors beside me fall at once, bleeding and

motionless from a single iron ball flying over the deck. Had I been standing just one step farther right, I'd be dead too. More shot strikes the *Faithful*'s planks, and the ship bucks in agony, the deck dropping from beneath me. I hear the dull thud of my own head hitting a spar. The pain comes with the next heartbeat, but by now, I'm already grabbing a line and forcing myself to my feet. I want my people to see me standing.

As I do, another Tirik ball rushes just above Captain Fey's shoulder, so close that he must feel the rush of air in the ball's wake. He spares it but a calm, passing glance as he reaches a hand to help a fallen middie back to his feet. "Stand tall, Mr. Jax," Fey tells the boy. "A ball either—"

I see it happen before I can scream. A stray shot strikes the mast behind Captain Fey's shoulder. The wood explodes in a bouquet of splinters that rises into the air and rains down across the ship. Captain Fey sees it too, the deadly jagged spears heading his way. He meets my eyes, a small smile on his calm face, and nods just as a piece of his own ship nails him to the planks.

"Captain Fey!" I don't remember moving to his body, but the sight of his lifeless eyes freezes the world around me. Wayward strands of red hair that escaped my braid obscure my vision. As the youngest child of the Ashing king, my place in the Ashing navy was always a certainty. But it was Captain Fey who taught me to love the sea, who showed me that what I do, even as a youngster, matters. With Captain Fey—

"Lieutenant Greysik!" Jax shakes my shoulder. The middie's voice is steady despite his pallor and the sprays of blood that speckle his uniform. "The lifeboats are ready, ma'am."

"Very good." My mouth is dry. Tucking my hair back behind my ears, I glance over the rail and survey the lowered boats. All in order, trim and neat despite the carnage.

Another young middie, a fourteen-year-old girl named Vast, is overseeing the final inspection and shouting orders, most of which I suspect originate from the quiet suggestions of the experienced sailor hovering beside her. As an officer, it's her job to know *what* the sailors should do, theirs to know *how* to do it. But she is smart enough to listen to experience, and the seamen are smart enough to subtly shore up the girl's authority lest the crew falls to chaos. Someone retrieves Vast's fallen hat. This is no game. This is the discipline that earns the crew's trust in its officers and keeps panic at bay. And it will keep us alive.

I force my voice to be calm and clear as I speak. "Very good. Inform Captain Fey we are ready to take the hands off, if you please." I realize what I said a moment too late and fight against choking breath. "My apologies, Mr. Jax. I meant the commander."

Jax's face falters. "I... He... The commander is dead too, ma'am. You're the most senior now."

2

Storms and hail. I focus on my breath. In and out. I am an officer of the Ashing navy. I've trained for this my whole life. I can do this. "The midshipmen?" We'd started the day with five officers in training.

"It is just me and Ms. Vast now," says Jax.

My hand tightens on the rope, long fingers scraping coarse hemp. "Very well." I make myself speak slowly, feigning the steel confidence of my late captain. "You and Ms. Vast will take charge of the lifeboats. Get every living soul out. The *Destiny* is close. She will pick up our boats within the hour, I am certain." If the Tirik Republic lets Ashing lifeboats live that long. The Republic's Committee for Patriotism has a habit of killing the families of "lax" Tirik officers, so we can expect few courtesies from their ships.

I scrub my sleeve across my forehead, wiping away sweat. I'm tall for a girl, but slender—nothing like the captain. Captain Fey's words echo in my mind. *"Keep the crew unified. Support your officers. Be worthy of their trust."* I raise my voice above the din of wind and crashing rigging. "The boats will shove off once every soul is accounted for, not a moment earlier. We are an Ashing ship. We are the best damn crew in all the kingdoms. We stay together, and we survive."

Jax runs off, shouting orders to petty officers. I pray he will see adulthood and push him from my mind. The captain's duty is mine now, and that means protecting the Tirik code book as well as the ship. The book lies below the deck, in the theoretical safety of what was once Fey's cabin. Captain Fey had warned against us carrying the prize alone, but the king—my damned arrogant father—had insisted. Ashing is the smallest of the Lyron League's six kingdoms, and the king wants us to prove ourselves to the League, show that our ships can do what others cannot.

And we held out longer than anyone could have.

But a seventy-two-gun frigate cannot survive against one with a hundred and ten.

Neither the *Faithful* nor my captain would now return, but the book has to. Its delivery to the Lyron League will save thousands of lives. Its destruction on an Ashing ship would submerge our kingdom in shame. *The book must survive.* I fix that thought in my mind as I fight my way across the slippery deck and dodge the raining debris. My sights are on the hatch leading below.

The Tirik Republic's great guns quiet, but the muskets continue to fire at the crew. The *Faithful*'s hull protects the lifeboats, but my uniform and sword draw the sharpshooters' attention. As if summoned by thought, a streak of raw agony sears across my left temple. I drop to a knee just as another musket ball streaks overhead. The deck rolls. My hand touches the wound and comes away bright red. My breath catches.

I crawl the rest of the way. Darkness stares at me from the hatch. The stench of copper filters through the opening. There is blood down there too. And the book. I swallow, steady my hand on the rail, and swing my legs down onto the ladder.

"You mustn't go below, ma'am!" A sailor's meaty arm blocks me. "The ship's taking on water."

I blink, calling up his name. Thomas. A gun captain. "I know." My words slur. "I must retrieve our package. It will take but a moment."

"I will get it."

A good man. I shake my head. The odds of surviving the trip are one in two at best. I am the *Faithful*'s captain now. The duty to fulfill the mission or go down with the ship is mine. "Get to the boat, Thomas. If I do not join you within five minutes, tell the middies to cast off." I shake off a spell of nausea and begin my descent. "That is an order."

"I can't do that, ma'am," Thomas says quietly.

My gaze flickers up in time to see him kneel, reaching for me. His hands grip the back of my coat and jerk me off the ladder. My feet dangle above the darkness, the coat digging into my armpits. My heart races. "What are you doing?" I claw at his sleeves.

Thomas heaves, lifting me higher into the air.

My boot strikes something soft.

The sailor grunts and pulls me closer. His hand clamps over my face. "I'm sorry, Princess," Thomas whispers into my ear. His breath is warm on my neck. "I have my orders too."

The hand covering my face shifts, and a noxious smell fills my nose before darkness comes.

3

I rise onto my elbows, my head throbbing. I'm in a bed. The sheets are clean and smell of lavender. Paintings of naval glories fill the walls, the wide brush strokes of blue and green hues matching the drapery. And, just in front of me, my favorite portrait shows my twin brother reaching up to pet a mare's dipped nose. He's still a toddler in the painting, his gaze not yet vacant.

Home. I'm home in the Ashing palace, with its paintings and high ceiling and flowing drapes. There is even a bouquet of fresh-cut tulips on the wooden table. Everything that is not the sea.

A figure sitting beside the bed stirs. "Nile. Thank the winds."

My mother's voice. I turn to her slowly, my long limbs sluggish to obey. My mother's eyes, the queen's eyes, are puffy and red. Even still, my mother is beautiful, with lush red locks framing her face and graceful curves that have just started developing on me. She brushes my cheek with soft fingers, her warm touch at once loving and possessive. I try not to wince. Officers shouldn't be coddled by their mothers. And they certainly should not enjoy the sensation if their mothers insist on doing it.

I sit up, blinking away the haze. I was on the *Faithful*, Captain Fey dead, smoke stinging my lungs. I needed to get the code book, but someone...Thomas...stopped me. "The code book."

"You took a wound, then two weeks of fever. You are fortunate t'ave lived." My mother's accent has a songlike grace I love, even though it's from the Felielle Kingdom, which likes to push us around. "All's well now."

All's well by my mother's standards means only that her children are safe.

I squeeze my fists. "We lost the book, didn't we?" Her silence tells me all I need to know. Captain Fey, the sunk ship, the dead sailors. All for nothing. My head is heavy and I want to return to sleep, waking to a changed reality. I push away my blanket, forcing my spindly limbs through unaccustomed motions. My usually trimmed fingernails have grown while I slept and, *oh waves and hail,* my mother painted them with a soft pink glaze. I ball up my hand, hiding it in my sleeve. "I need to see Father. There was a sailor aboard, Thomas, who may be in another's employ."

"You need nothing of the sort." Mother's back straightens at once. "I wish to hear nothing more of this wretched endeavor. None of the other five kingdoms put their daughters on floating buckets and paddle them off to war!"

"Mother, not now. I beg you, not now." My head pounds. In Felielle, daughters rejoice in raising families. In Ashing, all youngsters contribute to the kingdom's survival. Every Ashing adolescent serves the throne for two years, and at least part of the "throners" duty is spent at arms. Our whole tiny kingdom is an army, which the royal children are raised to command. After over twenty years of marriage to the Ashing king, you'd think mother would understand.

But she refuses.

She was young when she met my father, a dashing commander passing through Felielle. So she got it into her head that she wished to fix him, to make him see the absurdity in Ashing's notions. A handsome project. I think Felielle was more than happy to have Mother and her impossible project ideas shipped off to a different kingdom. As for Father... He wasn't yet the crown prince—my uncle had still been alive and Ashing's heir presumptive—and thus father had little political capital for refusal. My mother was the Felielle king's distant cousin, and when Felielle asks something of Ashing, it is difficult to say no. We can't survive without Felielle's subsidy.

Unlike the Ashing peninsula, Felielle is landlocked. Safe from the Tirik Republic warships. And, being central on the Lyron continent, they prosper from trade like no other nation. With large incomes and little resources demanded for naval protection, the Felielle excel at the arts and knowledge. And they know what their gold can buy.

And so do we. I swallow the bitterness.

Mother sighs. Her eyes are tearing again, which is embarrassing.

I love my mother. She is the only person left who loves me to my soul, who touches me, who paints my damn nails while I sleep because she wants to be close. I love her, but I pity her too. And I fear ever becoming what she is. Weak. Emotional. Irrelevant to Ashing. I need to get out of the sickroom, discover what happened, and get back on a ship. I swing my legs to the floor.

"Thomas is dead." My mother puts a hand out to stop me.

Even now, each of her motions is graceful and light. "Jumped from the ship and drowned. There is no threat. And you shall mention it no further."

I stare at her. Mother seldom recalls names of ships' *captains*. That she should speak of a common sailor with such certainty... *Storms and hail.* Thomas had claimed to have orders of his own. Orders from whom? A Republic agent would have killed me. Thomas saved my life.

And then took his own.

A growl rumbles in my chest. "You put a bodyguard on my ship?"

Mother's chin rises.

"Mother!" I catch myself and lower my voice. "Mother, how could you? If the Ashing people believe their leaders so cowardly as to hide behind bodyguards, they will give neither respect nor obedience to the throne. We lead from the front, Mother. If the king learns you broke the throne's promise—"

"Neither need learn of anything, dolphin. Thomas is dead. Who can say why in the Goddess's name he attacked you. Crazed from battle, no doubt." She crosses her long legs. Mother's dress of rose chiffon ripples with her graceful movements, as much an extension of her as a warrior's weapon. Her eyes glitter to match a teardrop gem hanging high on her neckline. "I do not regret my actions in the least. When you've children of your own, you will understand."

I ignore her bait. "What about Thomas's children?" I ask, turning Mother's notions back at her. "Who will provide for his two boys?" I'm shouting now. "Or did you not know he had them?"

"Three boys," she says with infuriating calm. "His wife was pregnant and has delivered since. And they will be cared for better than Thomas could have afforded himself. He made his choice with eyes wide open, Nile. He was a parent.

He understood. So will you."

I snap my mouth shut, cutting off the conversation. There is no point in rehashing old truths. Father doesn't need me breeding, he needs me to earn a place in the Ashing Admiralty, which commands Ashing's naval fleet. A position that my aunt, Father's sister, almost achieved when she died in action. And I too need to earn my place in the navy's command. I won't become the king's second great disappointment.

As if summoned by thought, the first great disappointment walks into the sickroom.

Tall and slender, with red hair and long, beautiful lashes, my twin brother, Clay, is the perfect doll our mother wishes I was. His skin is paler than my sun-kissed hue, his long fingers soft where mine are calloused from hauling rope and training with weapons. And where uncomfortable breasts and curves started morphing my frame in the past year, the lines of Clay's trim body are clean and familiar. "Hello, Clay," I say to my twin.

"Hello, Clay," he mimics, rocking and staring at the ceiling. On the table beside me, the metal pitcher and cup tremble once before toppling. I try to catch them, but I'm too slow. They slide off the table and toward Clay, hovering beside his waist. "Hello, Clay," Clay says again. "Hello, Clay. Hello, Clay."

4

My head hurts. The physicians promise the sudden pains will ease, but the fortnight since my fever broke has thus far proved them wrong. As I walk through the palace's open-air breezeways, I trace my fingers along the white plaster columns, a precaution in case that horrid pressure behind my eyes catches me unaware. It's windy here, as it always is in Ashing, which sits atop a small peninsula at the tip of the teardrop-shaped Lyron continent. The air carries the smell of salt and seaweed that coats the inside of my nose and tongue. Taking a final lungful of air, I open the tall door to the anteroom of my father's study and step inside.

My father's elderly clerk smiles sadly at me and scrapes his chair back to rise. Large leather armchairs and a small table with refreshments stand on the side of the room farthest from the clerk. I little bother heading there to wait for an audience. The clerk's smile had told me all I need to know.

There is no envelope with a new commission waiting for me, no ship to board, no sails to set. I wonder how much longer the king will make me wait. How much longer *can* I wait? Even Thad, my older brother and Father's heir, avoids me. *"You must rebuild your strength, Nile,"* he says each time I force myself into his chambers. *"Focus on nothing but that."*

An impossible mandate for a girl who draws her strength from the sea.

"Shall my father have need of me this day?" I ask for formality's sake, glancing at the tall wooden door behind the clerk.

"Not today, Princess Nile," he says with a rasp, as he does daily.

And, as I do daily, I leave the antechamber to seek out my Gifted twin.

Today, I must see ships and sea. I lead Clay down a back-roads path to the shoreline, sandy ground and low-growing thorny shrubs lining our way. The back roads are safer for Clay and shield him from curious stares and pity-filled looks, the kind people give a one-eyed horse or a deformed child. Or maybe I'm shielding myself. I'm not sure Clay can tell the difference.

"The Tirik are hypocrites, you know," I say, gathering my dress's hem into an undignified heap. I wore the bloody thing to appease my mother and I'm sorry for it already. "Their slogans may proclaim *We Fight for the People!* But they don't. They fight because if they stop, they must face their mistakes. Killing off the monarchy and nobility didn't make things better; it reduced their once-vibrant nation to ruins and fear."

Clay nods, his hand buried in the fur of the huge and very pregnant bitch who invited herself along for the walk and now trots by Clay's thigh. "Ruins and fear," he says, in a voice that's a perfect imitation of mine. "Ruins and fear. Ruins and fear."

"We have to protect ourselves." I sigh. "Father cannot continue to maroon me in Ashing like this."

"Ashing." This time, Clay mimics our mother. "Ashing needs stronger ties to Felielle."

The intonation is so perfect that I almost protest. Ashing needs to generate enough income as to make Felielle's subsidy irrelevant. And for that, we need to win this war. But Clay isn't speaking his own mind.

I squeeze his hand. It stays limp in my grasp but I hold it anyway.

Gifted. What a crock-of-shit name for a disease. *"Not a disease,"* the physicians take pains to say, *"Elemental attraction is a condition."* I think they say that to make themselves feel better for having no cure.

The Gifted have magic in their blood that turns their bodies into living magnets. Five types of magic are known: air, water, metal, stone, and fire. In each case, the afflicted Gifted's body attracts one of the elements. The attraction in and of itself is deadly only to fire callers, who burn themselves dead long before they have any hope of learning control. For the four other magics, a measure of control is possible but the side effects of having magic are gravely dangerous. Stone callers' muscles dissolve; water callers' blood refuses to clot; air callers succumb to fits and convulsion...and metal callers like Clay pay with their minds.

My brother is a cripple. The physicians say he will never get better.

I don't believe them.

One day, my Gifted twin will come back to me. I'm sure of it, in a way that only a twin can be.

We climb a hill toward a secluded cove, well away from

the main docks where Clay's metal calling is likely to cause problems. Like all metal callers, Clay little understands danger. If we walk through a busy market, he will inevitably send knives flying or overturn the fishermen's pails. No one needs that.

"Nearly there," I say, the climb taking my breath. My body is still weak and prone to sudden headaches that drop me to my knees. Despite my best efforts, the bloody dress catches on branches, and I leave a trail of ripped cloth in my wake. But at least I'm walking again. Even climbing the hill to the shoreline. And it's a good walk. Stray trees aside, Ashing roads are clean and tidy, even the little-traveled trails like this one. We run our kingdom like a ship, with every acre well employed and well maintained.

Clay raises his palm to his nose, watching two metal balls orbit each other just above his hand. I bought them for him after my last cruise.

Clay catches the balls and smiles at me.

My heart jumps with quickened beats. I step toward him. "Clay?"

His eyes stay where they were, the smile still in place. It hadn't been for me. It was for something only Clay sees.

"They are wrong, Clay," I whisper. "Once this war ends, I will find a cure for you, even if I have to sail all the way to the Diante Empire to do it. I don't care if they are hermits or hate women or anything else."

The hill gives way to a clean cove of sand. Waves foam as they rush around the stone wave break, and, in the distance, masts of warships rock majestically. All are anchored farther out than I'd wish, but the Ardent Ocean has an unfortunately shallow coastline.

Each of the six kingdoms on the Lyron continent—Ashing, Felielle, Biron, Spardic, Eflia North and Eflia South—has its own army and navy with a corresponding Command

and Admiralty to oversee the soldiers and ships. In addition, there is a large combined force known as the Lyron League Joint Force, divided into the Joint Army and Joint Fleet branches, to which all kingdoms contribute resources for mutual protection. The Lyron League Joint Force was formed after the start of the Tirik war, to defend our continent from the Tirik Republic's aggression. The Joint Force is a good idea, but Joint Army companies and Joint Fleet ships are notoriously poor performers, since every kingdom keeps its best people and vessels for its own forces.

The anchored ships speak to me through their hulls and riggings, telling me which kingdom's flag they fly, what their crew is like, and what station they hold. The masts of the Ashing ships swing proudly in the prime mooring slots, and a few Felielle ships anchor nearby. Being inland, Felielle has no ports of its own, so its ships rent mooring in ours. There is one new and trim Biron ship that never allows girls, and a few smaller slick vessels that run dispatches. The League's Joint Fleet ships, with their mixed-nation crews, anchor farthest out. They are second-rate, and we never grant them prime berths.

I coax Clay down toward the wave break. The hem of my useless garb again catches a root, and I nearly tumble down the slope. It's bad enough the unwieldy thing is impractical, but it also makes me feel naked. Mother insists that feminine attire is a uniform of its own sort. She's probably right, but it's a uniform to a service that I neither understand nor welcome. And the feeling is mutual. The dress clings to my hips, and my stride, while practical on a ship's rolling deck, makes me look like a waddling duck on land. A waddling duck dressed in frills and lace.

We stop at the wave break and squint against the sun. The main port traffic is always heavy but seems even more so today, as a small fleet flying Felielle colors settles into its berth and starts lowering a boat to bring the crew ashore. "Do you see the frigates there?" I ask Clay.

Clay cocks his head. "Frigates," he says. I recognize the raspy voice of my father's clerk. "Three Felielle frigates will dock today, my lord. We are still awaiting Prince Tamiath's ship."

I try again. "Remember when we used to sing? Come listen how rusty I've gotten."

"Yes." He stomps the lapping waves, ignoring me. "Yes. Yes yes yes. Yes yes." The metal balls lift into the air.

I bite my lip and pretend he's heard me. Maybe even promised to join me later. Sitting down, I reach for a sea song we used to love and send the melody into the wind.

The balls still. Clay sways with the song's rhythm. It's a piece for two, and it begs for accompaniment, like a void desperately calling to be filled.

Sing, Clay. I repeat the verse. Sing. Make it whole.

His mouth opens. His chest expands with breath in a mirror to my own. I lean toward him, and our gazes lock. In a moment, we'll connect our voices. My chest flutters. It is happening. Any heartbeat now. Just—

"Arrrrruffff!" The dog erupts in a howling bark. "Arrrf! Arrurrrrrr."

I curse, slamming my palm against the stone.

The dog barks again.

Clenching my jaw, I look up to see what has upset the bitch and feel my anger change to concern. Two horsemen are trotting into the far end of the cove. A third man hangs across one of the saddles. I curse again, this time softly, my heart quickening its beat. We need none of this.

Sliding off the rocks, I join Clay on the far side of the wave break. The wind seems to follow, ruffling my dress and carrying the voices as they draw closer.

The men are arguing. Then they stop. "This 'ere is far

enough, I tell you," a deep voice says in the songlike accent of my mother's Felielle people. "The patrols mill about the main market this time of day. Put him down. Domenic and I shall have ourselves a talk."

I wrap my arm around Clay's shoulders to still him. Water bubbles over the tops of our boots and wraps my dress hem around my ankles. "It's all right," I whisper, though Clay gives no indication he's aware of the activity on the other side of the wave break. "Stay down here for a bit."

I find a solid foothold and haul myself onto the perch to appraise the situation over a depression in the rock wall.

There are three men: two thugs wearing leather gloves, and their prisoner, who has been hauled down from horseback. The prisoner's hands are bound. All three men face the ocean, their profiles to me. The larger, bald thug hands off his pistol to his red-haired partner, whose own weapon is tucked in the small of his back. Red trains the pistol at the prisoner and steps back to hold the horses.

The animals dance. Metal-shod horses do poorly around Clay.

"Kneel," Bald commands and steps forward, giving me a better view of his victim. The bound man is three or four years older than me, with broad shoulders and a seaman's sturdy clothes. Dark hair frames a determined jaw, and his back is straight despite the bonds. My heart pauses for an instant, then resumes at a quicker pace.

"I said, kneel," Bald repeats.

I'd place my wager on the prisoner in a fistfight, but muscles stand up poorly to pistols. I watch his jaw tighten as he comes to the same conclusion and lowers to his knees.

Bald nods and adjusts his gloves, one finger at a time. "Much better. It would seem y'ave reached a credit limit, Domenic. One hundred seventy-four gold. My employer wishes to discuss a payment plan." His soft accent gives the threat an oddly polite tone.

That much gold in Felielle covers seven months' living for common folk; four in Ashing since we import most everything but fish. Little wonder Domenic has collectors on his tail. My mouth tightens. Whatever the sum or reasons, they have no business enforcing things on Ashing soil. With our economy dependent on safe ports, foreigners' dirty laundry hurts my people in the end.

Plus, two armed thugs against one bound man isn't exactly fair play.

Bald plants his boot into his prisoner's ribs. Domenic doubles over but makes no sound.

I slide off my perch. "Clay," I whisper. "There's a man with a pistol just beyond these rocks. Can you feel the metal? Can you push it back, into the water?"

"A backwater ship. No need to trouble over her," Clay intones in the king's firm voice. "Invite the other captains for a light dinner. Prince Tamiath will expect a banquet when he docks."

I sigh.

"Hurry it up, mate," calls a voice I presume is Red's. "Somethin's spooking the beasties. And I don't like it much either."

I wonder whether Clay is doing something or if Red simply fears discovery. Ashing has no prisons. We can little afford to sustain people for the sake of creating misery. As on a ship, punishment in Ashing is swift, with fines, lashes, and deaths handed down on natives and foreigners alike. The larger kingdoms had extracted many privileges in the name of diplomacy, but we held firm on these laws.

I hear the soft thud of fists hitting flesh and Domenic's grunts of pain. The man can neither fight back nor defend himself, and it is past time to put a stop to this. Or try to. I wish for the dignity and sword of my uniform. I have a rag doll dress and a rock instead.

Crouching, I wait for both the thugs' attention to fix firmly on their prey. Red's pistol wavers. He frowns at his hand, and I draw a breath. Clay's presence alone can trigger a misfire. If—

I startle as the pistol's report booms through the beach. Red jumps back, drops the gun, and stares at it in betrayal. Bald and Domenic duck. The horses neigh, their noses raised to the sky.

The momentary pandemonium offers the chance I need. Recovering ahead of the men, I sprint for Red's second pistol.

5

My breaths come quick, my side vision a blur of sand. The horses rear, showing their bellies and hooves. When Red turns to the beasts, I crash into him. The impact ricochets through me. I drop my rock.

Red staggers but remains standing.

I wrap my arms around Red and draw the other pistol from his waistline even as he throws me to the ground. I land in a heap and breathless, but my hands still clutch the gun.

Inconveniently, the bloody weapon is as much a danger to me as to the men. It bucks in my hand, yielding to the natural pulse of Clay's uncontrolled magic. Rising to one knee, I move the barrel between Bald and Red. "Stop," I command. "All of you."

Three sets of eyes grip me. None give a sign of recognition. I little blame them—having spent most of my life aboard an Ashing ship, the only people who'd reliably recognize me are those I've served with. This Felielle trio is unlikely to recognize even Thad outside the throne room, or think twice if they heard my name absent salutation.

My palms are moist, but I know better than to let the fear slip into my voice. "I believe the man has understood your message," I say.

Clay's dog chooses that moment to run up beside me and bare its teeth. Its low growl leadens the air between us.

One heartbeat stretches after another, punctuated by the break of waves and the horses' snorts. My breaths come quick and shallow. I'm unlikely to miss at this range, but the pistol is good for one shot only.

Bald squints. "What's your stake in this?"

"A broken law and a bound man." I shake my head. The constant foreign presence in Ashing is a necessary burden for now, but I hope to see it end after the war. "One pistol has fired already, gentlemen. I expect the Ashing patrols are en route to investigate."

Red scowls at me, likely calculating whether he might knock me to the ground before I squeeze off the trigger or the horses scamper. He probably can.

I scowl back, hoping the thugs' employer paid them too little to risk their hides so greatly. "I would wager you will pay with your horses and backs if the patrols come upon us now."

Bald snorts and makes a decision. "Is the lady correct, Domenic? Has the message penetrated?" He lands a vicious knee in the man's abdomen.

Domenic's jaw tightens, and he has to draw a breath before he can speak. "I have a debt." His voice is steadier than I had expected. "I will pay it."

"Why, that is all we wished to hear in the first place." Bald pats Domenic's shoulder and turns away, then twists back and punches Domenic's jaw as an afterthought. "A pinch of a memory aid." He chuckles at his joke and, accepting the reins from Red, swings into the saddle. The horses neigh and pick up a gallop, eager to be away, and I raise my free arm to shield my eyes from the flying sand.

I toss the pistol into the waves. My head hurts, a throbbing pressure behind my eyes. I want to sit down and cradle it, but instead, I double back to check on Clay.

My brother is still on the other side of the wave break, occupied with his metal toys as if nothing had happened. I hope that in his world, nothing has.

Returning to Domenic, I find him working his wrists free of the rope. Good enough. He and his debts can take care of themselves from here.

As for me, I don't think I can stand much longer. Turning my back on Domenic, I brace my arms on my thighs and gulp mouthfuls of air as the beach swims before my eyes. *Storms and hail.* I hate my body.

"Are you unwell?"

I look up.

Domenic crouches in front of me, his broad shoulders blocking out the sun's glare. Blue eyes frown as he takes hold of my elbow. His grip is firm, as if he is used to using his hands, and the steady pressure beneath my arm is a great deal more stable than my own balance. "Your face is white as foam." He frowns at me. "Sit."

My body obeys, though I only go so far as to lower myself to one knee. With the energy burst of the fight melting away, I want nothing more than to crawl into a dark hole and nurse my aches in private. "I'm fine." I sound more confident than I feel. At least I've retained control over my voice. I pull my elbow free from his grip and immediately feel the loss of support I shouldn't have needed in the first place. "Would be even better if you left."

Ignoring the request, Domenic reaches out to brush my hair away from my face. I stupidly wore my hair down in deference to the dress, and by now it's a tangled red mess. I wince as Domenic's firm fingers press the lingering bruise on my left temple. He shakes his head. "That was a stupid thing you did, going alone against two armed men."

My eyes snap up to him. "You've got to be jesting." I push his hand away from my face. "The bruise is not from today, and the proper response for my protecting your hide is 'thank you.'"

Domenic winces. "Thank you."

I rub the heel of my hand over my eyes and sigh. "I little changed the course of affairs. Those two sought to deliver a message, not leave a corpse."

"You spared me several fractured ribs or worse." He pauses, his handsome eyes studying me. The gaze is too piercing for comfort, though, as if Domenic is trying to unravel a puzzle. "May I ask why you did it? We know nothing of each other."

"It seemed like the right thing to do at the time," I say, but his gaze remains on me, expectant. I shrug. I'm too tired to make up something wise and mysterious, the way Mother would. The truth it is, then. "Because I want to live in a world where thugs don't get away with beating bound men."

His face twitches. In thought, perhaps. Or in surprise. Or maybe he just thinks me odd. I don't know. If I've just made myself sound the fool, I'm too exhausted to care properly.

A corner of his mouth rises in a hint of a smile. "You are a dreamer."

I'm an officer in the Ashing navy and the king's daughter. I shrug. "I have my principles."

Domenic cocks his head again, the sea breath messing his hair. "What if I deserved it?"

"Did you?"

The thoughtful humor flees from his face like a toppled wave, and I regret asking the question. I'm about to tell Domenic that he owes me no answer when he sighs, tightening his jaw. "My father forged my name on his gaming tab a year ago," he says, rocking back on his heels. "I'm yet to make the debt whole. Please accept my apologies for having endangered you in addition to myself today."

"The collectors will not take truth for an answer?"

"I don't know. I never told them." Domenic's lips press together. His loose shirt billows from beneath his coat, and the ends of the leather lace flap like small flags in the wind. When he speaks next, the words are distant, like a thought often visited but seldom said aloud. "The old drunk has no funds to pay. A beating would only prevent him from earning what he can. Plus, I wish none of this in my mother's sight."

"I understand," I say softly.

He arches a brow. "Do you?"

I give him a half smile despite myself. "I understand the part about keeping things out of Mother's sight." I rub my hand over my face. "I understand *that* better than I wish I did."

Domenic laughs. It's a deep, genuine sound. But it ends sharply as his eyes focus on something beyond my shoulder. "You, there! Stop!" He bellows. "The current will pull you under like ballast."

I spin, my stomach dropping as my eyes register the reason for Domenic's shouting. Clay is no longer behind the wave break. He is wading chest deep in the ocean.

6

CLAY IS DROWNING; HE JUST doesn't know it yet. The sea is treacherous here, with rocks that trap feet and currents that bend and hold victims beneath the surface. A tall wave crashes over Clay's head. He yelps as if realizing where he is.

The dog whimpers. She's too pregnant to go into the waves after her master.

"You deaf, man?" Domenic roars over the waves as if cutting through the fog of battle. He grabs a stone and skims it over the water, clipping Clay's shoulder. "Get yourself back ashore."

"Bloody imbecile," I yell at Domenic as Clay jerks and the balls spinning above his palm fall into the waves. Kicking off my shoes, I sprint into the ocean. Frigid water rushes into my clothes. My breaths come in quick, short bursts. Clay can't swim, not even in calm currents. My feet slip on the stones and my dress drags behind me like a wet sail. But I keep my focus where it belongs. On my brother.

Clay stops howling at his now-empty palm and clamps

his hands over his ears. He twists frantically round and round, moving deeper with each step. He's looking for his lost toy, and he won't ever stop. And there is nothing but water around.

"Ahhh!" Clay claws his face. "AHHH!"

It feels like years before I manage to reach him, and even then my relief is half-felt. I make myself stop within an arm's reach of him. Clay is strong, and he is scared. He can—he will—fight. I must be calm. Must keep him calm.

"It's all right now," I say softly and touch his shoulder. "Will you come with me?"

He slaps me. Salt spray hits his scratched face. He slaps himself.

"Clay." I call. "Clay. No. It's me."

"I will help." Domenic wades up to us. The water hitting my chest only reaches his waist.

I block his path. "You've done enough," I hiss before softening my voice. "Come, Clay. I will find new spheres for you. Take my hand."

Clay hits me.

My head explodes with pain, and I gulp salt water before regaining my balance. "Clay..."

Domenic shoves past me and weighs Clay with his gaze. The next instant, he grabs my screaming brother in a bear hug and hauls him to shore.

Clay's frightened wails jump across the waves, cutting my heart.

&

Clay sits on the sand and rocks back and forth like a wet pendulum.

I kneel beside him. My body shakes with cold, and my head hurts so much, I might pass out right here on the sand. "Clay."

He jerks away, his arms covering his face.

"I'm so sorry, Clay," I whisper.

He ignores me. His dog, now quiet, curls up beside him. When I try to reach for Clay again, she growls.

Right. I step back, rubbing my face and trying not to cry. Clay had been within a breath of connecting with me, and now I am back to the basics of keeping my twin alive. Of earning his trust. I pound my fist against my thigh and shudder as the wind pierces my wet clothes.

"Are you both all right?" Domenic asks.

"We *had* been before you came." My eyes sting. Stepping away, I wring the water from my hair and dress, which clings to my body like a soggy sheet. The clouds are shifting to uncover the sun. At least it will get warmer soon. At least...at least I'm not Clay. I lower my face. We'd worried about my getting sick when Clay's symptoms first showed, but four years have passed since.

Sand squeaks behind me as Domenic steps close and lays his coat over my shoulders. He apparently had the foresight to throw it off before plunging into the water.

The residual warmth wraps around me, mixing with the musk of sea salt that clings to the fabric. The relief is so great that, for a moment, I can do nothing but soak in the heat and scent. When I can force my body to obey again, I reach up to slide off the coat. "We're fine."

"Keep it." Domenic catches my wrists, his strength contained to a gentle touch. "You are shivering."

"Yes. I noticed."

Domenic catches my eyes. When he speaks, his voice is soft, as if calming a skittish horse. "You came to my defense against two armed men. A coat is the least I can offer. Plus," a corner of his mouth twitches as he reaches around my shoulders to straighten the collar, "it looks better on you anyway."

His coat *looks* better on me? Why would— Oh. My face heats, Domenic's words finally penetrating. Me. He is complimenting me on my looks. Apparently, the man finds that wet-rat look appealing.

"I mean no disrespect," Domenic says quickly.

My blush deepens, which I didn't think possible. "No, I didn't..." I stutter like a bewildered rabbit. "I mean, thank you. For the compliment. And the coat. You can have the coat back." No, not a rabbit. An idiot. I turn away from him. I'm not used to flattery. Ashing men don't compliment an officer of His Ashing Majesty's navy on her appearance.

Domenic clears his throat. "So, do you improve the world often, then?"

"What?" I turn back and blink.

"When I asked why you helped me, you said you wanted to live in a world where thugs don't get away with abuse." He walks around to kneel beside Clay's dog, rubbing the beast's ears. "That seems a bit grand a mission. Don't you think?"

"No." I shrug and sit down. "One battle doesn't win a war, but it's still a part of it."

Domenic studies me again but busies himself in petting the dog when he catches me looking. The dog rolls on her back, throwing her paws into the air. Obediently, Domenic rubs her belly. "Ah. You've pups coming, don't you, girl?"

I'm on my feet instantly, my heart pounding. "Now?" The word comes in a croak.

Domenic throws his head back and laughs. The bloody bastard. "You will take on armed thugs with your bare hands, but the notion of *puppies* sends you into a panic?"

"I'm regretting my earlier actions more and more each minute."

He makes a noise in his throat, though I'm certain he's just biting back a chuckle. "No, not now. But soon, if I remember anything from the farm. You may breathe again if you wish. And once you do, you could tell me your name."

I hesitate a moment. My father is ashamed of Clay and I hardly present the image the Ashing throne would wish to show foreigners, but I think giving my name is safe enough. Even if Domenic remembers that the king in the small kingdom of Ashing has a pair of irrelevant younger children, he unlikely knows anything beyond that. Given Clay's absence from all public functions, few outside the palace believe he still lives here. In a way, they are right. "Nile," I say, wringing out my hair and braid. "And I'm not scared of puppies. I'm scared of what Clay will do if the bitch dies in delivery."

Domenic's face softens. The question I know he wants to asks hangs between us.

I sigh. I seldom speak of my twin. There is no place for such talk on duty, and at home there is no one to speak with. "Clay is Gifted. He has some control of the magic that attracts metal to him, but it's hard to say how much."

"Ah." He averts his gaze. Few Gifted live anything resembling a normal life. "I've seen Gifted of course, but from afar. I've never met one. Has he always been...like this?"

I shake my head. "The magic usually lies dormant until another illness or injury weakens the body's defenses," I say, settling down a few feet away. "For Clay, that was a fever four years ago. We'd had thirteen years together before it happened, before the magic awoke."

Thirteen years of having a friend in a world of subordinates and superiors.

"Nowadays, Clay acknowledges no one," I say into the silence. "But I'm certain he knows me." I hug my shoulders with my hands, the memory of our friendship salting the hurt of its loss. The one guilt I feel over wanting to leave Ashing quickly is that Clay must stay behind. Just as our time together is the one grace of my imprisonment ashore. A chance to bring my brother back to me. "I think, though, that if the magic was dormant once, there is no reason it can't return to slumber again." I turn to stare at the sea. A cure is somewhere out there. "I've heard the Diante are making headway in understanding it. In the Metchti Monastery."

Domenic winces, and I know what he will say before he speaks. Tales of the Diante having one thing or another have been around for decades. When you close your borders to foreigners, said foreigners quickly develop a healthy imagination as to what you might be hiding. I happen to think the Diante are hiding a cure.

"I think we will not soon find out," Domenic says diplomatically. "The Diante Empire is so determined to stay neutral in the Lyron League–Tirik Republic conflict that it refuses entry even to ambassadors." He shakes his head. "It baffles me how the Diante don't realize that they'd be the Republic's next target if the Lyron League falls."

"The Diante have been self-contained and self-sufficient for three hundred years," I fire back. "They likely believe they can weather a Tirik offensive."

Domenic raises a brow. Maybe women in Felielle don't have opinions on military matters. In Ashing, everyone has an opinion. On everything.

"The port is seething with people this time of day," I say, changing the subject. "I am surprised those thugs were able to grab you."

He tenses, but after a moment, his shoulders settle, shifting beneath his shirt. "I avoid the main docks in Ashing. The youngsters are courteous enough, but the market takes pride in overcharging sailors, while most eateries crawl with women and royals selling wares of equal disrepute."

Not the description of our main port life I would have offered.

Domenic rubs his forehead. "My apologies, that was

inappropriately crude. I meant to say that with six kingdoms in the League, there is always someone trying to position a cousin or nephew to a post they've no business occupying."

"Because the privilege of a royal birth leads to certain incompetence?" I arch a brow. "Perhaps you'd find a happier home in the People's Republic of Tirik. I hear they are all about tearing down royalty."

"That is uncalled for." His nostrils flare, and it takes a moment for him to pull himself together. "The Republic murders people in the name of liberation and sows fear while calling it freedom. My words implied that there is little incentive to labor when promotion relies on relations, not skills."

I don't bother responding. It's an old argument, put forth by more than one commoner. The king and Captain Fey expected me to labor more, not less, than my peers. But nothing I say will convince Domenic of it. It is one of many reasons I've not had a friend since Clay.

I glance at my brother, who has settled to muttering, "I will not lose any more children! Don't do this," in our mother's voice. Ever since my youngest brother Shayn died at sea, we hear this declaration each time my father draws up orders for either Thad or me.

I pull off the coat and hold it out for Domenic to take. The wind hits my wet dress, and I fight off a shiver. "Thank you. I believe my brother is well enough to walk home."

"Keep it. The weather is chill yet." Domenic rises and offers me his hand, pulling me easily to my feet. "May I escort you and Clay home, Nile?"

"We can take care—"

"Nile," Clay says loudly in our mother's Felielle inflection. "Nile is prime for marriage."

My cheeks heat again.

Domenic laughs and steps away. "Stay safe, my friend."

"Nile. Nile is a princess and prime for marriage," Clay repeats. "Prince Tamiath is a good man. His wish for Nile's hand is an honor. We must accept. Ashing needs to strengthen ties with Felielle. Ashing needs Felielle." Clay's tone changes again to the king's. "Ashing needs Felielle." It changes again to one I fail to recognize. "Ashing needs Felielle."

I jerk around. "Clay, when did you hear this?"

"Ashing needs Felielle. Ashing needs Felielle. Ashing needs Felielle."

My hands tremble. I twist to study the masts, counting the ships flying Felielle colors. There are several. More than usual. My body tenses. When my gaze returns to Domenic, I see the sudden tension in his face. He'd read the implication of Clay's words. And in my sudden accounting of vessels.

Domenic backs away from me.

The coat, still in my hand, hangs between us like a poisonous snake. I let it fall to the sand.

7

THREE HOURS LATER, I STRIDE to the king's anteroom. My breath comes quickly, as if I am heading to battle. I'm not. I'm going to examine the barrel of a pistol already aimed at my head.

"Nile!" my mother's voice spins me to a stop. "What in the Goddess's name are you wearing?"

My pressed uniform trousers snugly wrap my thin waist, and a white silk shirt buttons high up my neck. It isn't comfortable, but it is familiar. And right now, I want any advantage I can get, protocol be bloody damned. "Not now, Mother."

She tsks. "How is anyone to see the woman you are when you dress like a boy? More importantly, how are *you* to see the woman that you are?"

I stop. Turn. Meet her beautiful brown eyes. "The woman that I am is a naval officer."

My mother takes a step toward me and catches my chin with her fingers "You are not any one thing, Nile. You are a daughter and a sister, a princess, a dreamer. You are many things that you've yet to consider. To experience."

Such as what, Mother? A bride? I jerk out of her grasp and quicken my pace, reaching the door before Mother can continue her line of thought.

The clerk looks up, giving me the same sad smile he had earlier. "Good day, Princess."

I glance over the same empty leather chairs and untouched refreshments and stop my gaze at the wooden door behind the clerk. "Might I beg for a moment of His Majesty's time?"

The clerk wavers a moment until his eyes land on my face. Whatever he sees there makes him turn on his heels and knock twice on the doorframe. He sticks his head inside, speaking softly. Moments later, a tall, immaculately dressed young man strides out. Thad.

"Did Father die without my knowledge?" I ask. The *majesty* title is reserved for the king alone, and I'm in no mood for politeness.

"He's away just now." Thad motions me to one of the leather chairs in the waiting area. With his wide chest and coal-black eyes and hair, Thad favors our father as drastically as Clay and I take after the queen. Also unlike me, Thad puts muscle on easily. That muscle, combined with Thad's significant height, gives him an aura of strength most believe born of hard physical training. I know better. Not that I care how tall or large or imposing the bastard is. Especially not today. Thad frowns at me. "Sit down, Nile. What is the matter?"

I stay standing. "Are you and Father conspiring to marry me to Prince Tamiath?"

Thad motions for the clerk to leave. "How did you hear

that?" he asks, taking the other chair for himself.

No denial. Clay was right, then. The blow of Thad's words pushes me back. My face heats, my fingers curling into fists. I step away.

"Nile. Wait." His large fingers pinch the bridge of his nose. "No, Nile, Father and I are not conspiring to marry you to Tamiath." He sighs. "Mother is."

"Crock of shit, Thad. Since when do either of you entertain Mother's opinions?"

"Since a Felielle prince asked us to," he snaps. Thad closes his eyes as if he, not I, is the victim in the conversation. "Tamiath may not be the heir to the throne, but he is important. And yes, Mother has her notions and ideas for your future, but this request originated with the prince. Whatever you heard, however you heard it—it isn't what you think. We all agreed that you should meet Prince Tamiath before anyone broached the subject with you. Even you must concede that acquaintance is material to the matter. There is little sense in debating anything before then."

We all agreed. Anger chokes me, and several heartbeats pass before I can speak.

Thad beats me to it. "There is something else you should know, Nile. Laila and I are expecting."

I blink, the directional change momentarily muddling my thoughts. Father had arranged Thad's marriage to Laila, one of the Biron princesses, three years past. So far as I can tell, she and Thad know each other little better now than when they first met. "Congratulations."

"You don't fully understand." Thad rests his elbows on his thighs and leans forward toward me. The chair sighs beneath his weight. "Ashing will have an heir."

I shrug. "You speak as if I have my eyes on the throne instead of the sea."

Thad throws up his hands. "Damn it, Nile, why do you

think Mother has kept her grip off you the past years? Because she's reformed to Ashing ways?"

I tense, certain I will little like where Thad is heading.

"Don't be daft, Nile," he snaps. "If Laila was unable to bear children, it would become vital that you marry an Ashing man to continue the lineage. Now that she is with child, a foreign marriage would prove of greater value. And with Ashing's reliance on Felielle's subsidies, we can't simply ignore their prince's request."

The room shrinks in on me. Have I always been nothing but a commodity? My body coils, my head pounding. My words come in a whisper. "I'm not a goat, Thad."

"No, you are an Ashing royal."

I gather myself. "I am an officer in the Ashing navy. My place, my *value*, is aboard a ship of war."

"You *were* an officer in our navy. That sank with the *Faithful*."

I freeze. "What?"

Thad rises and walks the few steps to the clerk's desk. Removing a new leaf from a drawer he brings it back to the sitting area, holding it toward me. "This ran three weeks ago, while you lay fevered." He pulls the paper back, just out of my reach. "You should sit."

I stare at the headline, *Faithful Treason*, and sink into a chair. My fingers are numb as they accept the print.

"One week past," I read aloud, "the glory-seeking officers of the Ashing Ship Faithful defied the king's orders and attempted to transport a valuable intelligence package by themselves through Tirik-infested waters. Unsurprisingly, the hubris ended in failure when the seventy-two-gun Faithful encountered a Tirik vessel of one hundred ten guns and sank in subsequent battle."

"You can read to yourself, Nile," Thad says. "I know what it says."

I ignore him.

"'While the Faithful's zeal for victory is reflective of Ashing ideals,' King Greysik of Ashing told the Lyron League Joint Fleet Admiralty at the Cloud Palace in Biron, 'this glory ride was a misguided scheme of a too-proud crew. Captain Fey should have waited for reinforcement.' The king vowed to discipline all involved. The—"

I glare at my brother. "These are lies, Thad." The words squeeze past clenched teeth. "Father had ordered the Faithful to forge ahead alone. He is the one who wished to show off before the other kingdoms. He lost the book and killed my captain and my crew."

"The Republic destroyed a third of the League defenses in the last year," Thad says, tapping a spot in the middle of the Ardent Ocean. "Let us see who the League will feed to the Tirik if the war fails to turn, shall we? Eflia North and Eflia South." He points to the fat part of the teardrop in the east. "Corrupt and dumb as rocks, but they have iron deposits in their mines and gold by their riverbeds, which no one else in the League does. Felielle?" He jabs at the inland kingdom. His voice rises with each word. "Too difficult to carve a slice from the middle, so the Goddess worshipers there are safe. Biron?" Thad's palm covers the kingdom in the northwest, the largest in the League. "They *are* the League. We need them, not they us. And the bastards know it. Are you visualizing this with me? What have we left on the map?"

I keep my mouth shut.

"Spardic and Ashing," Thad answers for me, spitting the words. "The warriors and the sailors." He jabs the point of the teardrop. "And who is here, at the western tip? The smallest, the closest to the Tirik, the easiest to amputate? The one whose military expenses are so high, it can't afford its own survival? Which kingdom is that, Nile?"

Thad draws a breath and steps back, his anger gone as

quickly as it had come. When he speaks again, it is with softer, conciliatory tones. "Ashing can ill afford a sour reputation and can afford to offend Felielle even less. League resources are scarce, and we are the smallest of the kingdoms. A peninsula jutting into the Ardent Ocean. If the cost of defending us outweighs our contributions, the League will expel us. If the Felielle halt our subsidies, we will starve. If the League expels us, the Tirik will strip our land. And as for Clay... I hear the Republic experiments on the Gifted. Part of their People's Committee for Prosperity's Greater Good plan. So, what would *you* do in Father's place?"

"Heeded Captain Fey's advice and held the *Faithful* back until reinforcement caught up." Thad doesn't get to lecture me on consequences of the war, and as for the reference to Clay, that was a low, crafted blow. Thad cares as little as Father does about my twin.

Thad shrugs. "It was a calculated risk. Had you succeeded, Ashing would have come out the hero."

A headache strikes me, and I sway, tightening my fingers on the desk's edge for balance. The candles flicker. I pull the newsprint from beneath the map. "This isn't true."

"Truth is irrelevant." Thad's voice grows hard. "Perception is what matters."

The door behind the clerk's desk swings open, and my father's graying head shows through the opening. The king who was *away just now*, according to Thad.

My stomach clenches. Pushing myself straight, I bow and scrape up strength for a confident voice. "Good day, my lord."

The king's gaze fixes on Thad. "I require the charts of Felielle royalty and the noble court."

The door closes.

I bite the inside of my cheek. A few heartbeats pass in silence, then Thad sighs. "Your ship failed one of the most important missions of the war, Nile," he says quietly. "Did you honestly expect a hero's welcome?"

My body shakes, my fingers trembling at my sides. "This isn't fair," I whisper.

"You're right." He holds my gaze. "But your duty is to Ashing. Whether you carry it out on the quarterdeck or in a bedchamber is secondary."

8

I WAIT UNTIL DARKNESS. WHATEVER Thad said, I'd have no choice. Never did. I have always been a pawn in the throne's game; the only change now is that I know it.

My future in the Ashing navy is over. I will never become an Ashing admiral. I will never hold any Ashing command. My hands tremble as I dig a seabag from my dressing room and stuff it with the bits of my life that lie close at hand. Three sets of sturdy clothes, some coin, my spyglass. Nothing that marks my lineage. There is no need for a uniform. I have lost my right to the quarterdeck, the sacred place where the ship's officers walk.

The last thought stings as it penetrates. I shake myself. I am expelled from Ashing already. The only question remaining is whether I'll leave to Felielle as an exotic toy, a pampered prisoner of a spoiled prince or... To the sea, as someone else. Someone free.

I sling my bag over my shoulder, take a candle, and slip out of my room. There is one last thing to do. Edging into my twin's chamber, I sit on Clay's bed and take his hand in mine. When he opens his eyes, I lock my gaze to his. I can say nothing to him for fear he'll repeat it. No explanation, no apology, no good-bye. We sit in silence as my candle burns. *Had you told me Mother's words on purpose, Clay? Were you looking out for me? Do you understand?* My eyes begin to sting. Whatever else, by leaving, I am betraying him.

No.

In that moment, I know what I will do once I walk away from the palace gates. I will leave, not just for me, but for *us*. The only *us* there is. Ashing be damned, I am going to save my twin. Two years of duty as a common seaman on any Joint Fleet ship will get the Letter of Service I'd need to join a civilian merchant vessel. I'd find one that trades with the mysterious Diante Empire. A few small merchants still do in the backwaters. And then I will go into the Diante Empire itself. Will find the Metchti Monastery. The cure.

I have to go. I rise. "Be safe," I whisper to him.

"Be safe," Clay whispers back.

And then I am gone.

Dawn is still a half hour away when I step onto the docks. The smell of fish hangs thick in the air even with the market closed. The fishermen go about their morning business with practiced briskness. The occasional youths who'd drawn the short straw of night duty patrol the pier, stepping around the few foreign sailors who lie passed out drunk on the ground. I try to paint each scene into my memory, to take with me. I do love the Ashing people. They judge each other by skill and effort, and they want every child to grow into a master. We've no people to waste.

Except, apparently, me.

I find the ship I need anchored in the least convenient of

all slots. Her name is the *Aurora*, and she is one of the ships in the Lyron League Joint Fleet. Fodder. Second-rate fodder. That's how I've always thought of the ships under Joint Fleet Admiralty's control. But what the Joint Fleet lacks in quality, it makes up in quantity. However second-rate, rat infested, leaky, or poorly handled the League's Joint Fleet ships are, the Joint Fleet itself is ten times bigger than any kingdom's private armada. And the Joint Fleet Admiralty, comprised of representatives of each of the six kingdoms, knows how to wield its dull but large weapon for the greatest effect against the Tirik Republic.

So the *Aurora* it is for me. She is a small man-of-war with twenty-six guns and no history of past glory or consequence. A bit of loitering in search of a midshipman who'll invite me into the *Aurora*'s company, and it is done. At the last moment, I realize I still wear a pendant with the royal insignia. When the middie girl turns away, I toss it into the sea. I had spent a lifetime building a worthy Princess Lieutenant Greysik. The change to a common sea-dreamer girl takes less than an hour.

The growing wind troubles the sea. The boat carrying the middie and me to the *Aurora* is obliged to make constant turns to avoid capsizing. Dull gray sky promises rain, and I huddle around my seabag, bracing myself for my new life. A common sailor with neither rights, nor rank, nor friends. Well, the latter isn't new. I haven't had friends since Clay fell ill, except perhaps the short-lived illusion of one with the stranger on the beach. But I have had the privilege of courtesy and trust, which I can enjoy no longer. I am no one. I am scared.

"Have you spent much time at sea?" the midshipman sitting across from me asks with a Felielle accent and a kind smile. Her name is Ana Lionitis and she is a mousey girl of sixteen. Her narrow shoulders fold in on themselves, her hair hanging limply in the moisture-laden darkness. When the shifting light of the lantern catches her hands, I see the nails painted with pink glaze. In the eyes of the navy, Ana and I are as far apart in status as a royal and a stable boy.

"A bit, ma'am." I cling to my bag. "Not enough. And you?"

Ana nods. "Six months."

I turn down my face before it gives away my thoughts. Sixteen is much too late a start for a midshipman. Most middies go to sea at ten or twelve, learning the ways of sailing and command. I went to sea at eight.

Most middies are not Felielle girls either, I remind myself. Women do not take up arms in my mother's homeland, but Ana has. From Ana's defeated posture, I doubt her reasons for doing so are pleasant. And I'm sure they are none of my business.

Ana too has avoided asking my reasons for enlisting. Those who love the sea sign on with captains directly, choosing leaders known for adventure and glory. Those signing up by night want to escape their life, not drag it to ship with them.

"Is the sea to your liking, ma'am?" I ask, because I don't know what else to say.

She looks away.

"It may grow on you," I say quietly.

"Not with our officers," she whispers.

I wisely avoid pointing out that she is part of "our officers." As a middie, she is an officer in training, the lowest of the breed, but an officer nonetheless.

We both sit alone for a while, silent until the oarsmen pull the bucking boat within a cable length of the frigate's looming hull. My stomach flips, and, for the first time in years, the sickness of sea motion clutches my throat.

"Here we are," Ana says. "The *Aurora*. She's a fine ship."

I seize the chance to study the frigate from the outside. The *Aurora* is as far from a "fine ship" as one can get. She is too old to upgrade, too small to join fleet-level engagements with large ships of the line, and too slow for use for dispatch. And her heading to the backwaters station in the Siaman Sea speaks to all that. I'd wager she'll see duty no more exciting than escorting merchantmen back and forth between the small islands in the archipelago of Lyron's southern boundary.

The *Aurora* is also my best chance to survive. Far away from the mainland and its eyes, the *Aurora* will be a world in and of herself. And her particular backwaters station is fortuitous to my needs, which is not a small part of the reason I chose her.

The Siaman Sea, where the *Aurora* is assigned, flows between the archipelago on Lyron's southern border and the Diante Empire's north shore. It separates the Lyron League and Diante Empire in the south the same way the Ardent Ocean separates the Lyron and Tirik mainlands in the west. Unlike the Lyron mainland, however, the archipelago's population is so tiny and unimportant that the islands are Joint League protectorates. No kingdom wants them, not with their lack of fresh water and redundant resources. Even the native trees, which would make valuable timber for building ships, are of little use since the same trees grow all along the Ardent coast on the mainland, where they are infinitely easier to harvest.

To get to the Siaman Sea, the *Aurora* will be obliged to sail south through the Ardent Ocean and traverse the narrow Bottleneck Juncture into the Siaman. The Lyron archipelago in the Siaman Seas is as close to the Diante as anyone from Lyron ever gets. That far out from capital cities, there is even some trade between Diante and Lyron merchants. With villages, drinking water, and goods as scarce as they are, people are flexible. For my purposes, the *Aurora*'s post in the Siaman Sea is perfect.

I hold the reins of my life now. Perhaps for the first time since birth.

Clinging to that thought, I climb aboard in Ana's wake and survey the deck. The wood planking is old and, by *Faithful*'s standards, filthy. Few sailors move with a will; fewer still do any work outside a petty officer's supervision. Eyes turn to me, hostile and predatory. Men's eyes. I search for the women and find few, with gazes harsher than the men's.

I force myself to stay steady. I knew it would be thus, did I not? The *Aurora* is a ship of the League's Joint Fleet, not Ashing's private armada, where women sail as readily as men. Fortunately, as far as regulations go, the Joint Fleet's are similar to Ashing ones. Equality between genders, forbidden sexual relations between officers and enlisted seamen, and castration of anyone who forces himself on another. I will be all right. At least on that front.

Forward, on the largest part of the deck, a detachment of black-coated marines goes through drill. The even columns move with the signature crispness of their profession but... My brows rise as I realize that none of the boys are old enough to shave.

"Where are the marine adults?" I ask Ana.

"Adults?" She follows my gaze. "Oh. The *Aurora* carries only a training unit of Spades, Spardic Kingdom's elite marines."

A young man in a black uniform shoves Ana from his path and keeps walking without a pause, much less an apology. A scarred black dog trots behind him. Arrogance trails in the pair's wake, tangible as gunpowder. His polished boots, dirty-blond hair hanging loose to his shoulders, mint-green eyes, and the feline grace with which he moves are at odds with the ramshackle ship around us.

"And that is Mr. Catsper," Ana whispers, biting her lip. "The Spades' lieutenant. Twenty-two-year-old violence incarnate. I'll wager my life there isn't an inch of him that's not pure muscle. And he knows it."

A Spade officer. That explains it. Catsper, like his young Spades, are from Spardic Kingdom's private stock. I watch the lieutenant a moment longer, wondering how he and his found their way to this ship, who he pissed off to get this assignment. My gut tells me the list would be too long to write out.

Ana tears her eyes away from Catsper and pulls her hair back into a bun. "I must deliver the mail to the captain. Speak to the bosun for your assignment." She points to a bony man tapping a rattan cane against his palm. "Mr. Dana, that's the first officer, will enter you into the books when he comes up." She starts to walk away but hesitates. "Keep your head down and steer clear from the officers' way," she whispers. "Dana hasn't flogged anyone in a week. He's searching."

I suppress a shiver. Does this ship run on lash and fear?

Ana slinks away, keeping as much distance between herself and the male crew members as the confines of the ship allow.

"Whatcha gawking at, *girl*?" a man beside me demands. He is stocky and muscular. His foul breath descends from his tattooed face, above which his hair is shaved into an Eflian crescent moon. "You think your little self a passenger?"

I turn to him. The dirt on his hands matches that on the great gun beside which he stands.

He crosses his arms.

"Dana on deck," someone beside us whispers urgently.

My new friend's posturing melts at once. "Make yourself busy if you know what's good for ya." He shoves a swabber into my hands and throws himself into an impromptu gun inspection. "You owe me."

Heeding the warning, I position the great gun between myself and the officer who is taking the deck. Once sure of my footing, I carefully lift my face enough to see the happenings. The man I presume is First Officer Dana stands with his back to me, towering over the others. He moves stiffly, as if someone has sewn a metal rod into his uniform. The seamen bend from him as grass from wind, only their burning eyes betraying their hate. Dana turns in a tight circle, and the men shuffle themselves from his way and sight.

Eventually, his turning faces him toward me. And when it does, I know his stiff motions have more to do with a recent pounding than any uniform rod. My heart squeezes once, then beats like thunder over waves. It is too late for me to hide.

Domenic Dana has seen me.

9

MY MOUTH DRIES. ONE WORD from Domenic will destroy me.

He moves toward me, and my breath stills. I give my head a tiny shake.

His eyes narrow.

Say nothing, I beg with my thoughts. Please. Just say nothing. I can explain. I will explain.

Domenic's gaze is locked on mine. Three steps away. Two.

No, I mouth to him, *please.*

He hesitates, then turns suddenly, stepping around me as if avoiding a piece of rigging. "Mr. Kazzik, let us prepare to weigh anchor!" Domenic calls. His deep voice carries clearly across the deck. "We will be making sail for the Siaman Sea to take a merchant fleet under escort."

Relief floods me. Whatever happens next, it will happen at sea, beyond Ashing's recall and Felielle's reach. And, for the time being, beyond my father's wrath. Princess Greysik of Ashing has disappeared, and Nile Ash is setting course as far south as one can get in Lyron and still be somewhere. A place that even the Tirik Republic cares little about, where the threat to the merchant traffic comes from pirates and similar opportunistic parasites.

"Captain on deck!" the bosun shouts, and I snap straight before remembering that this captain expects nothing officer-like from me. Common seamen like me don't even wear a uniform. So I knuckle my forehead like the other deckhands.

As many of the *Aurora*'s crew, Captain Rima is Eflian. If his yellow eyes didn't give his heritage away, the absurd amount of gold jewelry and the tribal tattoos climbing his cheekbones would. He strides onto the deck, smiling benevolently at the crew. Thin and slightly pigeon-toed, he looks more like a kindly uncle than a man who holds supreme reign over the *Aurora*.

"Johina," Rima addresses a large bosun's mate who knuckles his forehead in reply. Both men wear their hair diamond-shaved, a symbol of a shared clan. "I'd like you to dine with me this evening."

I hide my surprise. The privilege of dining with the ship's captain is typically confined to officers and middies. *Not your ship,* I remind myself. *Not your customs. Not your concern.*

Getting my name officially entered into the ship's book, on the other hand, is. But that's Domenic's job. The thought of that conversation quickens my heart all over again. I try to shove down the worry by focusing on learning my way around the *Aurora*'s deck.

I make it all of two steps before the mountain that is Domenic plants itself before me. I'm tall for a girl, but next to him, I might as well be a housecat staring up at a lion. His sea-blue eyes are ice as he meets mine and says, very, very quietly, each word rumbling with constrained fury, "At. Your.

Convenience."

I knuckle my forehead and look at him blandly. We can't exactly be having this conversation on deck, so unless he wants to drag me below this second, it will have to wait. For a heartbeat, I fear that is exactly what he'll do and bring unneeded attention to us both. But Domenic turns on his heels and strides away to his duties. I release a breath and go about learning mine.

The *Aurora* is smaller than the *Faithful* was, but the basic layout is similar. The top open-to-air deck is divided into four parts: the poop, a raised part in the back where the marines are currently training; then the quarterdeck for the officers; the main deck with the ship's boat strapped along the middle; and finally the forecastle at the very front. Great guns line the sides, their black barrels pointing to the sea. And, rising high toward the clouds, tower the *Aurora*'s three masts. I watch sails spread majestically before the wind, the patched canvas straining under the gust of a northerly wind.

My face is still raised to the blowing sea air when the headache returns, sudden as a rogue wave. Pressure builds behind my eyes and drills my ears. I'm aware of the crew's movements, of Ana's return, of Domenic bending down to speak with Rima, but the hurt twists down the canals of my ears like a corkscrew. My swabber clatters to the deck, and I sway, unsure if I'll follow it down.

Whatever damage the Tirik musket ball had done to me, the problem is getting worse.

The deck tilts toward me.

"In Gods' word!" Rima calls as Domenic grabs the back of my tunic, holding me like a child's toy. "Who is this?"

I try to answer, but nausea crawls up my throat, and I dare not open my mouth for fear of vomiting.

"Ms. Lionitis's volunteer, sir," Domenic answers, still holding me up. His voice is <u>nonchalant</u>, a mix of boredom and indulgence that I know not what to make of. "Nile."

Rima purses his lips.

Finding my footing, I swallow and touch my forehead. The headache is easing as quickly as it came, and heat is flowing to my cheeks. At least I fit the part of fish bait.

"If you are going to be sick, do so overboard, not on my deck," Domenic barks, shoving me away. I land hard on my knees and stay down until the two move away.

"You know what they say about women sailors, Mr. Dana?" says Rima. "They are neither women nor sailors." He chuckles, tapping his finger against Domenic's chest to punctuate the joke.

A blaze of hot rage scours through me. Captain Rima knows nothing of me, but one of his own middies and almost a dozen of the crew are female. As are two of Ashing's most prominent captains. Beside their ships, the *Aurora* would shame herself beyond redemption. What had Thad said of Eflians? *Corrupt and dumb as rocks.* The Eflians are only in the League because of their natural resources.

"When permitted to talk, dimwits say many things," I murmur under my breath.

Not quietly enough. The captain's face swivels toward me, and my stomach sinks with fear that he'd heard. But Rima only smiles. It isn't the kind of smile that touches the eyes.

I look anywhere but at Domenic, but I'm aware of his every movement. The hands that had placed a warm coat around my shivering shoulders are now clasped tightly behind a stiff back. Sea-blue eyes that looked into mine as he listened and called me a dreamer are glacier cold. There is no laughter in Domenic's face, no kindness. The very air around him ripples with harshness. The man I'd met on the beach so little fits with the cold-eyed officer on the *Aurora*'s deck that I feel the fool for believing the earlier game.

And... I *had* believed it, I realize. Had enjoyed it. The conversation, the coat, the thoughts exchanged in blissful ignorance of rank and standing. Domenic had made me feel as if being just me, just Nile, might be something special in itself. My having bought into such foolishness makes reality that much crueler.

Unlike me, the *Aurora*'s crew plainly knows what they are about with regards to their first officer. The few women on the ship give Domenic as wide a berth as the men do, his looks be damned. Not even a lingering glance at his back from a single soul aboard.

I force myself to push Domenic from my mind. I need to wait until he gets off deck before I can speak to him, so for now it's best to focus on getting settled, hopefully without humiliating myself again. Spotting a cluster of female sailors, I find a blonde woman in her thirties who appears to be in charge and, judging from the snippets of conversation, is named Sandra.

"I am new to the ship's company," I say with a bow. "Might you show me to the women's berth?"

Sandra ignores me.

My jaw tightens, and I force my way into their circle. "Good day," I say again, this time firmly. "I am to share your berth. Shall I swing my hammock at a spot of my choosing, or do you wish to guide me in this?"

Sandra steps in front of me. We are of a height, but she is stronger, her muscles taut from working the canvas. "You are not in our berth. Scat, fish bait."

A bloody lie. "There is but one women's berth," I say through my teeth.

"We're full." Her voice is hard. "Don't you go thinking that pissing sitting down makes you one of us."

The women turn their backs and leave. I can't help feeling the sting, even as I tell myself to pay them no mind.

I'd heard the lower decks as often abuse newcomers as welcome them, but an ocean of difference lies between knowing and living. Gathering the shards of my shattered dignity, I step away. I need their company as little as they want mine.

Ana intercepts me. "You can sling your hammock in my berth if you'd like."

She'd heard the exchange, then. I tighten my jaw. "Thank you, ma'am, but I need no charity."

Her eyes widen, making her look younger than her sixteen years. "No, it is no such thing. We are the only girls our age here... I would welcome the company."

I hesitate, but the offer tempts me into a grateful nod. This isn't proper, but nothing on this bloody ship is. "Thank you, ma'am," I say, meaning it. "Might I also see the ship's physician?" I don't need the recent dizziness making a reappearance.

Ana shrugs an apology. "We have none. Our doctor left a month or so ago. Mr. Dana has the medicines locked in his cabin, however, and Mr. Catsper is handy with setting a bone. Will that do?"

I stare. What sort of captain leaves a large port with his ship's sick berth unattended? Ana doesn't appear to comprehend the problem. What does she expect to happen in battle? For the marine lieutenant to lay down his musket and rush into surgery? I choose my words carefully. "Has the *Aurora* seen combat since you came aboard, ma'am?"

"No, thank the Goddess!"

I force a smile and decide I need no medical aid after all.

I wait a full bell after Domenic leaves the deck before seeking him out. He's played along with my ruse thus far, but the game hangs by a thread. I owe him an explanation sooner than later...and would not be altogether averse to getting one in response. He'd played me on that beach. Smiling and—

and *flirting*—for stars' sake. I might be the liar and fraud, but the man isn't altogether innocent. My face heats as the insult of being made the fool sinks deeper with each step toward *Aurora*'s gunroom.

When the gunroom door looms before me, I will my heart to slow its race and rap my knuckles firmly against the wood.

"Enter," a voice calls at once. Catsper's, I think.

I slide inside to find the marine lieutenant sitting alone at the end of the wooden table stretching the length of the officers' narrow common space. From the murderous look in his eyes and a stack of papers before him, I'm certain I've caught him in the midst of catching up on overdue reports. Sleeping cabin doors line one side of the room, the other side hosting several viewports and a nine-pounder gun. The familiar sight calms my nerves, and, despite myself, I run my hand over the gun. Cool black metal. Heavy and faithful and familiar.

"Do you two want to be alone?" Catsper asks, cocking a single brow. His dirty-blond hair is tied back with a leather thong now, underscoring the square angle of his jaw.

I yank my hand back from the nine pounder.

He chuckles, muscles in his left forearm shifting as he plays absently with a knife. Self-assured mint eyes weigh me from head to toe. The marine's gaze dances with more life than I've yet seen aboard the *Aurora*, and Ana's longing gaze clicks into place. She would not be the first middie to stare wide-eyed at a handsome young officer.

I straighten my back, touching my forehead in a formal greeting. "My apologies for the intrusion, sir. Might I impose on Mr. Dana for a moment if he is available?" Now that the words are out of my mouth, I can't help hoping Domenic is somehow away.

The humor in Catsper's <u>eyes</u> morphs to silent laughter.

"If you *really* wish to." He throws his knife, its blade sinking into the endmost cabin door. "In there."

The knife trembles where it juts from the wood. That is that. My stomach churns, but I can hardly back out now. Sets of opening words run through my mind, each better than the next.

I'll keep your secrets if you keep mine.

Thank you for not packing me off back to the palace, can we leave it at that and never speak again?

Or, my personal favorite thus far: It takes one liar to know another, doesn't it?

I stop before the closed door. Coming here was a mistake. Domenic had done as my gaze had begged and kept my secret. As the *Aurora*'s first officer, if he wished to discuss the matter now, he'd have sent for me. Yes, he said we would talk on the matter, but perhaps waiting until he broaches the topic is the wiser course.

"Unlike wine, meetings with Dana seldom get better with the passage of time," Catsper's dry voice says behind me. "I also imagine that he is not so deaf as to have missed the dagger banging into his door. He knows *someone* is here for him."

I wince. Right. Schooling my face, I rap my knuckles against the frame.

Like Catsper, Domenic is busy with paperwork when I enter. Watch rotations, supply reports, and sailing logbooks fill to capacity the small desk that hangs from the bulkhead. A short pace away, Domenic's bunk is tightly made, each corner tucked beneath the mattress. His sword and a pair of pistols hang beside the bunk. Quality weapons, but inexpensive. The few other items secured to shelves are League issued and, though well cared for, worn. Despite his being alone in his cabin, Domenic's uniform is pristine, the high scratchy collar buttoned to the end.

I feel naked without rank of my own.

Domenic looks up at me, his stare hard and unwelcoming.

A trickle of fear slithers through me. One word from him and I'm finished, bundled off back to my mother and marriage bed.

"Shut the door," he orders.

I do. As if on cue, my head starts to ache with the closing click of the door. *Not now,* I order my body, my fingers curling into a fist to ward off the coming migraine. *Not now.*

10

Domenic dips his pen into an inkwell, the silence between us punctuated by the tap of the quill against the glass. "Who are you, precisely?"

"I am Nile."

His eyes flash in anger, the pen clattering into the inkwell.

I cross my arms. "You know who I am, Domenic. You heard my brother correctly, I saw you put two and two together on the beach."

Another pause, his face stone cold and unreadable. "Nile Greysik, Princess of Ashing," he says finally. Flatly. "The prospective bride of Prince Tamiath of Felielle."

So I'm already a *bride*. My shoulders tense. I say nothing.

Domenic's lips press into a thin line.

The pressure behind my eyes builds, and I think I feel a breeze cutting into my skin, despite being belowdecks. *Not now*, I bid my head again while meeting Dominic's eyes. The faster we can get this conversation over with, the better. "Do you wish to know why I'm here or not?"

"Oh, I trust I've put that together as well." He shuts the sailing journal with a loud snap. "You are here because Your Royal Highness became upset with her parents and decided to run away from home."

Fine. Good enough. "Tell me you will continue keeping my heritage to yourself, and I will be out of your hair."

"Out of my hair?" Domenic throws the journal atop a pile of others and wheels around to face me squarely. "I am the first officer of this naval ship. You were firmly *in* my hair from the moment you stepped onto my deck and will be until the moment you leave."

Fair enough. But my question still stands. I wait.

Domenic snorts. "You need not worry about me destroying your cover story, Princess. You will cry foul yourself at about the second time a bosun's mate lays a rope's end across your shoulders. Do you know how much that hurts? Do you know what it feels like to haul on a rope in the midst of a storm?"

Oh, for stars' sake. I little expect someone outside Ashing's armada or palace to know the details of my training and occupation, but to presume that I've spent my life pampered in silk—as his tone plainly implies he does—is downright insulting. Maybe that is the way of female nobility in Felielle, where Domenic is from, but that excuses nothing. Gripping my hands behind my back, I meet his cobalt eyes stare for stare. "I've an idea of what it feels like to face a loaded gun," I say dryly. "I expect the experience might somewhat translate."

He has the decency to flinch, but the reprieve is short-lived. "My problem with you, Nile, is that when you're done playing sailor and decide you want to go home, you are going to cause this whole ship to abandon her mission to ferry you back."

"That won't happen."

"Of course it will." Domenic braces his powerful forearms against the edge of his writing desk and leans toward me. "I'll keep your secrets. But I'll also ensure you are never tempted to repeat this farce again. On my ship or any other."

Anger pulses through me. *Your ship is the bloody definition of dysfunctional laziness, and it's me you peg as your problem?* I grip my hands behind my back. I had come to Domenic's cabin to ensure the secrecy of my identity, not rekindle a friendship that never existed to begin with. I hold his gaze. "May I have your word on that, Domenic? That you will do nothing to compromise my identity? And that in two years' time, I can leave with a Letter of Service, like any other enlistee?"

His gaze flashes. "If you last that long. And while you are here, you will address me as Commander Dana or sir."

"Aye. Sir." I touch my forehead. As I do, my vision blurs. The dizziness is worse than it had been on deck, and I turn quickly to hide my face from Dominic's eyes. As the spell ebbs, I focus on the bulkhead where Domenic's slate lists the location of friendly fleets.

Without asking permission, I pick up a chalk and correct his work before walking from his cabin.

Fortunately, the gunroom is empty. I imagine I feel a bit of an air current again and shake myself. The sensation gets worse. My head pulses in pain, as if in vengeance for being ignored in Domenic's cabin.

I stagger, catching myself on the table's edge.

A breeze touches my cheek again. Which is impossible down here. I—

I gasp, the pressure in my head redoubling. The deck tilts and disappears from under me. I hear a thud inside my skull and realize I have fallen. The pressure is so great now that I know something has to give. __

And *something* does.

Air rushes at me, filling my mouth and nose until I choke on the flow and my fear turns to terror.

That *something* that gave moments ago was magic awakening in my blood. And the reason for the wind in the gunroom is me. I am air-calling.

11

OPEN MY EYES WITH A GASP.

A small trickle of blood creeps from my brow, which I must have cut when I fell. The gunroom is still mercifully empty. I roll onto my knees and rest my forehead on the deck to keep the dizziness at bay. My head is heavy and stuffed with cotton. But my heart races and my lungs burn as if torn from the inside.

Which they nearly were.

I've just air-called. I'm Gifted. Like the fever that awoke Clay's magic four years ago, my post-wound fever had awoken mine.

Nausea seizes my throat, my imagination already supplying the pity-filled looks, the averted gazes, the regretful mumbles of *oh, I hadn't realized* said while backing away. No. No. No. *Storms.* Please no. I can't be a cripple. I've a life. A plan. A mission. I've a Letter of Service to earn. A cure to find. I can't be a cripple, because I must save Clay.

My hands shake. My whole body shakes. I must save *me.*

At least it is air, not metal. A small voice penetrates my thoughts and leaks guilt. Convulsions, the air callers' symptom, are better than mind loss. I can hide convulsions. Have to hide them if I want to stay at sea. The afternoon after Clay's diagnosis grips my memory.

"Don't believe them, Clay. It might go away or be different for you than others. Maybe... Maybe you will even like it. You need your knife, and ta-da, you call it over to you."

"The knife always wants to come to me. If I pay it no mind, it will come and impale itself in my flesh."

"You'll learn to control it, then. We'll work it out together. Tell me what it's like. Do you think about it?"

"It's like pissing. You have to do it, and you don't really think on the how. Relax your hold on the pee, and it all comes."

"Well, we piss every day and we're no worse for wear. Clay? Come now, that was at least a little funny."

"Funny funny. That was a little funny..." He rocked. "You said something, didn't you, Nile? You said something, and I don't know what you said." Tears welling in his eyes spilled over. "I don't want to be a freak, Nile. Make it stop."

I gasp, pulling myself back. I had lost my twin within a week. How long until I lose myself? The physicians were right to have worried about me once Clay's symptoms showed. Elemental attraction runs in families. And then my wound, my fever...

I sink my teeth into my hand to keep from whimpering. No one must learn of this. They will put me off the ship. They will send me home and hide me away from pitying eyes, like they do Clay. There will be no cure, no future, no life.

Bile creeps into my mouth. I sprint from the gunroom, barely reaching the deck and the ship's rail in time to vomit overboard. Behind me, the sailors on watch erupt in laughter.

A seasick fish bait. My body bends with heaves. I grip the

rail until my stomach has nothing more to bring up and then sink to the deck in a quivering heap.

A boot nudges me. "You are in my way."

I swipe my sleeve across my mouth and look up at Domenic. It's hard to believe he's the same man who'd given me his coat on the beach. Now, his face is stonelike except for something lurking behind his eyes. An expectation. Here I am, my princess self, suddenly and unceremoniously exposed to life at sea. Domenic is waiting for my plea for return to the Ashing palace. He isn't angry. Not even annoyed. Just expectant.

I wish what you think you see was true, Domenic.

I rise to my feet only to scramble back to the rail to vomit anew. That over, I straighten again slowly, holding on to the ship for support. But I do straighten. I will not be fulfilling the first officer's expectations today. My secrets—all my secrets—will remain mine.

"Aye, sir," I gasp. "My apologies."

Domenic's brows twitch in surprise when I touch my forehead, but he says nothing more.

I spend the rest of the day white-faced. When night settles, I receive a thin hammock from the *Aurora*'s quartermaster and sling it in Ana's cabin, which the small girl has transformed into a shrine of homey impracticality. A tangle of pretty lace and cosmetics fills the box where others keep pistols, an embroidered blanket covers her sea chest, and small bright pouches of apple cinnamon incense hang from the overhead.

All my belongings fit into a single seabag I hang from a peg with shaking hands.

Lying in that darkness, smelling the dried apples native to Felielle, I burrow in the rhythmic swaying of my hammock. The tentative hold on my panic snaps like a twig. My heart runs. My breaths come quick and shallow, but I can't seem to get enough air into my lungs no matter how hard I try. My hands tingle, constricting into stiff, painful claws. *I can't do this,* I whimper silently. *I can't live as a Gifted.*

Do you want to give up and die, then? asks my mind's voice. It's cool and confident and reminds me of Captain Fey.

No, I tell it.

Are you certain?

I think awhile. There is too much I have to do still. Too much I'd promised Clay. *Yes, I'm certain.*

Then you better start figuring out how you'll handle your magic, before it makes the choice for you.

I agree with the voice and dig my nails into my arm, the pain giving me something to rivet my mind to. My breaths quiet slowly, painfully. My mind's voice is right. If I don't get myself under control now, I may die before I have to worry about living.

But how? My thoughts race beneath the surface of consciousness. *Evade. Resist. Refuse.* Yes. That's right. I will let this go no further. No air calling. No experimenting. No raising suspicions. I shall do nothing different tomorrow than I did yesterday. I will not give one inch of indulgence to the magic until I must.

Perhaps today's episode was nature's odd mistake, like a rogue wave, and will trouble me no more.

Mind over disease, I tell myself. Life one secret day at a time. Starting now.

Releasing my forearm, I draw deep, even breaths and listen to the ship's sounds. The lap of water against our hull, the quiet calls of the watch above, Ana's subtle snoring. These are the sounds of my new life on the *Aurora*.

In the morning, Captain Rima declares an end to my acclimation period and orders a bosun's mate, the yellow-eyed Eflian Johina, to put me to work. Work is never in shortage on a man-of-war that requires a thousand tasks a day to keep it trim. The main deck is filled with people under the notional supervision of the two oldest midshipmen, Kederic and Ana. Two more middies, twelve-year-old twins, Song and Sand, chase each other in the shrouds. They wear their hair shaved in a diamond, like the captain, and someone tells me the boys are Rima's nephews. In truth, many of the Eflians have diamond or crescent cuts. Ten-child families are common on the east side of the continent, so it's possible—even likely—that many of the Eflian crew are at some level related.

I've just registered the light drizzle and a favorable wind blowing toward south southwest, when Johina shoves me between the shoulder blades. I fall neatly onto my hands and knees beside a row of similarly positioned sailors. A stone used in daily deck cleaning is thrust into my hands.

"Push forward, pull aft." Johina little bothers to conceal his opinion of my intellect. The wave of tattoos decorating his face falters when it crosses the bridge of his nose, which has obviously been broken at least once. "Forward. Aft. Repeat."

I glare at him. I've given the man no cause to think me a dimwit or a shirker. A short, respectful instruction would have sufficed. I clench my jaw and break away from his gaze. This isn't personal. It is the common crudeness of the lower deck that I had thought myself prepared for. Nile Ash has yet to earn the privilege of courtesy.

Keeping my mouth shut, I bend to the task I'd once supervised each morning. A pair of men dump a bucket of seawater on the deck before me, leaving the front of my shirt and the knees of my britches soaked. Another pair of seamen sprinkle sand. The combination grinds my skin as efficiently as it does the *Aurora*'s planking. The stone itself proves heavier than I expect, and my back and arms soon burn from the effort. I roll my shoulders to relieve the pressure and glance at the men beside me. They work in the effortless rhythm I am used to seeing. What trick have they for the task? Surely I am missing a small, vital technique that makes the hour-long chore bearable. I lean forward, studying their movements.

The line of fire across my shoulders catches me unprepared. I cry out, arching my back and searching for the source of the assault.

Johina stands over me, hefting a knotted rope's end in his hand. "Slide the stone forward and aft." The mate's eyes gleam with righteous satisfaction. "Gawk at the men on your own time. Or better yet, from ashore."

My face heats, my fingers curling around the stone to keep my tongue in check. The rotted sadistic goat's son probably can't find his own rear without a map and guide flags. And now he's adding insult to pain, enjoying his bite of power. I've seen his kind before.

Johina shifts his weight, seeking a reason for a second strike.

My heart beats faster than I wish. I resume scrubbing. Beneath my shirt, the filling welt burns. I don't want another one. *Storms and hail,* I really don't want another one. Is this the trick of the men beside me? Fear? I feel Domenic's eyes on me and, instead of whimpering, keep my face as still as Captain Fey taught me to. I'll lick my wounds later. In private.

Domenic walks away.

The wind comes then, soothing my back with its cool embrace. It brushes against my magic. *Let me in,* the air seems to say. *I will feel good. Like wine down a parched throat.*

Gritting my teeth, I push my stone forward and aft.

Once the decks are stoned and rinsed to Domenic's satisfaction, my watch is permitted to breakfast. I follow the rowdy mob down to the gundeck, where the ship's men sleep. The hammocks have been piped up already, and tables now hang between the guns.

I hesitate.

As a midshipman and officer, I took my meals with others of my kind. The common seamen all eat together, dividing themselves into messes of eight or ten. Will any of these ready-formed groups welcome—or at least tolerate—my presence? My gaze sweeps the room. The ship's divided sects are plain here, where the crew has their choice of companions. The Eflians occupy the prime tables. They make up about half the ship's company and speak loudly. The women have their own mess. Seeing me, they turn their backs. The Biron and Felielle natives fill a couple of tables each. Only the foremast jacks—the highest-skilled seamen who work at the top of the rigging—form a mess that transcends nation lines.

In short, I have no place to go.

But then, I'm not looking for friends. In fact, in light of my new Gift, the farther the crew stays away, the safer I am.

The black-clad marine boys go silent as I approach their table. I would be a supplicant to any sailor mess I approach, but here I am simply an intruder.

I sit.

The Spades' glares threaten to push me off the bench.

I reach for the bread box and retrieve a piece of ship's biscuit, tapping it against the table to evict the weevils. *Don't mind me, lads.*

An older boy clears his throat.

Heads all over the gun deck swivel toward us. I fill my cup with water and wash down the hard tack. I have as little to say to the marines as they do to me, and the sooner this is clear, the better. I may know little about life on the lower deck, but I've an abundance of experience living alone in a crowd. Another bite of biscuit. Another gulp. And soon the marine boys resume their conversation, giving me little more notice than they had to the empty seat.

12

EVERYONE IS WET, COLD, AND on deck. We've been sailing south from Ashing toward the Siaman Sea for a week, half of it under rain. Open seas, with no sight of land, span to the horizon in all directions. Lightning cracks across the waves, heralding thunder. Glorious white flashes break the drab afternoon sky. The weather teased us with a bit of sun this morning, but has worsened by the hour since. The southeast part of Lyron, where we head, sees very volatile weather, cold and stormy one day and warm the next. Without access to instruments, I've trouble tracking the *Aurora*'s movements. The middies' noonday calculations put us in the Felielle capital.

The wind calls to the magic inside me, demanding I let it inside. I turn my back to the wind and breathe on my hands to warm them. Three bells of the afternoon watch toll across the deck, announcing half past one in the afternoon. We last trimmed the sail a quarter hour ago, and my fingers are chilled stiff and raw from hauling rope.

But it's a comforting misery. It reminds me that I am at sea, alive, and, as far as anyone knows, healthy.

The *Aurora* rises and drops over the waves, the volatile gales flogging her sails. Both the captain and Domenic are on deck, which, despite the morning's efforts, is a mess of ill-coiled ropes, poorly furled sails, and hammocks shoved haphazardly into the netting. I keep out of Rima's way. Domenic flips up the collar of his oilskins and accepts a cup of steaming coffee from a ship's boy. I doubt Domenic has eaten today at all. He hasn't left the deck. And from what I've seen, it's he who has kept the Aurora afloat, even if he's employed a rope's end liberally to make it so. I'm careful to give him no cause to touch me with it. It was horrid when Johina struck me, but I don't think I could bear it if Domenic did. He is the one truly good seaman on this bloody ship. I don't need his friendship, but professional respect? I do want that. I have my pride, if not the quarterdeck.

"Goddess save us," Rory, a young Felielle seaman beside me, whispers to himself as he stares up into the shrouds. He's slipped descending during the last sail change, but fortunately, his hands held firm to the ropes and no harm came from the misadventure. "I can't go up there again."

Well, maybe some harm.

"You will be all right," I tell him.

Rory's gray shirt is soggy with rain. My own clothes likely look no better, and the wind chills me through wet cloth. He shakes his head, and I stifle a frown. Rory needs to get a hold of himself before his own thoughts spiral him into disaster.

We'll be changing sail again shortly, I'm certain, and I force my body to keep moving until then. Four of the middies are working up in the swaying rigging. Of the four, only Ana appears aware of the deathly danger, her movements slow and choppy in contrast to Song and Sand, who scamper like monkeys. A fresh wave strikes our hull, jerking the ship. I clamp on to the rail for balance. Ana shrieks.

My breath catches as I watch her hold on the ropes waver. "Hold fast!" I holler to her over a sudden pounding headache, but the wind steals my call.

Her grip trembles but holds, and I breathe easy again, though the headache remains. The pressure pains had disappeared for three days after I fainted in the gunroom, but then returned, laying siege, trying to catch me under stress or fatigue. I shake it off. It's just a headache.

"What was that noise, Mr. Dana?" Rima frowns up into the shrouds. "Has one of the piglets escaped and donned a middie uniform?"

A few men and women chuckle.

Bastards. I scowl at the captain's back.

Domenic checks the weather glass and shakes his head. "Shall we reduce sail, sir?"

Of course we should, but no one is asking me.

"Did you hear Dana?" Rory whispers. "The sadistic bugger wants to send more of us aloft to mess with the sails. We'll fall, one of us." He looks out at the angry sea the *Aurora* is riding, and his face pales. "We'll never pull a man up from overboard. Not in this sea."

"Reduce sail?" Rima barks. "You would make the *Aurora* late to the convoy, Mr. Dana? And what will you tell the merchants whose ships get ransacked while they wait? That the *Aurora* was so soft, it feared a bit of sea? That we failed to protect them because we were too frightened to set sail?"

"We'll be of little aid to the merchants if we lose a mast or steerage, sir," Dana says evenly.

"We shall lose neither," says Rima. "Not in this little breeze. If you care nothing for our charges, then consider the effect on your career if the Admiralty believes us so lazy as to stall our orders."

Domenic's cheeks redden, and several pleased smirks run among the deck crew. I think such disrespect toward a ship's first officer—the next in command after the captain—is disgusting. Especially before the hands.

Rima strokes his mustache. "One thing, though, Mr. Dana," he says in quieter tones. "These seas are unsafe for the inexperienced midshipmen. Recall Song and Sand to deck, if you please."

Rima's two nephews. My mouth thins. Not even a show of impartiality.

None of the hands look surprised. Or offended. I'd once had an Eflian diplomat advise me never to trust a man who showed no bias toward his kin, for a man with little loyalty to family would have none to a stranger.

"Tamim, Rory." Domenic calls out names without looking at the crew. "Relieve Mr. Song and Mr. Sand aloft."

Beside me, Rory jerks, takes a step forward, and freezes. His eyes widen, skidding between the shrouds and the sea. He teeters on the edge of refusing the order, and if he does… I tighten my jaw. I've *ordered* sailors aloft by means of lash, and their faces haunt me since. It is unjust but necessary. A ship of war demands work in the shrouds.

Domenic turns, seeking for the cause of delay.

Rory licks his lips. "I don't think I can just now, sir, just this once."

"You don't think you can." Domenic adjusts his hat. His voice is cold. "You may think on your own time. On mine, you will do what is needed."

Waves and hail, Domenic. Rory is young and strong, but he is too frightened to be of much use aloft just now—if he will go at all. I'm starting to doubt the probability of the latter.

Rory's face is ashen now, and his hands tremble at his sides. Domenic should have looked before he gave his orders. He hadn't, and that put him on a likely path to having to flog the young man.

Unless I throw them a lifeline.

I take a step forward and place myself before the first officer. "I volunteer to go up, sir."

13

A SMALL MURMUR RUNS AMONGST THE HANDS. Domenic looks down at me. "Ash. I was unaware I'd asked for volunteers."

Anger flashes in my eyes. Surely he understands where the mess with Rory is heading. I'm giving Domenic a means to avoid a flogging, to change his order before it's refused. And the damn man is hesitating. I long to yell as much back at him, but I square my shoulders and pierce him with my gaze instead. The pressure in my head grows, pounding in rhythm with my heart.

"Seaman Rory." The warning in Domenic's voice chills me. "Relieve Mr. Sand, if you please."

Nothing. No movement.

I shift my weight, blocking Domenic's view. I demand his attention.

Domenic's eyes snap to me, ice blue against the challenge of my gaze. His shoulders square in echo of mine. "Rory." Domenic's voice is low, and, despite directing his words to the seaman, it's me he watches. "I will repeat myself no further. Go."

My nostrils flare. *Is the crew right, Domenic? Do you savor blood?*

"I..." the young man stammers, and I know I have lost. A dark, scathing dread burns my chest. Rory's voice chokes, and he breaks into sobs.

The locked gaze between me and Domenic smolders.

"I cannot do it, sir," Rory blurts out behind me. "I won't go up there. Not now."

Damn you, Domenic. I turn my back on him and stare at the sea. Behind me, a pair of Spades escorts the sobbing seaman off deck, and Domenic calls out another name in Rory's place. I feel the weight of several eyes stray to me and ignore them. I want no conversation. Eventually, the men and women return to their business. All but one. When I turn back to the deck, Catsper is watching me.

That evening at dinner, one of the marine boys passes me the bread box.

Twee DEEE, the bosun's pipe calls across the deck. The weather is mockingly bright and cheery after yesterday's storm and rain. *Twee DEEE*. "Captain's Mast! All hands to witness punishment!"

I am nauseated, have been since last night. The magic in my body increasingly thirsts to call the air that I know will choke me. Holding the wind at bay is harder each hour. Dredging up a stoic face, I join the herd of the ship's company climbing up to the deck, where Captain's Mast will be held.

Catsper's Spades are already there, mustered on the raised poop deck to ensure order. They stand in two tight black lines, their backs as straight as their muskets. Each boy stares straight ahead and holds his weapon at an angle as perfect as his neighbor's. The captain, officers, and middies stand beside the marines. Dark blue coats with brushed tails, clean white linens, polished buttons. Domenic's perfect face is as cold as Ana's is pale. Captain Rima projects an impressive mix of determination and compassion.

Below the poop, the quarterdeck is clear except for a metal grating, rigged upright. The rest of us fill each square of the remaining space.

"Captain's Mast has begun. Bring forth the accused," Domenic orders, reading from Lieutenant Kazzik's list. "Rory, ordinary seaman," Domenic reads. "Johina, bosun's mate. Mic, able seaman."

The three men step forward, flanked by Spades. Rory's eyes are lined with the silver of unshed tears.

I despise punishment, as had Captain Fey. But hundreds of souls cooped for months and years aboard a ship need order for survival, and officers have precious few options for enforcing discipline. On land, the courts may jail a man or demand a fine. A ship can hardly run a prison, and, since men and women have no need for money aboard, a fine will only take food from their families. Unpopular duty answers for minor offenses but much of the ships' mandatory work is tedious and long. Ship discipline requires sharp reminders, quick to administer and leave in the past. A seaman who refuses an order has to be flogged. But a good officer knows when an order should not be given.

I glare at Domenic. This need not have happened to Rory, Domenic. Not when there was a choice. He was frightened, not insolent.

I have to calm down before I feel sick. Sicker. This isn't my ship. I've no word in these proceedings. I am Nile Ash. Fish bait. I am one face of two hundred in the crowd, and the less mind anyone pays me, the better. I can't help Rory, just as no one can help me. Biting my lip, I copy the half-curious, half-dread-filled posture of the seamen around me and disappear among them, alone on a cramped deck.

Captain Rima examines the trio. Johina stands tall. The black diamond on his head is freshly shaved, as is the crescent on Mic's. Rory's blond hair is pulled into a tight tail. "Bosun's mate Johina?" Captain Rima frowns at his clan mate. "Why is he in this crowd, Commander?"

"Dereliction of duty, sir," Domenic answers crisply. "On the second day of this week—"

Rima puts up his hand, cutting Domenic short. "Ah. Yes. I know now of what you speak. I have already addressed the matter with Mr. Johina and am satisfied that it stemmed from a misunderstanding. No man derelict of duty could hope to achieve the post of bosun's mate, not on my ship." The latter is directed to the crew and, I think, to the far off Admiralty. "The *Aurora* has the highest standards in the League." He turns to Domenic. "No need to further pursue a matter I have already addressed. Move on, Mr. Dana."

Johina touches his forehead in solemn salute. The captain has not surprised him. Or me. Or the crew. Being an Eflian has its privileges on the *Aurora*. Being an Eflian with the diamond haircut of Captain Rima's clan carries even more.

A few steps behind Johina, Rory watches his own feet and quivers. He has no diamond haircut. He is from Felielle.

My initial nausea still brews, but a buzzing now fills my ears. Even the minor excitement of indignation has made ignoring the wind's pull more difficult. But I have to ignore it. I've not had a single convulsion that is the signature of an air caller's symptoms, and I'm certain it's my refusal to give in to the temptation of air calling that's keeping the disease at bay.

The pressure behind my eyes threatens to burst my blood vessels. I focus on my breath. In and out. Steady and uniform. Just like the crowd around me. I should stop paying mind to the Mast. I can change nothing here. Unfortunately, after the years of standing with the officers, the self-mandate is more difficult than it sounds.

On the poop, Domenic moves on to the second man, Mic, who shares Johina's mess.

"Mic, rated able, stands accused of dereliction of duty. Three days past, Mic was found asleep while his watch was on duty."

Found is the key word in that sentence. Mic sleeps through more work duty than he joins. I watch as the man crumples the hat he holds in his hands. The wind ruffles his shirtsleeves.

Wind. I want it.

Rima's brows pull together. "A serious accusation. What have you to say, Mic?"

Mic licks his lips. "Aye, sir, I know the accusation is serious. But I never did the crime, sir. I swear on my mother, sir. Mr. Johina was the bosun's mate on duty, and I am certain he could vouch for me. I think perhaps there was a mistake made, begging your pardon, sir. With Mr. Dana being belowdecks at the time and all."

"How about it, Johina?" Rima asks the recently freed mate.

"Never a moment without doing his duty, sir," Johina replies. "May the gods strike me dead if I am lying."

Captain Rima sighs, rubbing the bridge of his nose. "Mr. Dana. How came you to learn of this alleged transgression?"

"It was reported to me by Midshipman Kederic, sir." Domenic nods to the youngster to speak.

Seventeen-year-old Kederic raises his chin. "Aye, sir. I found Mic asleep on the gun deck, facedown between two guns. I requested that he rise and return to his duty, but Mic ignored me utterly. I thought perhaps he was ill, sir, and reported the matter to Mr. Dana." More likely drunk than sick. The hat in Mic's hands deteriorates to a shapeless wad. He shoots a glance at Johina, but the mate's gaze is locked on the captain.

Captain Rima takes his time turning to the middie. "Mr. Kederic, you found a man facedown, belowdecks, in the gloom. How certain are you that you identified him properly?"

"I'm fair certain, sir," Kederic replies at once.

"Mr. Dana is about to have a man flogged on *your word*, young man," Rima snaps. "And the best you can give us is 'fair certain'? You better think hard, Mr. Kederic, as to whether there is any chance, however slight, that you may have been mistaken when you identified a seaman by the back of his head."

At seventeen, Kederic is getting ready to stand before a lieutenant's commissioning board. He swallows, but his shoulders stay square. He will stick to his guns. Good lad.

Rima rubs his goatee and leans slightly toward the midshipman. "It is difficult for a middie on a Joint Fleet ship, I know. You must prove yourselves to your officers and to the crew. You must lead men who've spent years more at sea than you have. Men whose reports may have seen you embarrassed or even punished. It is hard, I know. I've also known a midshipman or two who have tried to play out personal grudges during Captain's Mast. Or else enjoyed the power of seeing men hurt." The captain squares on Kederic now. "I warn you now. I will have no petty tyrants on this crew. These seamen deserve better. The *Aurora* deserves better. The League deserves better! Is that understood?"

Bloody waves and hail.

Kederic, whose face now turns crimson, touches his hat. "Aye, sir! But—"

"Let me thus raise the stakes for half-truths," Rima continues. "I shall take your word, Mr. Kederic, but should I later learn that you were mistaken, your uniform will offer you no protection. I will have you strapped to the grating."

Kederic's face turns from red to pale.

Rima holds the silence a moment longer. "Now then, is it possible you were mistaken in your report?" he asked kindly.

"Aye, sir," Kederic stammers. "It is possible."

I stare in stunned silence as Mic steps from the quarterdeck. Around me, the crew gazes on Captain Rima with loving eyes. To the Eflians, he is loyal kin. To the others, he is a savior and champion, the only protection they have from the hated officer who doles out savage discipline. In the land of Domenic's lash, Rima is hope. Rima smiles compassionately at his admirers. *I am here for you,* his eyes say. The bloody nepotist is supposed to be here for the *Aurora* and her mission.

Stop it, Nile. Stop looking, stop listening, stop thinking. I dig the nails of one hand into the soft webbing between the fingers on the other and focus my attention on the resulting sting. The wind bats at me. My knees buckle as I reject it. If I don't calm myself, I'll lose the fight.

Rory stands alone before the mast now, crying without a sound. He stares pleadingly at Rima, searching for any thread of reprieve as Domenic mercilessly reads the charge. Refusal to follow orders. Refusal to fulfill duties. Cowardice. I try not to listen.

"Very well, Rory," Captain Rima's voice drags me back to the proceedings. Rima's eyes are sad, as if the matter touches him personally. "Have you anything to say for yourself?"

Rory shakes his head pitifully. "It was only the once, sir. Just that once. It will never happen again."

Rima sighs. "I would aid you if I could, Rory, but I fear this is Mr. Dana's territory."

"Seaman Rory. You are guilty of the charges." Domenic doffs his hat. "Two dozen lashes. Remove your shirt."

Rory's hands shake. I look down at the deck.

"Nile Ash," Domenic says suddenly. "Come up to the front row, if you please. I believe you will have a better point of vantage there."

I jerk and stare up at Domenic. Is he bloody joking?

His gaze holds mine. Waiting.

Understanding dawns on me slowly, a burning that starts in my chest and grows until my body is aflame. This punishment is not just Rory's, it is also mine. Mine for interfering with Domenic's command. Fine. "Aye, sir," I say clearly and step forward into the passage the mob of crewmen opens before me. Two marines tie Rory's hands to the grating. A bosun's mate—at least it is not Johina—takes the cat-o'-nine-tails from its bag.

"Do your duty," Domenic intones formally, and the Spade drummer boy starts a roll.

I make myself watch Rory, as Domenic commanded. Blood comes with the third lash. Screams with the fourth. My knees shake. Several sailors glance my way, smirking. *Storms and hail.* I've seen floggings before. I know how to keep a straight face. Or at least, Princess Nile of Ashing had known. But right now, Rory's agony fuels my own. Each second I deny the wind is worse than the last. I sway, the pressure in my head unbearable.

Domenic stares right at me. Ensuring I am learning the meaning of ship's discipline.

I clench my fists but stare right back. My heart races as quick as the rolling beat of the drum. *It's not I who needs the lesson, Domenic,* my mind yells through clenched teeth. *It's you.*

And then I can't fight the pressure anymore. I drop to my knees and grab my head with my hands. The magic calls to the wind, and it rushes to me, a sudden gush that ruffles the deck. I choke on the flow, unable to hold the floodgates closed a moment longer. My lungs stretch and burn. I fold into myself. I'm drinking air so quickly, I can't breathe. The edges of my vision darken. I'm aware of the world a heartbeat longer, and then I crumple. The darkness finally stifles the piercing of Rory's screams and Domenic's eyes.

14

I SUCK AIR INTO MY BRUISED LUNGS, feel them expand and hungrily gulp down more. My pulse races in terror. Each breath threatens to gag me again. To suffocate. To kill.

"Nile."

I open my eyes. Ana and Domenic are leaning over me. With them, my memory swims into focus. Rory's flogging. The pounding in my head. My surrender to the unchecked onslaught of air and the quick, agonizing darkness. *Storms.* For the first time since I was eight, doubt about my place at sea twists my gut.

"It's all right," Ana says, her hazel eyes haunted as she strokes my hair. "I'll take you below."

Domenic says nothing, but he watches my every move from behind that gaze of cobalt blue. His wide, powerful body shields me from the crew. Not in kindness, I don't think. He's simply large and, apparently, interested in seeing my reaction up close.

I'm tempted to give him a vulgar gesture but am smart enough not to.

I push myself up. The pain eases, but my lungs burn as if I'd run for miles. I feel the bile rise from my belly a moment before it exits, and I leap to the rail to vomit.

"No place for women at sea," voices say to each other behind me.

"Lionitis's fish bait. What did ya expect?"

"A disgrace. I told you. Hard enough without that aboard."

The last is said in a woman's voice. I know my display little helped the standing of the *Aurora*'s women's berth. Heat fills my face.

"Don't listen to them." Ana takes my arm and whispers into my ear. "I've seen blood make many a seaman dizzy."

"Lionitis." Domenic's voice makes Ana flinch and sends others scurrying from sight. "Find employment elsewhere for the next few minutes, if you please."

I climb to my feet as Ana leaves, but keep a hand braced on the rail for balance. I want to be anywhere but facing Domenic right now. He tilts his head to the side, studying my face. The concerned look is unsettling.

"Nile, listen to me," Domenic says quietly, almost gently, once our privacy is secure. "*This* is life at sea. Your stomach will settle if you stay on, but the work, the danger, and the discipline—those will stay constant forever. You've done far better than I had predicted, but there is little more to gain from continuing the experiment. Have you something you wish to tell the captain now?"

It takes a moment before the words register. When they do, my body tenses like a coiled spring. My pulse quickens, and the color in my face is no longer from shame. There is no way in the deepest hell that I will surrender before Domenic. The sudden steel behind my gaze as I lock eyes with him surprises even me. "You are a goat's ass for flogging Rory."

Satisfying surprise flickers over Domenic's features before the mask of cold indifference snaps back into place. "Competence aloft takes years of learning," he says with condescending chill. "If you'd mounted the rigging in that storm like you'd wanted, you'd have been dead before you got useful. I don't expect you to understand."

Our gazes stay on each other in silent battle until Domenic turns on his heel. "Be about your duties, Ash," he calls over his shoulder. "And remember you are under the same discipline code here as your shipmate Rory."

I stalk to my berth and slam the door hard enough to make Ana's potpourri bags fall from the overhead beams and topple a lantern she's left precariously atop her sea chest. Our berth is large by ship's standards, meaning that with my hammock rolled up, there are two steps of space between her cot and the opposite bulkhead. Right now, it feels like an apple cinnamon coffin.

The anger boiling inside me is hot enough to burn the whole bloody ship to a crisp. The bastard threatened me. Worse, he accused me of knowing nothing of the sea. Of incompetence of all things.

"I don't think Dana meant insult on that front," Ana says carefully, and I realize I spoke my last thought aloud. She sits cross-legged on her cot, a book with diagrams of the human body spread on her lap. I originally thought her sea chest was filled with clothing, but it's mostly books. Anatomy, botany, biology. Mathematics, navigation, and naval strategy texts are conspicuously absent from her collection. "You've been at sea less than a fortnight. Goddess, I don't believe I just defended the Savage." She shakes her head, her ponytail swinging like a pendulum. "About what happened and the crew... Listen, Dana is the one who ordered the lashes. And he'll do it again next week, to someone else. And the week after that. No one should ever get used to brutality, but the crew has. Your feelings are sane, Nile. You are the one in the right."

Ana means the words to balm my spirit, but they remind me of the fraud I am instead. A part of me just wants to tell Ana the truth—that I've seen dozens of floggings; that I've ordered some; that I'm concealing a disease that would get me put off the ship faster than Rory can drown his pain in grog. At the very least, the truth would make her despise me now and save the trouble later.

Instead, I force a weak smile, as if her attempts to raise my spirits have succeeded, and steer the discussion away from myself. "What brought you to sea, Ana?"

She chews her lip, considering the question. Or her answer. I wonder if I've given offense before she finally speaks. Her voice is thin and lovely. A bit like my mother's, though without the self-assured confidence. "There was little choice in the matter, I'm afraid. My family's of noble birth, but the war brought about hard times. We owed tax we could not pay. It was my brother's duty to pay tribute by taking up arms, but he refused. So it was either me or shame." She pauses and wrings her small hands. "Greater shame. Anyone from Felielle who sees me would know my family's failures. But...but at least we will keep our birthright. My children will be of noble blood."

"Children?" The word feels odd on my tongue. Pregnancy would force a woman from naval service as surely as a cannonball. I'd never heard a middie utter it with anything but fear. "Children?"

Ana's face lights up into a rare smile, and she closes her book around a finger. "Oh yes, I shall have children as soon as I escape this floating bucket. You don't think I will be too old in a year or two, do you?"

"No." I press my palm into the bridge of my nose. For a

moment, I had imagined Ana and I had a bit in common, but I was wrong. Perhaps Ana is what my mother wishes me to be. "Certainly, not too old."

"I'd like to run a small apothecary too. There is a forest near my family's estate where you can find fifty different medicinal plants within half a day's walk. I used to sketch the leaves as a girl and compare them to texts back in our library." She swallows. "What of you, Nile? When do you wish to have children?"

The absurdity makes me blink. My contribution to the world can only come from the deck of a ship. It's all I have. "Never."

"Oh! Are you… Do you fancy…" Ana's eyes widen. She leans away from me, the tips of her ears as red as lip paint. "You don't fancy men."

Ah, yes. I had forgotten the cardinal sin of Felielle. Ashing cares for things more important than bed preferences. In Goddess-worshipping Felielle, people with too much time on their hands worry about others' bedchambers. I am about to reassure her, but hesitate. There is that chance again. One nod, and I can castrate this budding friendship before it hurts us both. I am not the girl Ana thinks I am. She wouldn't like me if she knew me. "I fancy men fine," I hear myself say instead. "They do not fancy me."

Ana's shoulders relax as if I had informed her of the war's end. "Of course they do. You are beautiful, especially if you forget to dress yourself as a boy. Truly, Nile. Seamen wear no uniform. It would take so little effort to add a bit of a feminine touch to your tunics." She tilts her head, assessing me like one of the drawings in her texts. Ana is a smart girl, I've learned, but smart in an odd way I'm hard-pressed to understand. "Have you never caught men looking at you?"

I give her a frank look. I've muddied the water with enough fiction for us both without Ana adding spice to the mix. "Men don't look at me, Ana." At seventeen, not only have I never been kissed, but the only man to have ever considered doing so had been a Tirik agent trying to lure me into a trap. Then, he tried to kill me.

Ana arcs a trimmed eyebrow. "Dana does. When he thinks nobody is watching."

Her words hit some target inside my chest. I flinch, my stomach clenching. "Dana is waiting for me to fall flat on my face."

She smiles coyly, but then the mirth fades from her face. "You are right, Nile, he is." Her voice lowers. "I know nothing of the sea, but men... I dare claim expertise on that front. The Savage is pleasant to look at, but there is a reason everyone on the ship stays away. You let your guard down with that one, and you'll be in for a world of pain."

の

"The *Siren*, *Maiden*, and *Solace* have made their signals, sir," Domenic says, naming the three merchant ships in the *Aurora*'s wake. Having passed through the Bottleneck Juncture and sailed east on the Siaman Sea to pick up the merchants, we will now escort them back west. This is our job here in the Siaman—protect merchant traffic. This means occasionally escorting convoys between trading ports and mostly patrolling the waters for threats to neutralize. Small privateers most likely, ones that will be poorly matched against the *Aurora*'s guns. Truth be told, just the sight of a League frigate doing its job will deter most problems. All we have to do is move around a lot. Safe. Repetitive. Boring.

There is simply nothing of great value out here. The islands' vegetation, though lush, is the same as the mainland's. And the Crystal Oasis—one island's unique freshwater source with easy frigate access—is of little use for its remoteness.

Domenic touches his hat and leans respectfully toward Captain Rima. I hate to admit it, but Domenic is crisp in his duties and tightens much of the slack his fellow officers leave behind. "The merchant convoy is ready to set sail."

The weather is with us. Like a horse fresh from the barn, the lively breeze is eager to pull us with the tide. In my mind, I call orders to the signals middie, setting the convoy into formation and letting loose the canvas. In reality, I am on my hands and knees, scrubbing the deck while the *Aurora*'s sailing master is deep in his cups.

Rima puts his hands behind his back and frowns. I can't fathom what has our fearless leader concerned, but instead of setting sail, he sends Song for a spyglass.

The salty air caresses my cheek. I can taste it. The longing to call it becomes an ache, as if I've waited too long to relieve myself. Sooner or later, I will have to. The memory of choking sends echoes of panic through my body. Perhaps if I give release to the attraction before it overwhelms me as it had at Captain's Mast, the effects will be more tolerable. I will have to try it soon. But not just now. Not yet.

I feel Domenic's gaze touch me and become acutely aware of how pathetic I look now, after mere weeks of working with my hands. The abuse from sand and seawater have cut into my skin. My hands are awkward from swollen cracks as I grip the sanding stone.

Song returns with a glass, and Rima trains it on the sea. "Just as I expected. The merchies cannot differentiate their bow from stern. Mr. Dana, drill the convoy, if you please. I will not set sail until I'm satisfied the skippers can handle their ships safely."

My brows pull together. The convoy can drill en route, so Rima's words are a crock of excrement. After all the hurry to get here, why is he now dragging his heels?

Across the deck, Johina emerges with Rory in tow, the

latter pale and cringing but walking on his own. Domenic walks off toward them. Rory steps back, but there is no escape.

"I am glad to see you return to duty," Domenic says coolly and loudly enough for all to hear. "I imagine we've cleared up your misconceptions about who decides what said duty is?"

"Aye, s-sir," the seaman stammers.

"Good." Domenic puts his hands behind his back. "Just to keep Seaman Rory's memory fresh, Johina, please ensure his wounds are cleansed with salt every day for a week."

Rory's knees buckle as Johina grins.

Domenic continues aft to check sails and thus leaves Ana in lone charge of the cleaning efforts. Within ten heartbeats, the pretense of work within the scrubbers' ranks plunges like the weather glass before a storm.

Ana hugs her thin shoulders, working hard on not seeing the increasing loitering. It's a mistake. The commotion increases until a man at the end of my row grunts in pain. A quick glance confirms Domenic's return. He hands the rope's end with which he'd struck the loiterer to a bosun's mate and beckons to Ana. I can't make out his words, but Ana's eyes glisten. I want to punch Domenic in the nose just for that.

"Ten minutes," the sailor beside me whispers. "I will wager you a day's grog ration that I can make Lionitis cry all out within ten minutes."

Ana wouldn't last five, but that's not the point. My face heats at the perversion of naval spirit. I think of little Vast inspecting the *Faithful*'s lifeboats, the able seamen gently helping her along. "How long have you been at sea?" I ask.

"Six years. What's your care?"

I clamp my hand around his wrist. "Six years. You've been at sea six years, and your pleasure is destroying a middie who's stepped on deck six months ago? Coward."

He pulls his hand away. "This here is no charity ship, and I ain't her mama." He turns his face toward me. "And you ain't mine."

I snort and busy myself with my sanding stone. "What do you think Mr. Dana just whispered to her?"

"How in the bloody hell would I know? Probably told her to wear tighter trousers." He chuckles to himself, but I see his mouth tense for a moment.

I lower my voice. "Probably told her that he just beat a man because she failed her duty. Except she doesn't know how to bloody do it, because instead of guiding her, you're busy making bets. So go win your grog ration. You'll win today because she still cares."

The sailor rolls his eyes in reply. But he doesn't make the offer to the man on his right.

By dinnertime, we still have not moved. Captain Rima prowls the deck like a well-dressed hyena, snapping his jaws at weary seamen. Even Johina and Mic are stripped of grog rations for moving too slow. The wind is cool and healthy, and the *Aurora* fights her tether.

I wonder if Domenic knows what Rima is waiting for.

The *Solace* runs up a signal. *Ready to sail.* It's the merchie's third time signaling, and even Ana, doing a trick as a signals middie, knows what the flags say without needing to consult her code book. She looks from the *Solace*'s masthead to Captain Rima, presses her lips together, and keeps silent.

The flags scamper down, and new ones rise in their place. Ana opens her book, and her shoulders sag. She chews her lip, her eyes skid to me in rising panic.

"What is it, ma'am?" I ask, sliding up to her.

"The *Solace* is asking what we are waiting for," she whispers when I step closer. "I do not believe the captain would welcome the question from me."

No, I don't think he would. My jaw tightens. This is no way to run a ship, with the crew fearful of reporting the facts. I touch Ana's arm and march myself to the captain. I cannot do much nowadays, but at least I can bear the fire of Rima's wrath better than a middie with six months at sea.

"Sir." My voice is respectful but loud enough to carry to the crew. "The *Solace* requests reason for the departure delay."

Rima wheels around on me, and I see the distaste in his eyes even before they flash with anger. "Delay?" He spits the word, as if it's sour. "Is there some timetable to which only you are privy, Ash?"

I raise my chin and pretend he's posed a reasonable inquiry. "No, sir."

His brows narrow, the volume of his voice rising with each word. "And has a divine intervention poured naval expertise into your skull today?"

"No, sir. Not today."

"Then pray tell me what gives you the gall to question the operation of this vessel?" Rima is yelling now, and his face is red. He turns to Domenic. "Mr. Dana, I understand that the middie girl dragged this rubbish aboard, but I expect you to manage the crew to some extent, sir!" Beads of sweat gather around the diamond shaved on Rima's head. He looks back at me, his lips pulling back in disgust. "The League Articles mandate that I permit females to infest my ship, but there will be no dual standard or leeway or any other privilege you seem to believe yourself entitled to, Ash."

Privilege? Entitlement? In what bloody ocean is his diamond-shaved skull sailing? My fingers curl into fists, and I hide them behind my back. Striking a ship's captain is mutiny, and I'd be court-martialed and hung in a heart's beat.

"Ash." It's Domenic. He shifts his weight, interposing himself between me and the captain. "Take a trick in the shrouds."

A trick in the shrouds. A mild penalty handed out to wayward youngsters. My gaze cuts to him. I know he is just getting me off the deck. Fine. I turn on my heel and hoist myself into the ratlines.

I climb quickly into the wind, channeling my fury into my muscles. My hands and feet find their holds while the rocking ropes push and sway me with the sea. The burn in my legs is fiercely familiar. And calming. Rima had twisted my words into absurdity, and there isn't anything anyone can do about it. A captain is the god of his ship. But not all gods are created equal. And sometimes, even the best ones fall. Like Captain Fey.

It doesn't matter. I remind myself. Rima does not matter. The convoy schedule, the shipboard communication, the education of the middies—none of it matters. You are here for neither command nor glory. You are here for freedom.

Right. Freedom. Freedom from Ashing politics and freedom to find the cure. The deck shrinks. The sailors, the captain, grow small as children's toys. To the men on the deck, I'm little more than a dark shape silhouetted against the sun. They don't matter, the breeze whispers to me. The breeze thinks I'm here for it. Maybe it's right.

I climb higher, reach the first of three lookout platforms on the mainmast, and continue on quickly. The swaying shrouds make me feel real and alive. I hook my arms through the ropes as the ship sways, tipping me over the deep sea and back again. I breathe in the exhilaration and salt air of the sea.

On the second platform, I stop and hoist myself onto it. Swallowing my pride, I use the bit of rope I keep secured to my belt for small tasks to tie myself to the mast. Until I can predict my body better, it's prudent to be safe when I can. Knot dressed, I lean back on my arms as my legs dangle over the abyss of ocean.

The breeze strokes my face, stirring the magic in my blood. Begging. Demanding. An ache brews behind my eyes, growing with each second I continue to deny myself the release.

I can't hold out much longer. I am as alone as one gets on a hundred-foot ship swarming with over two hundred souls. Rima and his petty manipulations are far below. I close my eyes and breathe to the rhythmic whoosh of crashing waves until my nerves calm. It is time to let my magic off its leash.

15

M Y HEART RACES. THE GAMBIT of painful need and paralyzing fear opens before me. It's as though I am about to shove my face into the barrel of a loaded gun in hopes of resolving a malfunction without the resolution in turn taking off my head. I shift on my perch. Test my tether. Chew my lower lip. I have to do it. I have to do something, and this is the best I can conjure.

I close my eyes and allow myself to feel that magic inside me that keeps shouting *come come come* to the wind. A final breath, and I stop fighting down the magic, letting it play as it wishes.

That's all it takes.

The rush of air hits me like a pistol shot. I choke, writhing and struggling against the current. The air beats against my skin, flows inside where it can. Eyes, nose, mouth, ears. My windpipe and lungs threaten to rip open. I try to push the magic down again, but it won't listen, like a dog kept too long in a cage. *More, more, more.* My magic craves the element that's tearing my body apart. *Storms.* Panic floods my veins. This is how Gifted die every day, with their magic calling an element until it kills them. Fire callers burn to death. Metal callers impale their guts and hearts and eyes with accidently attracted knives. Me, I'll die with the wind ripping my lungs.

I'm scared.

How in the bloody hell did Clay live through this?

That thought seems vitally important, though it's hard to think through the pain. *Clay.* Clay lived. How? I think of him playing with the metal balls. Clay doesn't just attract metal toward him, he repels it too. Back and forth. A magnet. A balance. Control.

How do I control a flow of air?

I stare at the sails billowing all around me and know the answer. Or *an* answer. A sail pointed directly into the wind is ineffective, but one angled to shape the wind's course just so can move ships.

Except I don't know how to do any of that. The only two actions I've tried with my magic have been suppressing it completely and letting it loose. Off and on. Sail lowered, sail raised.

So, I start there. I imagine my body is a sail and push down on the magic on just one side of my body. The left.

The release is as sudden as the *pop* of a filling canvas. One moment, the wind is trying to blow me up like a balloon, and then next it's rushing in from the right to fill the void on my left.

My lungs draw breath, drinking from the fountain instead of choking on the flow. My vision clears. The air that my magic calls flows across my body instead of into it. And...and it feels good, to let the magic out, to use it up. Like emptying an overfull bladder, but a hundred times more powerful. A thousand times.

Even as I construct the puzzle of what's happening to me, I feel the wind rising. The magic wants to be free faster, all at once, *now now now*. The wind I channel whips itself toward a gale. *Storms and hail.* I might be the equivalent of a magical sail that creates its own wind, but I'm also on a mast of a *real sailing ship* with *real sails set*. And I'm going to capsize us if I keep at it.

I scramble to rein the magic back in, hoping I've burned off enough of it to make the shutdown possible. It's a messy affair, and I manage to nearly choke myself before I succeed in suppressing the remnants of my magic into inaction. Once I can breathe again, I collapse against the mast in utter exhaustion.

That was neither pretty nor controlled. But I lived. Living counts for something.

Several bells sound before I can sit up again. I check my tether, relieved to find it sound. That little piece of line connecting me to the mast saved me from toppling to the deck. I reach out to grip the shrouds and whimper. I ache. And while I'm done air-calling for the day, I know I will have to perform this exercise again sometime soon. The very thought makes me nauseous. I rub my hands over my face and watch the waves.

Sobbing is the first noise to shake me from my trance. A childish sobbing, too clear to be far off.

I lean back and look up the mast. Someone is up there, on the lookout platform above me.

I untie my tether and, gripping the ropes, haul myself into the shrouds. The climb feels good despite my muscles' protests. Captain Fey little tolerated his officers engaging in childish games aloft, and I've missed scampering through the ratlines, the exhilaration of shifting ropes, the excitement of soaring high above the world and sea.

I reach the next lookout platform and climb over the

edge into the crow's nest. There is an entry opening by the mast, but the sailor way is to scale the rail, leaning backward for a few moments over the roaring sea.

The boy on the platform is a marine, a young lad who sits at my mess table. He has a glass swung over his shoulder like a musket. Scrubbing his sleeve over his red face, the boy glares at me with all the friendliness of a savage dog. "What do you want?"

I sit beside him and tie myself in. The circular platform wraps around the mast, extending a pace in all directions.

His eyes fix on the line, and he licks his lips. His own hands grip the stays so hard, they tremble. "Tying in is for cowards," he informs me. "No seaman ties himself in."

He is half right. Before today, I'd tether in only if I wished to read or nap in the rigging, neither of which had been permitted after my middie days. But the lack of tether is a matter of logistics—little can be accomplished aloft on a leash. I shrug and lean back on my hands.

I wager Catsper had ordered the boy up here now, in calm weather, to accustom the lad to heights. Only time will alleviate the fear, but the presence of another sailor close by often helps.

The boy squints at me. The tension in his face is easing, and his fingers relax their grip. "You are Nile," he informs me. "You sit in my mess."

"Thank you for the report."

His mouth twitches. "I'm Penn."

"Deck there!" the foremast lookout shouts, interrupting what passes for conversation between Penn and me. "Sail ho!"

I jerk my attention to the sea. This has to be Rima's reason for lingering. "May I borrow your glass?" I ask Penn and feel the metal slip into my hand. I train the glass on the ship. *Who are you?* I wonder. ___

A merchantman by her size, albeit one with an unfamiliar design. A League Merchant flag runs up her mast. Then another signal to give her name, *Hope*. I look down to the deck. Rima is relaxed. I am not. I swing the glass back to *Hope*. Father had started drilling Clay and me on reading ships' hulls, rigging, and handling before he let us step foot on a frigate. I know ships. I remember them. And despite having spent years in the largest trading ports of the six kingdoms, I know I have never laid eyes on the merchant ship *Hope* before.

This is not terribly strange in itself as there are many ships in the League. But what bothers me is that I cannot even place *Hope*'s origins. Possibly the merchant is a Tirik prize, though she varies from their typical build as well. I lean forward, studying the curious little vessel. "We've a visitor, it appears," I say to Penn. "The LM *Hope*."

"The *Hope*?" Penn is little impressed. "She's attached herself to the past half dozen of our convoys."

I lower my glass, suddenly comprehending Rima's heist. Merchants pay a fee to the League Admiralty for a naval escort. If the *Hope* attaches herself to established convoys, she is likely paying fees to Captain Rima's pocket directly. No wonder Rima hurried to the rendezvous point but then, not seeing *Hope* among the waiting vessels, found reasons to wait.

It's disgusting. By taking *Hope*'s escort fees for himself, Rima is not just ignoring League law and robbing the Joint Fleet Admiralty of the fees it needs to maintain the fleet, Rima is also endangering the other ships. A convoy of three ships can move faster and be protected more easily than a convoy of four.

I examine our merchants. The *Siren* and *Maiden* are decent ships, Biron built and sturdy. The third, *Solace*, I peg as a child of an Eflian shipyard, with maneuverability sacrificed for greater hauling space. Those three are our true charges and should take priority. I know they won't.

Hope sails closer and lowers a boat. I wager it's her skipper coming over to give his golden apologies to Rima for the tardiness.

Beside me, Penn draws a sharp breath. I think he is looking down at the tiny deck beneath us, but no. His gaze is fixed on two figures making their way across the rigging. Johina and Mic. The men speak as they climb, the wind carrying bits of the sound.

"—*rat's up there,*" Johina's voice reaches Penn and me.

"I dunno."

"… ordered him up two bells past." Johina climbs a few yards closer. "…little shit… near got you flayed. …learn to keep his trap shut."

I raise my brow questioningly at Penn.

"I was the one to report Mic to Mr. Kederic," the boy whispers, his body tense. There is neither pride nor shame in the confession. A simple statement of fact.

Grunting breaths reach us from below. The shaved diamond and crescent cuts approach our perch. A few heartbeats later, the Eflians come up onto the platform, climbing on the outside of the railing like I had. Johina chuckles at my tether. "Get off, fish bait. I've some chores for the boy, and we'll need the space."

I pull my knot loose and step between Penn and the Eflians. My shoulders settle into a solid posture trained into me as an officer on the quarterdeck. I understand the Eflians' grievance. The lower decks despise rats, even ones whose job it is to maintain order. But no one is going to be addressing the issue seventy feet above the sea. Not on my watch. "Penn, return to deck."

Johina's tattooed face darkens. "You deaf, girl?" He says *girl* with the same foulness Captain Rima had.

"We are both leaving. Pe<u>nn</u>." I jerk my eyes toward the lad. True to his training, the young marine knows authority when he sees it and moves toward the shrouds. I keep myself between him and the Eflians. They'd have to leap around me to grab Penn, and no sailor plays such tricks in the rigging.

"Fish bait's got a mouth," Mic says pointedly.

I wait for Penn to get a couple of feet clearance, then grab onto the shrouds myself. I have nothing to prove, not to these two.

My foot is about to find its hold when Johina's hand snatches forward and closes hard around my wrist.

16

SHOCK SPURS MY HEART. I try to jerk my hand free, but my arm is little match for Johina's strength as he pulls me right back onto the lookout platform.

He grins, showing yellow teeth that match his eyes.

"What in the bloody waves are you doing?" I demand.

Johina bends my wrist painfully, forcing me to my knees beside the mast. "Why, I'm doing you a great favor, fish bait." His face hovers inches from mine, and the reek of his breath fills my nostrils. "I shall teach you to do as you're told and to show respect to our captain. Don't think I was blind to your insolence."

I have a moment to digest the threat before Johina's fist sinks into my gut.

I rock back, unable to breath. My eyes widen. I've never been struck with a fist before, never even fathomed a fight with my own crew. For waves' sake, a sailor would face a court-martial for striking an officer. *But you aren't an officer, remember?*

As if to drive home my thoughts, Mic's thick arms grab me from behind. They snake under my armpits and interlock behind my neck. The hold stretches my shoulders and forces my head forward.

I start flailing, pulling with all my strength against the iron hold. Which is stupid to do on a bloody platform that's barely wide enough to hold all three of us. A foot in the wrong direction and I will fall from the crow's nest and splatter on deck. I open my mouth to scream, but a calloused palm decamps from my neck and clamps over my mouth instead.

Johina backhands me across the face. My head snaps sideways, a trickle of burning blood filling my mouth.

The reality of my predicament finally sinks into my thick skull, and I stomp my heel into Mic's bare foot. He curses and loosens the hold on my shoulder long enough for me to buck my head back, hard. There is a satisfying crunch as the back of my skull connects with something breakable and a slew of curses fills my ears.

Johina's fist sinking into my gut wipes all that satisfaction away in an eye blink. I double over, unable to breathe, and receive another stomach blow for my efforts. Mic regains his hold, pinning my arms behind me.

I raise my head, the only body part I can move just now, and spit into Johina's face.

He elbows me in mine. And then it's Mic's turn for a swing.

By the time Penn returns with Catsper in tow, the Eflians have finished their instruction. I am curled up alone on the platform, the right side of my face burning and my eye already swelling closed. My pride flames as fiercely as my head.

"Were you born stupid or is it the height?" Catsper inquires coming over the rail.

"Both." Talking hurts.

"Get down, Ash."

I uncurl slowly, biting my lip to keep from gasping. My

limbs move because there is no choice. I can't stay up here, and I won't crumple further before the marines. The world frays around the edges of my vision, but my feet find the ropes and my hands tighten around the hemp. One step. Two.

Catsper and Penn stay beside me all the way to the deck. Here heads turn, and snickers rustle through the crew. They know what's happened.

I look straight ahead and follow Catsper's blond head. Step. Step. Step. Perhaps I'll get fortunate and some tsunami will swallow the ship.

I realize we are in marine country only when we approach the Spades' barracks. Catsper shoves me behind him before entering, as if we're heading into enemy territory.

The assessment is not far wrong. Inside the dormitory, black-clad boys chase, shove, and climb over each other like a mob of puppies. One lad launches himself at Catsper, who blocks the attack, tossing the boy over his hip with neither effort nor attention. The contrast between the hard-faced Spades I'd seen on deck and this jovial mob hits me like rain in drought.

The boys register my presence, and the din dies away. Catsper's dog, Rum, nuzzles between the boys' legs and growls.

My heart stalls. Dogs had started acting odd around Clay too, once he was ill. A coincidence. Rum growls at everyone. I take a step back.

Catsper blades his body toward me. He is taller than I and built like a panther. Strong, smooth, and deadly. "You are a guest in Spade's Cove, Ash," he says. "Everything you see and hear in the Cove, stays here. Clear?"

"Aye, sir."

He signals with his hand, and the boys return to mayhem.

Catsper leads me to a bench. Rum, following at his master's heels, continues to growl. Catsper frowns.

I hope Rum dislikes enough people that one more raises little suspicion.

The marine motions me to sit, which I do gratefully. As ironic as it is, the very essence of the crowded jostling of the Cove offers the kind of privacy one seldom finds on a frigate. I touch my face gingerly and wonder if Johina broke anything.

Penn, looking small and miserable, appears beside me with a medicine box, water, and some rags. Catsper dismisses the boy with a jerk of his head and examines my face. His gaze is calm and calculating. "You'll see problems with those two again, I think." Catsper lifts my swollen eyelid. "I recommend you prepare for it. Have you much training in hand-to-hand fighting?"

I blink my good eye. Did the lieutenant of the marines just recommend I seek out a scrap? Even if I had a prayer in taking on Johina and Mic, which I don't, I have little intention of sinking to their level. "Some, sir." I wince. "But I'd rather face the Eflians' wrath than Mr. Dana's in any case."

Catsper catches my chin, forcing my face up. His eyes laugh. "You don't fear Dana, Ash. You are the only sailor aboard who doesn't."

"Not for my lack of trying." Domenic's voice makes me jump. The door slams closed behind him. "What happened?"

"You can bloody well guess what bloody happened." Catsper does not bother turning around, and the general din of the Cove remains steady. I sit up straighter, curiosity battling pain. Domenic and Catsper never speak on deck, but he is plainly a common sight here. Common and welcome. "And then Nile injected herself into the middle of it, with bravery getting in the way of arithmetic."

Domenic removes his coat and neck stock and squats

beside me. His shirt collar falls open, reaching halfway down his muscled chest, where a tattoo snakes along the groove of his pectorals. Stripped of rank insignia, Domenic looks younger, his sea-blue eyes brilliant and piercing. He looks like the stranger on the beach who had shared his jacket and his thoughts. And had listened to mine.

"Are you unable to walk past trouble without sticking your head in?" he asks. With him crouching and me sitting on a bench, our eyes are level with each other, and I notice a small crescent scar marring his left brow. Domenic dips a rag into the water bowl and presses it to the gash along my cheekbone.

I realize it's *salt* water when I feel its harsh sting. I jerk away and glare with one eye.

Domenic's large hand cups the back of my head, locking it in place. Fingers calloused from ropes and weapons press against my hair. "Blame Catsper for the salt water," he says, resuming his task. "He think salt fights off infection and fever."

"The Spardic surgeons think salt fights off infection and fever," Catsper clarifies lazily. "I just parrot smarter minds than mine."

I want to smile, but the recent demonstration with Rory reminds me who I'm dealing with. I lean away. Cove rules or not, Domenic is still the first officer, and fighting is still not permitted aboard ship. "I fell, sir."

He sighs and looks to Catsper. "How badly did they hurt her?"

"Considering there were two sacks of Eflian scum and one her, less than they could have." The marine taps my cheekbone, which I fear will need stitches. "And less than I'm going to."

What in the bloody hell does he mean by that? I tilt my face up to regard the marine with my good eye.

There is a hint of a smirk in Catsper's gaze.

I'm weary, but somehow not frightened. "Is that a threat or a promise, sir?" My words are thick through the swelling.

Catsper's smirk widens. "A prediction."

"Let her recover first." Domenic speaks over my head as if I'm not there. He pushes the bowl of water away and stands facing the marine.

Catsper crosses his arms. "Pity you and your opinions are here in my Cove, Dana. Plus, I believe we can safely say that your methods have failed." He turns to me, and I am suddenly uncertain which of the two men before me is the greater force to reckon with. "All right, Ash. Since in your brilliant judgment the proper course of action upon being confronted with two thugs is to stand between them and the one person who is actually trained to fight hand to hand, pray show me what you are capable of on your own."

"You..." I rub my temple. Are hallucinations a side effect of air calling? "You want me to *fight* you?"

"It won't truly be a fight," Domenic says darkly. He sits on the deck with his arms crossed and shoots a dagger-filled glance at the marine. "He'll knock you about until you can't see straight and then tell you to return tomorrow."

Catsper shrugs. "On your feet, Ash." Despite an amused expression, there is nothing light in the marine's voice. "I wish to see what you know. Besides how to find fights."

No, he's not a hallucination. Just a lunatic. I wonder what he'd do if I refuse, but in the back of my mind, I know. If I refuse, Catsper will shrug and leave me be. And he will never invite me into the Cove again. *And this matters because...?* I ask of myself even as I rise from the bench.

I'm truly unsure who I'm trying to impress, but having tasted the inside of this place, I am prepared to trade a few bruises for right of entry. My head feels heavy, but I don't deceive myself. Domenic is right—I won't hold my own in this fight no matter what state I start in, so the bruises are a moot point. Halfway to my feet, I launch myself at Catsper.

The marine pivots from my path, and my surprise attack ends with my face in the deck. My puffed eye throbs. I push myself to my hands and knees, and then to my feet.

Catsper slams the side of my head with an open palm. "Hands up, Ash."

I cover my head and focus on his hips with my good eye. If I can land a single strike, I will consider this fight a victory. I circle, looking for my opening. I feign to my left and throw my right fist into him. Blind and hard.

Catsper parries my punch and slides forward. He twists as he moves until his back is to me, his shoulder jamming into my abdomen.

I have a second to gasp as I am lifted into the air. The overhead beams rush toward me, and I brace myself.

Catsper drops to his knees in midthrow, and my body avoids striking the overhead beams as I sail over the marine's shoulder.

There is nothing to soften my landing, and my back thuds flat against the deck. I have enough sense to tuck my head, but that's of little comfort. The reverberation of the impact echoes through my bones and knocks my breath away.

"Storms and hail, Catsper," says Domenic, his anger washing over the Cove.

Catsper merely cocks his head at the first officer. "You need not watch, Dana."

"And how in the bloody waves would *that* help?"

He has a point. This little match is going to continue until I'm unconscious, because there is no way I'm either winning or quitting. I collect my limbs and ready for a return attack. In a small way, sparring with Catsper is akin to standing on deck in battle. You can't think of what might become of you.

You must focus on what you can do. And right now, I can get up and try again.

Or perhaps not.

Catsper's knee drops onto my abdomen before I can rise and pins me to the ground. I writhe like a fish, unable to breathe as he grips the fabric of my tunic and pants and pulls up against the pressure of his hold. I shove his knee with both my hands. It dislodges slightly, but now presses my rib. My side explodes in pain, and I scream.

"Enough." Domenic shoves Catsper away.

The marine rocks gracefully onto his heels and cocks an eyebrow at Domenic, whose face turns crimson. The men's eyes lock in silent conversation, the kind only friends can have.

I clear my throat. "How did I do, then?"

"Bad but workable." Catsper rises and walks off to gather the abandoned medicine chest and water. "If your guardian protector permits me to train you without his sage advice, that is," he adds over his shoulder.

I'm unsure what just happened, but I am grateful for the reprieve. Sitting up, I grip my middle.

Domenic kneels beside me, catching my chin between two fingers. I try to pull away, but he holds fast, his gaze examining every bruised and cut inch of my face. "Are you all right, Nile?"

Everything hurts, but no worse than it had. Spectacular as Catsper's attacks had been, he'd not injured me. "I'm not petitioning to be returned ashore, sir."

"Yes. You've made that point clear by now." He frowns at my swollen eye. "Though I must point out that you are unlikely to worry about black eyes as Prince Tamiath's bride."

I struggle up to my feet. "I didn't think I'd need to worry about them aboard a naval vessel either, sir. Not from my own crewmates." It's a shot across Domenic's bow. A properly handled crew does not ambush its mates—and it's the first officer's job to make it so.

I expect a tightened jaw and a dagger-sharp look. But Domenic flinches and turns too quickly on his heels before leaving the Cove.

17

N ILE?" ANA, WHOM I THOUGHT safely on watch, sticks her head into our cabin. It's been three days since my encounter with Mic and Johina, which I told Ana about in detail, and my initiation into the Cove, which I didn't. Three days of her worrying about me and jumping at every creak the ship makes. I'd appreciate the concern over my well-being, except that it comes with unending advice and admonitions. "What's going on here? Why aren't you resting? Did something happen?"

I lift my head, clamping down the magic I'd been slowly releasing, and choke on air. I'm sitting on the deck, my hands braced against my knees. The cabin looks like it had hosted a storm. Which, to be fair, it had. A cough until I get my breath back. The magic in my blood grumbles its disapproval at being cooped up again.

Ana squats to pick up the scattered clothing and papers while I try to convince my body that I am still alive and breathing. I thought letting the magic free in a confined space with less air to attract would be a tame experience, one less likely to kill me and the ship. I was somewhat right, if not nearly as inconspicuous as I'd hoped.

"What happened?" Ana demands again. "Does your head still hurt? Did you fall?" She crouches beside me, her small hands pushing my braid away from my face.

"I fell," I say between breaths. "But it was my own fault. Was trying one of Catsper's tricks. Didn't end well."

She scowls. Catsper has taken to training with me every afternoon but won't give Ana the time of day. A sin of the grandest proportions in Ana's world. She sits back on her heels. "Find some other place for it. Dana heard the commotion from his cabin and was little pleased."

I keep my face still. Domenic has been avoiding me ever since I told him off in the Cove. I think I actually hurt him. Which is as ridiculous a notion as my fretting over its possibility. Domenic couldn't care less about my opinion. Or about me. And yet... The worry in his eyes as he pushed Catsper away and knelt beside me seemed more than genuine—it seemed personal.

But it had seemed just as personal on the Ashing beach, hadn't it? And I remember how that ended. With the truth of my birth mattering more than I did.

I grab onto the bulkhead and pull myself up. "Please pass my apologies to Mr. Dana," I mutter. "It won't happen again."

"Good," Ana says neutrally, though her eyes sparkle with unsettling curiosity.

"Good." I nod, and shuffle past her into the passageway.

"Deck there!" We are at the foot of the companion ladder to deck when the lookout's call sounds.

I straighten at once, listening for more.

"Sail to starboard!" the lookout's voice calls.

The familiar prickle of excitement wakes my senses. "Sail to starboard," I repeat to Ana, who seems to have only marginally registered the words. "Come quickly."

I rush to the deck, Ana trudging behind me. The moment I'm in the open, I turn to the sea. Fog hangs thick under a graying sky, but I can tell the amorphous shape in the distance is large. Too large for a merchantman or one of the small sloops the League favors for carrying dispatches. My blood warms, coursing through my veins with renewed vigor.

Midshipman Kederic scampers up the mast with a glass.

I hold my breath.

"Square rig," Kederic calls down.

Man-of-war. I knew it. My hands tug straight the ghost of a uniform I no longer wear, and I twist back toward the deck, already tasting the order to prepare for battle.

But instead of a crew readying to sprint, I find the deck awash with uncertain whispers. Second Lieutenant Kazzik, the third in charge after the captain and Domenic, has the watch. Kazzik now shifts his weight from foot to foot instead of clearing the ship for action. The wrongness of it all crawls through my skin. I want to shake Kazzik, to grab the drum and beat it myself. *Not your ship, Nile.* I clench my jaw tight. *Not your call.*

Ana scampers over to me. Her hands are white where they press against each other. "What think you?" She bites her lip. "Surely not the Republic. They've caused us no mischief here before."

Oh bloody storms, of course it's the Republic. We are in the middle of a war, and an ally would have signaled before now. Moreover, with the juicy convoy of merchantmen the *Aurora* has in tow, the Tirik skipper probably has his eye on the gold already. The Republic needs the money. Butchering off nobility in the name of equality and the people's power may sound righteous on a public square, but it also left the Republic with no one to properly run commerce. And since taking from the rich is a short-lived source of income, one must forever find new rich to impoverish.

Hence the Republic's mission to liberate the subjects of the Lyron League kingdoms from oppression.

"I think it would be safer to presume the ship is Tirik and be proven wrong than to act otherwise," I tell Ana.

She stares at me blankly. Which isn't entirely her fault. She has too little training for this, and Kazzik, the officer who is supposed to be guiding the middie, is too busy clutching a spyglass in an attempt to divine details he cannot hope to see.

I lower my voice. "You may wish to ensure your division is in order, ma'am."

Ana nods readily, eager to have a task she can manage.

My attention returns to Kazzik, my empathy ebbing to irritation. The man has the deck; it is his duty to call the ship to quarters. That he's unlikely given the order alone before is his problem.

Or mine, it seems.

I give him to a count of five to locate his wits. Kazzik's silence grates on me like nails scraping slate. An amateur ship playing war. Stepping forward, I knuckle my forehead and say, a bit louder than necessary, "Shall I inform the captain and Mr. Dana of the sail, sir?"

Kazzik stares, then jerks his head *no*, dispatching one of the middies for the task. At least he remembered that little of the protocol.

The second officer handled, I turn my attention to the convoy. Four gray outlines in the fog. Hundreds of souls entrusting their lives and livelihoods to us. We should signal the merchants to scatter so that at least some survive if the Tirik overpower our defenses. The Republic can chase down only one runner.

"They are hoisting a flag," Kederic shouts, his voice breaking with excitement. "Red and black. Tirik colors! It's a Republic frigate. Enemy in sight!"

"Thank you, Mr. Kederic." The booming confidence of Domenic's voice precedes his appearance—clean, perfect, and composed, as if he'd not just been awakened. "In the future, a single description will do."

The crew's mumbling ceases such that the creaking of the ship's timber sounds loud in the silence. Even I find myself unable to look away from the first officer.

Domenic puts his hands into the small of his back, surveys the deck, and scowls. His face stays stone still as his chest fills with breath. When he calls out, Domenic needs no speaking trumpet to carry his voice. "We shall beat to quarters!"

18

BOOM, RATATATAT. BOOM, RATATATAT.

The rousing din of the marine's drum reverberates through each plank of the ship. A stampede of bare feet erupts around me.

BOOM, RATATATAT. I fall in with the wave of sailors rushing the deck, clearing anything not nailed in place. Gun crews loose the ropes of the few main deck guns, their counterparts doing the same on the gun deck below. Boys spread sand. Somewhere inside the *Aurora*, carpenters break down the makeshift bulkheads separating the cabins. At the rail, Catsper's marines take up places.

BOOM, RATATAT. Seven minutes and we are still at it. Domenic is giving instructions that should be unnecessary. Rima is nowhere in sight.

The *Faithful*, with near triple the *Aurora*'s armament, cleared for action in three.

I secure a stray bucket another sailor left behind. In the back of my mind, a different marine drums the same beat, different crews man their guns, different boys spread sand. On that ship, the captain stands tall on his quarterdeck, staring at three decks of approaching guns. He must know there is no chance of surviving the attack, but his face says nothing of that. On that ship, I have charge of the gun deck, not buckets.

That ship is gone.

"Captain on deck!" the bosun cries out.

About bloody time. I snap toward the companionway, ready to make a report this captain would never ask me for. The crew whispers. We watch Rima's shoulders emerge from below and his boots stride across the quarterdeck, cleared and ready for battle. What's coming, I wonder, praise for the final result or reprimand for the sloppiness we went through to get here?

Rima puts his hands on his hips. "What is this racket about, Mr. Dana?"

The slap of the words forces me back a step. My jaw tightens.

Domenic's face is a mask of cool calm. He holds his spyglass out to Rima. "A Republic man-of-war on starboard, sir."

Rima brings the glass to his eye and studies the mist. "I do not know her," he declares. His tone is a mix of surprise and offense. "Who has command of her?" He waves his free hand at Domenic before the first officer can respond. "Do not trouble yourself, Commander, you would not know." Lowering the glass, Rima taps it against his palm. "The Tirik Republic has no interest in the Siaman Sea. They will take no action."

My eyes widen.

Domenic shifts his weight and looks into the distance. "Twenty-two guns on her, I believe. Four fewer than us."

"When I want your beliefs, Commander, I shall ask for

them." Rima snaps the glass shut. "Our duty is to our convoy, Mr. Dana. We shall not glory-seek at their expense and I would thank you not to overheat the crew."

"Aye, sir." Domenic touches his hat. My own hands are trembling with cold fury, but his mask of cool indifference stays solid. "Shall I signal the merchants to scatter?"

Captain Rima's cheeks darken, a sharp contrast to the unflinching officer beside him. "The waves take your soul, Commander! Am I speaking for the pleasure of hearing my own voice? My convoy will not act the prey to a ship whose broadside is inferior to ours. We will stay our course. The Republican cowards will maneuver to avoid our guns."

That last bit hits the crew just right. The tension around me shifts fast as a snapped bowstring. There will be no battle, no blood, no death. Some of the hands feel righteous. Their ship shall neither cower nor glory-seek. They are above such things. Others care only that they won't face battle with a ship ill prepared and a crew ill trained. Either way, the men and women around me nod, safe in their understanding.

Not the marines. The boys' gazes are locked, but I find Catsper's. His jaw is tight. He's read Rima's words for the self-serving manipulation they are. Rima wishes to risk neither his hide nor the merchant fees a scatter order will cost.

With a nod and a smile, Captain Rima begins his inspection of action stations, shifting several sailors between posts—more often than not sending diamond-cut Eflians to the safer belowdecks tasks. Apparently, Rima's confidence at avoiding battle does not preclude his preparations for it.

Then there is nothing to do but wait. The day is late, with dusk just a few hours off. The Republic frigate has the weather gage, the favorable position wind-wise. They will dictate the timing of the action, if there is to be any. While all is still calm, Song and Sand replace Kederic on the lookout platform, and Rima orders the cook to bring sandwiches to the crew. I wash my bread and cheese down with water and sit tight, though my blood boils with the scent of coming danger.

As soon as I judge the frigate close enough for meaningful inspection, I beg a glass from Ana and train it on the closing ship. The name painted on her hull reads *Devron* in Tirik, and she handles well in the water. A nimble ship. I swing the looking glass back and forth across her deck, movement along the *Devron*'s ports catching my eye. My chest clenches in recognition. *Waves and hail.* Are the twins bloody sleeping on the platform? "Sir!" I call out, my glass still trained on the enemy. "The *Devron* is opening her gun ports!"

As if it had waited for my announcement, the report of a gun roars from the distance. The ocean rises in a fountain of spray off our starboard quarter.

Several hands whoop.

"Just like the Republic!"

"Cannot hit the beach if they were stranded on it."

Idiots. I snap the glass closed.

"Silence fore and aft!" Domenic orders, then lowers his voice to an even timbre and addresses the captain. "Warning shot across our bow, sir."

The cheering stops.

Fear creeps across the deck in the form of shuffled feet and muffled prayers. Rima's face is pinched.

"Replace the youngsters on the lookout platform with a solid hand," he snaps at Domenic. "I shouldn't have to tell you such basics, Commander." Rima's gaze sweeps the incoming frigate, our merchants, and the *Aurora*'s tense deck. His fingers drum his thigh. It is disgusting and disgraceful, what Rima has done. The man-of-war has caught our captain off guard, and he knows it. He had been so certain his backwater post and lack of previous engagements would translate into continued tranquility, he went to sea without so much as a surgeon aboard. I'd feel glad the Eflian is getting his due, if the crew and merchants were not about to suffer for it.

A heartbeat ticks. Then another. And then Rima raises his face high, reclaiming the poise of the confident—even arrogant—master. "'Tis but a single ship," he announces. His voice is not so deep as Domenic's, but it carries remarkably. "We've no cause to fret. The *Aurora* can easily take a ship of thirty guns, and I'd wager this little scoundrel has but twenty-two to offer us mischief! Is that not right, Mr. Dana?"

A muscle twitches in my temple. If clearing for quarters is any indication of this crew's battle readiness, the little scoundrel will give us plenty to worry about. But this isn't the time to say so. Whatever else Rima might be, he is the *Aurora's* captain. The crew looks to him for survival.

"Aye, sir," Domenic says calmly. "Twenty-two guns on her at the most."

Good answer.

But not good enough. The seamen stay silent. Uncertain.

Rima puts his hands on his hips and smiles. "Is there any man jack on here who doubts the League's honor outshines that of the Republic's dogs?" he demands of the hands.

Scant shouts of "No, sir!" pelt deck.

I add my own voice to the ragged chorus. It's all I can do. Honor will not turn the tide of the coming battle, but a unity of spirit may. And our captain knows it.

Rima feigns to be hard of hearing. A child's move but effective. The hands call out again, louder, in greater unison. *"No! Republican dogs! League honor!"*

The seamen's eyes focus on their captain. They may obey Domenic's orders from fear of the lash, but a goodly number—if mostly Eflian—actually trust Rima to have their best interests at heart. And even those less certain of their captain's holiness are swept along in the vibrant energy of the crowd. The rising din of two hundred voices joining together will wake the most timid spirit. And it does. Even my own heart pulses in reluctant accord with the brewing excitement.

Rima rides the wave of energy just long enough before adding fuel. "Who shall see victory this day?"

"Us!'

"Who will make the Republic cowards regret entering the Siaman?" he shouts.

"The League!"

A moment's pause as he grips the hungry eyes of the crew. "Who will do me proud this day?"

Fists pump the air, and I find mine among them. "The *Aurora*! The *Aurora*! The *Aurora*!"

19

THERE ARE TWO PREPARATIONS for battle any ship makes. The first is the official, practiced routine of sailors and officers attending to their battle stations, readying their weapons and ordering the workspace just so. The second is internal, happening within the soul of every man and woman as they brace themselves to meet gazes with death. Some pray. Others chatter incessantly over things that little matter. Still others face their fears in stoic silence, feeding an illusion of total confidence. As an officer, I've seen it all and have been drilled extensively in the latter.

Which is why the sight of two Felielle seamen opening their wrists with a knife sends me into a frenzy.

I'm about to shout alarm when Ana's small hand touches my shoulder. "It's all right," she whispers quietly. "They aren't trying to take their own lives. They are becoming blood brothers. It's one of the more archaic Felielle rituals, but it counts."

"Counts as what?" My eyes are riveted to the flowing blood as the men press their opened wrists against one another. One of the two has plainly misjudged the depth of the cut and is slowly turning pale. If this keeps up, we won't need the Tirik's help to kill ourselves off.

"It makes them legal brothers, so if one dies, his family will come under the other's care."

"Can't they just agree?" I shake my head.

"An agreement is a word of man. Brotherhood of blood is protected by the Goddess and the law. If we were on land with a Felielle army, a priestess would have been summoned to oversee the rite, but here..."

"Quiet on deck," Domenic commands, ending my conversation with Ana and pushing me aside as he ascends the quarterdeck. "You are a messenger, Ash. Stay out of the way. Mr. Kederic and Ms. Lionitis, join Lieutenant Kazzik on the gun deck below, if you please."

Kederic touches his hat and jogs to the companionway. Ana starts after him, then hesitates and steps toward me instead. Her hand clasps my wrist. "Stay safe, Nile," she whispers. "All right?"

I shift my weight uncomfortably, the warmth of Ana's hand creeping through my sleeve. The fear in her eyes is so raw, I feel that I must say something to cool the fire. Preferably, something true. "The lower gun deck is safer than here. The ship's hull will protect you some down there," I say, nodding toward the ladder. "So help the rest of us out and fire quickly."

A ghost of courage touches her mouth, safety's promise fueling her resolve. "I will." Giving my wrist a final squeeze, she starts toward her station.

"Ah, Ms. Lionitis, one moment, if you please!" Rima smiles as Ana turns toward him and touches her hat. He puts a fatherly hand on her shoulder. "You've impressed me with your improvement since coming aboard, I must say."

I tense.

Ana smiles.

"Point of fact," Rima continues, "I believe you would do well with the upper deck guns. You have it in you, and you must find it. Yes?"

Ana's smile falters.

The bastard pats her on the back, propelling her toward the small battery on *Aurora*'s main deck. "Song! Sand! Down to assist Mr. Kazzik on the gun deck, if you please."

My nostrils flare, and I squeeze my fists tight to keep my tongue in check. At least in this arrangement, Ana will be under Domenic's command and might learn something, though the first officer will have to split his attention with other duties.

As if aware of my thoughts, Domenic beckons the middie to him. "Lionitis, stay with me," he says calmly. "We shall—"

Rima's arm bars Domenic's path. The captain waves Ana away and squints. "You aren't fearful of the battle, are you, Mr. Dana?"

What? I stiffen, my nine years of naval discipline the only barrier to answering the insult on Domenic's behalf. If anyone on the ship is a coward, it's the bloody captain himself. Domenic—

I take a breath. Domenic can take care of himself.

Domenic's shoulders tighten. "No, sir. I hope I've never given you cause to think otherwise."

Rima smiles again. "Very good, Commander. I shall leave this little scramble to you. We well outgun that small ship, and I believe the learning experience will serve you well." Rima taps his thigh. "Do not take too long however, as I hate for the merchants to lose time for the sake of your education."

He has to be jesting. The captain of the *Aurora* did not just decide to hide the battle out in his cabin.

Or perhaps he did. My gaze follows the manipulative bastard as he descends the companionway ladder, and this time I can't help the low growl escaping under my breath. "The captain's confidence in the *Aurora*'s crew is bloody inspiring."

Not low enough.

Domenic spins around, the back of his hand sailing at my lip before his eyes even meet my gaze. He pulls the strike, though the narrowing of his brows promises the next one will land.

"Give my compliments to Ms. Lionitis." A formal naval instruction telling me to deliver a message to Ana. Domenic's voice is cold and the command not strictly necessary, as Ana stands only a few steps away. Still, since I'm to be the messenger during battle, it is best to stay consistent. "And inform her that she shall take charge of our four carronade guns."

Ana. I pull my mind from Rima's antics and turn to her. She doubtless heard the first officer's instruction, but protocol mandates I repeat the command anyway. With the Tirik frigate bearing down on us, its gun ports open and its carnage minutes away, we can't afford to just assume that others heard orders correctly.

Despite first Domenic and then me having informed Ana of her station, the girl makes no move toward the guns. Ana's face is too pale for comfort. I stifle a frown. Ana needs to pull herself together. *Now.*

"No," Ana whispers to me finally. "I cannot do it, Nile. Tell Mr. Dana… Tell him to choose someone else."

"There is no one else." I find her frightened hazel eyes and hold them. "This is your command. Your first. And you will do well. Trust yourself."

"There has to be someone else." Ana's voice catches in the

chasm between panic and despair. Already petite, she seems even smaller now with her shoulders hunched and her lower lip between her teeth. "I don't know what to do."

Waves and hail. I will my voice to calm confidence, as if there is all the time in the world for this conversation. "Listen to your senior men, then. They'll guide you."

Ana blinks from me to her crew. The four sets of men mill about their guns, with much motion and little result. There will be no help from them. My jaw tightens. This isn't my ship. Isn't my crew. But it still is my war, no matter how far I've run. I draw breath. The decision I am about to make is a bad one. But somehow it is the only one I can make. Because even if the men could guide her along, Ana is in no condition to lead.

I thrust a neckerchief into Ana's hand. "All right, then. You will do what *I* tell you. Put this around your ears and straighten up. Taller. Head up."

Ana steps back, wide eyes staring at me. Hers and the gun crew's both. On the quarterdeck, Domenic is maneuvering the *Aurora* in front of the trailing merchants. Whatever else, he's a good seaman, even by Captain Fey's standards. And he will bring our starboard battery to bear soon.

"Lionitis, *now*." My voice isn't that of a friend any longer, but of an officer addressing a middie. "Cover your ears, straighten your back, and pay attention."

And after a heartbeat, Ana nods.

As do I.

"Load the guns," I tell Ana, letting her shout the orders to the men. They'd heard me, of course, but we might as well do things properly. The hands set to work with tolerable efficiency. I hope their resolve will remain in the face of fire.

One at a time, my four gun captains raise their fists. They are ready, but I hold fire. The *Aurora* is only now reaching the outer envelope of her range and the fog makes aiming difficult. It is a game of nerves now, both ships wanting the opening volley. My heart picks up speed.

The *Devron* closes.

The gun captains shift their feet and throw expectant glances at Ana, at me.

I ignore them. We are not close enough. Not yet. It would do little good to send shot harmlessly to the ocean floor only to receive a harsh blow while reloading. Firing well will trump over firing first.

"Fire!" Ana calls out suddenly and much too soon.

So much for nerve.

The gun captains jerk their lanyards. The starboard carronades belch and buck, discharging in unison. The deafening crack of the cannon still echoes in my ears as smoke engulfs the deck. I cough.

The shots fall short of their mark, of course. I want to strangle Ana, but I raise my brow at her instead. The consequences of her order will teach her more than my chastising.

Or they *should*. I don't think Ana, pale and shaking, even sees me.

Domenic does. In the time it takes me to yell, "Reload," Domenic takes in the scene. Our gazes meet over the heads of reloading men and scurrying boys. His eyes are deep and startled, and the sudden comprehension in them sends a shock through me. Then, through the roaring din of action, he mouths two words before turning away. *Carry on.*

For a moment, I stand there, quiet and satisfied.

And then it is the *Devron*'s turn.

A terrible report of great guns shatters the air as the *Devron*'s full broadside discharges at once. Fountains rise where two balls fall short into the sea. Two more pass through the *Aurora*'s sails, leaving clean holes in the canvas. The rest smash our hull. My ears are still ringing from the cannon's harsh boom when, three paces away from me, a man screams as splintered wood rips through him. A moment later, he is still.

Ana crumples to the deck.

My gut clenches. I drop to a knee beside her, the sharp tang of gunpowder filling my nose. "Where are you hurt?" I ask, my hand roving her body.

"I want to go home," Ana whispers. Tears stream down her face.

I continue searching. The ship rolls beneath us, slowly and rhythmically, as if soothing itself. "Where are you bleeding, Ana? You need to tell me."

She shakes her head.

"Ana, are—" I cut myself off. She isn't hurt. Not in the flesh, anyway. Relief washes over me. And fury. And sympathy. I feel them all and have time for none. Grabbing Ana's coat, I haul her to her feet. "You want to live? Then fight."

She ignores me.

The gun crews are staring at us now. Several of the men cower on the deck. Half of those still standing have eyes closed in prayer. Their trust in the command cadre is disintegrating to bilge water, and that *will* get everyone killed. I let Ana go and step forward, my head rising high and facing the wind. "Guns! My guns!" My voice carries over the deck. Heads turn at the declaration, Domenic's among them. The energy of command crackles in the air beside me, and I drink deep, twisting to face my men. "On your feet! Sponge out your guns!"

The crews jump to the task, the drilled motions a shield against terror.

"Load cartridge!" I snarl. "Run out your guns!"

Powder cartridges and wads are rammed down the cannons' throats. The gun captains choose shot to feed their beasts.

A small voice clears her throat behind me. "I'll..." Ana whispers. "I'll—"

"Go help the wounded," I snap, sparing her a shooing motion with my hand. My attention belongs to my crews, and I nod as they finish reloading and push their guns into place. "On the up roll," I call, raising my voice for the captains to hear over the deck's commotion. "Fire as you bear."

"What do you make of our enemy?" Domenic's voice catches me by surprise as the boom of the cannon subsides.

I turn my head to find the first officer behind me, watching as my crews fire and reload the carronade guns again. I wonder how long he'd been there beside me. He asks nothing of Ana.

I reach for my nonexistent hat and touch my forehead instead. Between the fog of cannon and nature, our sight of the enemy frigate is limited to muzzle flashes. "She is moving toward the convoy, sir."

"Yes. But for what purpose? She cannot take them unless she disables us first." Domenic frowns. I do not think he expects an answer, but I give him one anyway.

"Perhaps the *Devron* has something else in mind to amuse us with? A sister frigate hiding in the fog?"

He squints into the mist, but there is no time to reply as a shrill cry from larboard spins Domenic and me around.

"Boarders! Boarders to larboard! Repel boarders!"

I see the grappling hooks clamped to the *Aurora*'s side. Making use of the smoke, fog, and carnage, the Tirik rowboats had caught us unaware. *Devron*'s seamen pour over the side, shouting like rabid animals. Dressed in shirts of faded red, the Tirik men and women lean toward tan skin and light shades of thick hair. More crimson flashes in forms of makeshift armbands and neckerchiefs. The Tirik literally wear their allegiance on their sleeves. As far as I'm concerned, it makes knowing who to kill easier.

"I'm duly amused," Domenic growls under his breath as he draws his sword.

I've time for a half smile before one of the Spades thrusts a cutlass into my hand and Domenic disappears from view. The deck swarms with weapons and bodies. Song and Sand are here, having somehow found their way back to deck with a pair of pistols. One of the boys fires into a man's stomach and stands frozen as the foe looks down at the wound and falls atop another body. One in a middie uniform.

A shove from behind jolts me. I spin. A Tirik sailor swings a cudgel at my temple, the whites of his eyes shimmering with the fever of the fight.

I throw myself down, and the cudgel strikes someone else.

"Ash! Look high," Catsper calls as I scramble back to my feet.

I look up to see a mountain of man rushing me with an axe.

"Be still," Catsper commands and points his gun over my shoulder. The weapon discharges with a sharp *crack*, and the axe wielder staggers away, still swinging wildly despite the hole in his chest.

The marine discards the pistol, now useless.

I gasp shakily, uncertain whether I love Catsper for saving my life or despise him for trusting said life with a pistol's uncertain aim. No time to decide. Two men rush Catsper at once, and I circle around to cut one of them from the back.

"Tolerably good, Ash," Catsper says as my target falls. My lungs burn too much to answer even if the pounding of my heart would allow me to form words. The magic in my blood rumbles but fortunately stays put.

The Tirik are pressing us inward. The black-uniformed

marine boys rush about, fighting with skill and vigor if not size. I wonder where the other members of the *Aurora* crew are. Surely our numbers surpass what I see on deck.

A shrill pipe calls in three bursts. A signal. Not ours. The pipe sounds again, this time accompanied with shouting in Tirik. *Retreat. To the boats.*

I jerk. I speak Tirik tolerably well, but I can make little sense of the command.

"We can take this ship!" another voice answers. I think he is right.

"Keep to your orders. Retreat."

The crimson-clad Tirik seamen dissolve from the *Aurora*'s deck, and I fall to my knees as the last man throws himself over the rail into the waiting boat. *What has just happened, exactly?* my racing thoughts ask. *Or more accurately, why?*

20

I STAND OUTSIDE CAPTAIN RIMA'S CABIN, the muffled voices of Domenic and Rima escaping from the closed door. I'm fatigued to the bone. The morning air-calling practice in my cabin is as distant as the horizon. Disappointment soaks through me, a heavy layer beneath ripped clothes matted with grime and dried blood. We've failed. The Tirik have taken not one but two of our charges as prizes.

"The boarding party was never intended to take the *Aurora*," Domenic's low voice explains behind the door. "It was a diversion to occupy us while the *Devron* cut out the merchants."

"Dishonorable cowards." Rima spits the words. "Attacking civilian vessels while shying from our guns."

I roll my eyes. Does Rima ever get tired of his own rhetoric? If the Tirik captain had had an inkling of our incompetence, he would have taken the *Aurora* first, despite our heavier armament. And then he'd have two frigates with which to lasso our charges.

Rima sighs. "You are certain it was the *Siren* and the *Maiden* that were taken?" The relief is sickening. The Eflian merchant is safe. That is what matters to him. "Very well, bring in the girl."

I straighten, not wanting to be caught slouching against the bulkhead when Domenic opens the door. My stomach knots at the approaching footsteps. I'm little savoring explaining how I came to learn how to command a gun battery and understand Tirik.

Domenic sticks his head into the passageway and motions for me to come inside. As I cross the threshold, he gives me a hard look, warning me to behave.

As if I need to draw any more attention to myself than I already have.

"You wished to see me, sir?" I bow formally as I take in Captain Rima's living quarters. The cabin spans the width of the ship and is filled with rich carved wood furnishings, good china, and medals. A window shows the ocean and the two ships left in the *Aurora*'s wake. My gaze stops at a painting hanging beside Rima's worktable. It's a portrait of a woman. She wears a gaudy purple dress I'm certain I've seen before. On second glance, the pointed nose and dark eyes are also familiar.

I sift my memory for her name. Lady Madeline. Yes, Lady Madeline from Eflia North, who spends her days lavishly prancing between courts to inspire people to charitable deeds—preferably ones that bolster her prestige without the inconvenience of work. She also owns the *Lyron Herald*, a news press with all the integrity of a hungry hyena. When Thad threw her out of Ashing, the *Faithful* took her back to an Eflian port. The carpenter was obliged to remove one of the bulkheads to accommodate her luggage. Last I heard, she had gone to Felielle and made herself comfortable at court, befriending Felielle's Queen Leanna in the process.

Rima follows my gaze. "My wife," he says. For the first time, I hear genuine adoration in the captain's voice. "Lady Madeline Rima."

Lady Madeline *Rima*? I hope the captain reads my surprise as awe. "She is beautiful, sir." And expensive. A captain's year's wages would barely cover a fortnight of Lady Madeline's style. The *Lyron Herald* must be faring better that I thought.

"Divine," Rima agrees, smiling at the portrait. His smile fades as his focus returns to me. "Well then, girl. You claim the Republic leader ordered a retreat?"

Claim? Domenic spears me with his eyes, and I oblige him by checking my voice before speaking. "That was the order I heard, sir."

"In Tirik. How came you to speak our enemy's tongue?"

"I learned it during my two-year throne service, sir." The grain of truth soothes the words along. I decide against mentioning that I've a passing knowledge of Diante as well. "The Palace trained me to translate Republic newsleafs."

Rima's mouth thins. "I hope you'll find no more employment for it on my ship. Republic newsleafs may amuse the Ashing Admiralty, but aboard a man-of-war, they are nothing but enemy propaganda. You will keep that vile language to yourself and confine your intellectual pursuits to learning your naval duties. Is that understood?"

I itch to ask whether Rima imagines I've plans to hold language courses for the crew, but curl my fists and give the appropriate "Yes, sir." The more Rima indulges in this absurdity, the less he will worry about my heritage. Plus, the insult to Ashing should mean little to me. Not that the waste of the uniform sitting before me has any right to insult the best bloody navy in the League. Perhaps the marriage of Lady Madeline and Captain Rima is not as outrageous a notion as I had first thought. The pair are abysmal human beings and thereby well suited for one another.

Domenic shifts his weight. Although his feet stay in place, he seems to have moved between Rima and me. "Ash handled herself admirably during battle, sir. She took charge of carronade division."

If anything, Rima's scowl deepens. "*Took* charge?" he growls. "If I recall correctly, the chain of command does apply to women in the Lyron League Joint Fleet. So, pray tell me, Ash, did I give you leave to issue orders to my men and toy with my ship's armament?"

My skin heats, the audacity of this bigoted, manipulative coward pushing my common sense to its breaking point. "No, sir. I do not believe you were on deck at the time."

"That's enough, Ash." Domenic's hands flex behind his back, but his voice reclaims its calm as he addresses the captain. "Although she is already making me regret it, I field-promoted Ash to master's mate during the battle, sir. I intended the position for Mic, but he was indisposed."

Domenic... Wait, what? I fight to keep my face straight. Domenic is playing on Rima's absence. The captain will find it difficult to reverse a promotion awarded during a battle he *wasn't at.* Harder still to put the equally absent Mic into the slot. My stomach churns. I don't want to be a master's mate, and I know Domenic will pay dearly for this fiction.

Rima turns to Domenic, whose eyes remain straight ahead. The captain's face is tight and calculating. He taps his hand against his thigh. I expect a voice of cold fury when he speaks, but Rima sounds like a disappointed parent.

"Ah, yes, Commander. Your handling of the *Aurora* was..." Rima trails off, his head shaking. "I need not tell you how disgracefully you served this ship, Commander Dana." He rises from behind his desk and paces the room. "You lie and assure me of your ability, lull me into entrusting you with my ship, and proceed to hand over half the convoy to the enemy. An enemy with half our broadside, no less! If you had not the wit to fight a ship, you should at least have ordered our charges to scatter safely as well as informed me of the situation. Even I cannot rescue you from your folly if you wait until the enemy has departed before confessing the problem."

I've no words. Which is probably a very, very good thing. Especially since the weasel isn't done talking.

"I dislike stating the obvious, but facts are facts," says Rima. "You may rest assured that my report to the Admiralty will conceal none of this sloppiness." He stops at his desk, his tone conciliatory. "I will, of course, emphasize your youth and inexperience to the Admiralty... That should provide you small leeway. But it would be a mistake for you to rely on such charity in the future."

I hold my breath, but Domenic's stoic face never wavers. I fight to keep my mouth shut before I talk myself into irons.

Rima waves his hand in dismissal.

Domenic turns on his heel and walks from the chamber.

I follow in his wake, jogging to keep up with his greater stride. "Wait. Please."

Domenic stops, his foot already on the companionway step, his muscled arms bracing the rail. He is too large for this small space. In more ways than one.

Meeting his eyes, I realize, with unexpected surprise, how exhausted he is. And that despite the cool face and stoic façade, the dressing-down from the captain had hurt. Rima *would* write the report he promised. And that would hurt even more—not just Domenic's pride, but his career. Yet, through the whole ordeal, Domenic had protected me.

I draw a breath. There is much I want to say, if I could just find the words. That he handled the ship well. That he is a true seaman. That I saw through Rima's manipulative speech and so will the Admiralty. That the *Aurora* and the League are lucky to have Domenic on their side. But most of all, I want him to know I'm grateful. "The promotion—" I start, but he holds up his hand.

"After your deck exhibition, I had little choice. It was either promotion or punishment." He shakes his head, and his hair sways over his eyes like a shaggy dog's. "You've played me for a fool since you came aboard. I've not the energy to speak of it just now." Tugging down his uniform, Domenic climbs the steps.

His retreat leaves me with a sudden and inexplicable emptiness. Then anger, slow and viscous, trickles into the void.

I hesitate by the sick berth, by the door separating my world from the one of moans and bitten-back screams.

Death little scares me. At the core, an enemy's ball either has my name on it or it does not. There is nothing I can do for it but stand tall on deck and pretend myself immune until I'm not standing any longer.

Injury is different. That monster haunts my thoughts. A life without a leg, an arm, an eye. Beyond the door of the sick berth, that is someone's new world. *Someone else's. Not yours.* I draw myself up. Captain Fey insisted on knowing the human cost of battle, and it's time for me to face the butcher's bill.

Inside, blood covers the deck. In the far corner, men hold down a sailor while a carpenter's mate in a leather apron applies a bone saw to the remnants of a leg. Bile rises in my throat. I want to look away, but I see Ana there by the surgery, squeezing the poor sod's hand. She speaks in a soft, hypnotizing voice. I'd never seen someone speak to a man during amputation, but the sailor clings to Ana like a lifeline.

The carpenter's mate, who appears be fulfilling the role of the *Aurora*'s missing surgeon, steps away. I catch sight of the bloody stump and spin away, leaning my hands on the bulkhead. I'm dizzy.

"Nile?" It's Ana. "Are you all right?"

I'm not. I need to leave. Maybe that makes me a coward, but I signed on as a seaman, not a surgeon.

And so had Ana.

Ana smiles, and fury, as harsh and sudden as a rogue wave, flashes through my blood. How dare she smile? How dare she feel anything but shame and regret? Ana's actions on deck were a hair short of cowardice. She had fallen apart. She took responsibility for neither her duty nor her people. Her incompetence and fear had turned her into such a liability that I actually sent her away.

And she cares nothing for it.

"I need to go." I walk out the door. I can't look at her. She's befriended me, and I'd let her. I should have paid better attention. This girl isn't the company I wish to keep.

Ana trots after me to our berth and puts her foot into the door before I can slam it. "What's wrong?"

I don't know what to say, but I want to say something. I want her to understand the importance of battle and duty. There is much good in Ana's heart, and I want her to be the girl I like. "The Tirik boarded us," I tell her. "They diverted our attention while the *Devron* cut out two of the merchants."

"Dear Goddess." She closes her eyes. "I pray we shall never see that ship again."

My nostrils flare. "That we never see her again?" I'm tired. And I'm angry. I spin around and slam my knuckles into the wooden bulkhead, just shy of her ear. "The *Devron* bloody took our people from under our noses. And all you want is to make certain no danger befalls you? What kind of officer are you, Ana?"

She takes a step away. Her eyes widen. The tears I expected don't come. Instead, Ana crosses her hands delicately. "You forget yourself, Nile."

Oh waves and hail, if you knew how right you were. I shake my head and dig clean clothes from my seabag. Ana can go back to holding hands in the sick berth. I have work to do.

"I little worry about the war because I worry about my family first," Ana says into my back. I don't know why she is bothering. "My mother, my younger sisters, the children I will one day bear. How well I handle a gun or set a sail or calculate a course, none of it matters. I will never stay in the navy long enough for my skills to make a difference. A life I help in the sick berth will. The hurt sailors are sons and fathers and husbands. Those are the important things, Nile. For someone so fervently in love with the navy, I do not understand how the basics of family are lost on you."

The fight leaves me like a deflated sail. Ana is right; her values are lost on me. Just as mine are lost on my mother. And maybe Ana's are the right ones, the ones normal people should have. But I've never been normal. Perhaps friendship and compatibility are reserved for those who aren't me. I rub my eyes with the heels of my hands. "Just…just ask the captain to rate you surgeon's mate. We've no physician aboard to object. You'll be doing your assigned duties, and none rely on you for anything different."

Ana shakes her head. "I asked, but the captain refused to rate me mate as I've no experience in the matter. He offered to make me a sick-berth attendant, but such a post is so junior, it would do nothing for the status of my family name. I could not accept that."

I throw up my hands. There is nothing more to say. I was an idiot for letting myself believe there would be.

"People concern me more than gun batteries," says Ana. "Speaking of which, who are you, exactly? You knew your business with the guns."

I rub my fist. "My life is my own."

She looks at me with hurt eyes that bother me more than I wish they did. Turning my back to her, I walk out and slam the door shut.

21

By the following day, the *Aurora* resembles her former self, except for the dead sailors lying on deck, each man sewn into his hammock. Sand helps sew shut the hammock of a middie boy Lucas, who's died from injuries during the night. At supper, the marine boys sit quietly and avoid glancing at the two empty spaces at the table. I keep my eyes on my food. My break with Ana lingers like a bitter aftertaste. And Domenic... That scorches. My own fault for getting too close. I won't be repeating the mistake.

I rise from the table, leaving the remnants of my salt beef ration, and walk away.

I climb onto the deck and pull myself into the shrouds. My muscles protest, but the exhilaration evens the score. I time my steps to let *Aurora*'s motion propel me up, higher and higher until I reach the main yardarm and hoist myself atop it. Straddling the wood, I lean back against the mast and stare out to sea. The waves roll along, the occasional crowns of white foam bubbling at the crests. We continue heading west toward the Bottleneck Juncture and the nearby Diante port, though now only the *Hope* and *Solace* bob along in our wake. The sea stretches around us as far as the eye can see on larboard—Diante—side. On starboard, the occasional landmass of the Lyron archipelago interrupts the horizon.

The wind teases me, and I wrap my elbow around a rope, unsure if I should let open my magic. I still choke every time I try, either at the beginning or end of the exercise. Sometimes the whole time. But I'm still alive. And not a single convulsion yet.

"You are quite comfortable in the rigging, Princess." Domenic's voice sounds from right behind me. I'd been so focused on my own thoughts, I'd not seen him approach. *Him* of all people.

I jerk to face Domenic, spinning on the ropes so quickly that my balance falters.

Domenic's arm clamps around my waist like iron. He draws me against himself as the *Aurora* crests a wave and falls back, her masts leaning out over the open sea. The salty musk of his coat fills my nose. His body is hard and steady. And close enough that I'm certain he can feel my heartbeat.

I pull away from his chest and find steady footing, but his hand stays gripping my elbow.

"Your charade ends now," he says. "I will accept that an Ashing princess would learn Tirik from her tutors, but I know perfectly well that even Ashing has no cannons in the palace ballroom. You will tell me how you know your business and how well you know it. Now."

A growl forms deep in my throat, but I stop its escape. I'm not about to let Domenic think I care one way or the other about his interrogation. "You rated me master's mate. You tell me." I shake off his hold, but the solid feel of his hand stays on my skin. Rolling back my shoulders, I grip the ropes and lean away. "I've been at sea since age eight, if that is what you are asking."

Domenic steps in, looming over me. It's a calculated move, designed to intimidate. His body is large and lethal, made hard by years of sea life, and he uses it for all its worth.

I raise a brow.

"Why did you keep as much a secret from me?" he demands.

"In what world are your erroneous assumptions my fault? I don't expect you to keep track of the chosen occupations of all the six kingdom's heirs' younger siblings, but the assumption that I knew nothing of work was your mistake alone." My nostrils flare. "Until the *Aurora* revealed herself to have but one sea officer capable of commanding her in action, the point was utterly irrelevant."

With the next breath, the unintended compliment in my words registers with us both.

Domenic stares at me.

I grit my teeth and stare back.

"What exactly was your assignment prior to enlisting on the *Aurora*?" he asks, softer now.

"Second officer on the AS *Faithful* of seventy-two guns," I fire back, daring him to so much as blink at my ship's name.

"The Ashing flagship." Domenic blows out a long breath. His hands flex around the shrouds. "Goddess. The finest ship in the six kingdoms' finest fleet. Little wonder you—" He stops himself and looks out at the horizon.

Little wonder I what? I want him to finish, and when he says nothing, I'm disgusted with my own desperation. How easily kind words about the *Faithful* make me forget reality. "So then," I ask, crossing my arms and sitting down on the rope, letting my legs dangle through open air. "Are you enjoying watching a royal get her comeuppance, *sir*?"

"No, I'm not." He turns, sees me sitting, and climbs down a few feet of rigging so his face is close to mine. One muscled arm hooks around a line to keep him balanced. His blue eyes hold my gaze. "And what of you? Are you enjoying your recent career move?"

I chuckle humorlessly. "Do I enjoy scrubbing the quarterdeck instead of walking upon it? No."

"Then why are you doing it?" His gaze deepens. "I know what I said when you came aboard, but this is about more than escaping marriage, isn't it?"

"No." I swallow. "Just that."

"No." He shakes his head, his brows furrowed in thought. "You made me promise you a Letter of Service. Why…Goddess. You *told* me why." His eyes widen, the words coming in a whisper. "Back on the beach in Ashing, you told me. You are looking for the Metchti Monastery. You are the girl who believes all is possible. And you want to cure Clay."

My mouth is dry, my heart pounding quickly. It'd been a private outing to the Ashing beach. An accidental meeting. A conversation with a stranger that drew its fuel from anonymity. And with that, I'd discounted how deeply that stranger had peered into my private world. Now, Domenic's words strike a wound more raw than he knows, but I will not let him make it bleed. I won't.

"Nile," he says softly.

"The line is worn, sir." My voice is all business. I hop to my feet and reach past Domenic's head to tap a fraying buntline that helps furl the sail. "It should have been replaced before now. I'll see it done."

Domenic sighs. "I did you little service with the promotion, you know. Finding fault in the crew's work earns few friends."

"Yes, making friends is certainly worth the risk of the line snapping in the middle of a storm." Anger bubbles under my skin again, and I latch on to it. Better anger than fear. "I'm not interested in feigning blindness so I can lounge about and bloody make friends."

Domenic rolls back his shoulders, his muscles shifting beneath his coat. His expression straddles a fine line between amusement and rage.

I don't think I could bear the former.

"Very well," he says finally, his voice mercifully hard. "Allow me to give some advice. A master's mate is not a lieutenant. I spent ten years on the lower deck. Trust me when I say that the code of conduct you've learned as an officer elite does not apply to you now. The seamen will not care how well you know the fleet or plot a course or set a sail. They will care how hard you can haul on a rope or lay it across another's shoulders. And you do neither of those things well."

"Is that your reasoning behind flogging frightened sailors?"

He ignores me. "You are small, you are weak, and you are friendless. And you've injected yourself into a world where those things matter. Either adapt or go on believing that you can convert wolves into vegetarians."

"The crew fears you, Domenic. And you know it. You do it on purpose, turning anything you can into apparent torment. Work that needs to be done regardless, salt on Rory's wounds. The crew fears you, and you *want* it that way."

"Yes." He doesn't flinch at the accusations. Any of them. "You should fear as well."

"No." Shaking my head, I step close to him. Our faces hover inches apart, our breaths mixing. The muscles in his jaw tense, rippling beneath freshly shaved skin. The heat from Domenic's body wraps around me, caressing my neck, snaking through my tightly braided hair to touch my head. My heart quickens, and I lick my wind-dried lips. "No, Dominic. You will have my obedience and perhaps my respect. But I've been at sea too long to fear you."

"Then you are daft," he says quietly and climbs down.

I let him get ahead before swinging into the ropes.

I am three steps from the deck when a surge of sudden anxiety races through me. The confusion of it freezes me in place. My stomach tingles, my pulse sprinting ahead. Something is about to happen. I've no notion what. But something terrible. My head turns to the right of its own accord as green splotches of light flash in my eyes.

Not real. I know the lights aren't real, but they are painfully bright nonetheless. I shut my eyes tightly against them, but it little helps. I bite my lip, some primal part of my brain remembering that I'm still in the shrouds and thrusting my arm deeply into the ropes. Just in time. A heartbeat later and my body refuses to obey my will. My right arm jerks in small, rhythmic ticks I can do nothing about.

My first jerking spell. I wonder whether I will fall, but the thought is distant and muffled.

The convulsions end as suddenly as they came, leaving fatigue and nausea in their wake. I climb down the few remaining feet of shrouds and barely make it to the rail to vomit. The few crewmen who bother to take notice, laugh.

I slide to the deck, my body aching as if beaten.

Domenic takes a step toward me, then thinks better of it and finds employment elsewhere.

I'm too spent to be humiliated. My heart gallops in my throat, and I wipe moist palms against my trousers. Did anyone see the jerking spell take hold? I study the seamen on deck but find only the deep gray moons that fatigue has painted under the crew's eyes. Now that they've had their laugh over my lost breakfast, no one is paying me any mind, thank the waves. The convulsions must have kept themselves discreet, even if the nausea did not. How considerate of them.

I draw a shaky breath and find a reason to get off the

deck. My limbs are heavy, and my belly aches with dread. The grace period—if being suffocated on a regular basis could be termed that—is over. I knew it would be, sooner or later. Blood from my bitten lip drips onto my tongue, and I swallow copper saliva. I knew this would happen when I first realized myself an air caller. I did. So how can I be so damn surprised nonetheless?

Climbing into my hammock, I bury my face in my hands and fight back tears.

By late evening, when the ship's bell warns me of Ana's imminent return, I know I want to spend the night alone. My muscles cramp, my stomach heaves, and my thoughts are so heavy, I can hardly see through them.

Taking a lantern, I descend to the lowest deck, my light little scaring the darkness. Here, in the hold, the *Aurora* accommodates the stores of sailcloth, ropes, water casks, and provisions that can be trusted to remain out without a guard. The hold also houses millers, ship's rats who forever make their way into the flour. One of the ragged creatures scurries across my foot, and I jump. My lungs fill with the horrid, stale air that always hangs here, far below the waterline.

I climb onto the pile of coiled ropes. The nest lifts me from the grit and damp of the deck planks and gives me a fighting chance of kicking millers free from my spot. Arranged just so, the ropes are comfortable. I wonder when the next set of convulsions will strike. Whether one day soon I'll be uncovered and hidden away in disgrace, like Clay.

I feel very mortal. And very much afraid.

I close my eyes. My pulse is loud. Too loud. I focus on it, trying to relax my aching shoulders, my arms, my mind. The coiled ropes are rough beneath me. The air is thick, heavy with the stench of the ship's bilges and the rats' small snorts. And...and something else.

A rush of alertness cuts through my fatigue. I listen

harder. There. Scraping. There is scraping and a sharp intake of breath. It comes again. Someone is here.

I lift my lantern. "Who's there?"

No answer. I frown. I'd found sailors in the lower hold before, usually sleeping off extra drink they had managed to procure through one sort of contraband or another. But this feels different. The back of my neck tightens. "I hear you," I call again. "Make yourself known."

Silence. Dead silence. Then a short gasp, quickly stifled.

Another rat runs across my boot. Likely one of its mates had sunk its teeth into my visitor.

I consider climbing up to call the marines, but the hider will likely find a new hole while I'm gone. Plus, I doubt he's a soldier. The little noises sounded frightened, not predatory.

I stand still and listen. There. Under the spare canvas covering the water casks. I hop up on the casks and make my way toward the corner. The intruder's breathing is evident now, coming from beneath the sailcloth.

I squat atop a water cask and grip the corner of the canvas. My palms are moist, and my heart is quickening. I tighten my hold on the lantern in my left hand and, with a quick jerk, throw back the cloth.

It is a boy. He is about my age, but skinnier than me. Starved skinny. He curls into a fetal position, his arms covering his head.

I nudge him with my foot.

The boy's crop of blond hair shifts, and a dirt-streaked face with frightened eyes looks up at me.

"Who are you?" I demand.

"Please," the boy says in Tirik as his palms rise in surrender. "Please do not hurt me."

22

"WHO ARE YOU?" I REPEAT, THIS time in Tirik. If the boy is a spy, he is the worst one in the history of the war. If not a spy, then what? A sailor who never made it back to the boats? A defector? A coward? It's all happened before.

The boy's eyes widen. "You speak Tirik." What little color he had in his face drains, and he presses away from me. "No. Please. Please!"

"You are aboard the League Ship *Aurora*." My voice is cool. "Surely you hear my accent?"

He lifts his eyes. The point registers, but whether he finds the assurance a comfort remains to be seen.

"Talk," I order him. His pathetic frame and palpable fear eat at me, and I wish I was offering him blankets and food instead of interrogation. But I cannot. It is important to get his answers now, before comfort makes lying easier.

"I am Logan Price," the boy whispers. "From the *Devron*. I stole aboard. With the boarding party."

"And forgot to leave?"

He shakes his head. "No. I stayed on purpose. Because I wish to live." He holds out skinny wrists and speaks quickly. "Take me as a prisoner of war. Please."

I believe him. At least, I believe his desperation. My tone softens. "Are you one of the old royalists, Price?" The Republic's rule started with the extermination of entire royal families as punishment for the oppression of the workers. The kind of people who kick off their reign with child killing are unlikely candidates for building a humanitarian nation, no matter what they proclaim about the rights of man.

"No." Price draws a breath. "Not a royalist. A Gifted."

My gut clenches, but I manage to keep my voice steady. "What has that to do with it? Are you a danger to my ship?"

"No! Not at all. I swear it." Price shifts slowly to a sitting position. Bruises and cuts and burns cross exposed skin. "You've heard of the Republic's People's movement?"

I nod briskly. The notion is that man is capable of anything—ruling himself, sailing through any storm, defying nature. The Felielle and the Eflians take a deep offense to People's Power since it necessarily scorns all divinity. Personally, I hope the Tirik will try to defy gravity and get themselves killed. "What of it?"

Price licks his lips. "The Republic runs an institute... A research facility, studying elemental attraction. The condition is too unpredictable... Uncontrollable. The science men in the People Over Nature Bureau want to harness it." With the initial wave of terror subsiding, Price's voice becomes void of emotion. "I was one of their Gifted subjects. Most do not survive."

Breath leaves me. If Price is telling the truth... He can't be. *"And as for Clay... I hear they are experimenting."* Thad's voice surfaces through my memory. I wonder how much more Thad had known of the Republic's dirty little secret. I look at

Price's skin. Really look. It is a lot of pain for a farce.

"What element does your magic call?" I ask.

"I...I can't call anything," he says.

I lean back, shaking my head.

"I *feel* air and water both, their movements and pressure. But I call neither." Price adds quickly, "I'm unusual. I'm...interesting."

A shiver of fear trickles down my spine. The wounds tell the story of just how interesting the People Over Nature Bureau had found Price. It's all I can do to keep the nausea at bay. An institute experimenting on the ill. On boys like Clay. On girls like me. I see my twin, my beautiful, gentle, animal-loving Clay, cowering in a dirty corner, never understanding what shattered his world, what he did to deserve to suffer. I see him crying and rocking and begging as a science man in a bloody leather apron burns his skin.

A fire kindles in the pit of my stomach. My face is hot, and my fingers curl into fists until the nails draw blood. "What price do you pay for your Gift, then?" I ask, as much to know as to interrupt the frightening spiral of my thoughts.

He shakes his head in confusion.

I search for a different word. "What are the side effects of your magic? What effects does your odd Gift have on your body? Have you convulsions or..." I stumble. It is difficult to say the words with cold distance, as if the disease was not spreading its roots through my body as we speak. "Or thin blood? Or both?"

"Ah. I understand now," says Price with unsettling neutrality. "I've none of the traditional effects. Instead, I do not feel most emotions. But that is a blessing, not a price. It allowed me to survive."

"You feel fear." It isn't a question.

"Yes. I feel that. And pain."

I dislike that word. "How did you escape?" I ask.

"I'm a living weather glass. The frigates use me when the Institute lets them. I was on the *Devron* when I heard the boarding ordered. And I came along."

"All right." I rub my forehead. It is time to pass Price to the marines and make my report. I snatch a small piece of rope. "Show me your hands. Slowly. Now face away from me and stand up." Price flinches as I bind his wrists. The rope is cutting into already raw flesh. He needs salve and bandages. Instead, I search him for weapons and find none. Only the skin and bones of a shaking boy.

The fire in my stomach is blazing hot now. I want to swing the *Aurora* around, find the Institute, and destroy it. Each minute we do nothing, another lash or hot iron touches an innocent's skin. I think of Clay again and feel sick. "Price." My voice is quiet. "How do the Tirik permit this to happen to their own people?"

He looks down at the deck. "They do not. Mostly, the Institute uses...others."

"Others?" Ice slides through me.

"Prisoners of war," Price says after a moment's hesitation. "The Institute goes through a lot of non-Gifted subjects for comparison."

I freeze. Prisoners. Such as the crews of the *Siren* and *Maiden* we had just failed to protect.

I stare at Lady Madeline's portrait again, although this time it's illuminated by lantern light. Even painted on canvas, her jewels sparkle. I don't understand why Rima is at sea at all if his family enjoys such wealth. It's clearly not for the love of service.

"How many Republic vessels cruise these waters?" Rima demands for the fifth time.

I stifle a growl and translate. The questioning had exhausted its usefulness three hours past. Price knows nothing of naval value. He was on land three weeks ago but can mark neither the Tirik harbor nor the Institute's location on a chart. The questions Price might speak to—questions about the Institute itself—Rima avoids. We are wasting time. Time that might save the lives of the merchant crews.

"I do not know," Price says in Tirik. "I only sailed aboard the *Devron*." Price may experience neither annoyance nor irritation, but I feel both adequately, and my sentiment leaks into my voice as I translate.

Domenic cuts me with his eyes. He is sitting in a chair while Captain Rima paces the room. Price and I both stand beside Rima's desk, and Catsper lounges by the door.

Rima scowls and drops himself into his chair. "All right, boy." He sighs. "Go eat and rest. We'll have the doctor take a look at your wounds."

I translate. Catsper steps forward and takes Price's elbow. If the lack of the doctor Catsper is intended to find bothers the marine, he keeps the thought private. Price's eyes remain on me as Catsper motions him from the room.

"You will have no wind by morning," Price tells me quickly in Tirik.

"Ash..." Domenic warns. Rima hadn't given Price and me leave for private conversation.

Catsper shoves Price toward the door.

The Tirik boy twists back to me. "What is to happen to me?" he asks. Price feels fear just fine. "What will he do?"

"Nile!" snaps Domenic.

I'm not about to let Rima's lack of the Tirik language add to Price's suffering "'You will be all right," I assure Price in his language as the door closes. "The marine will not abuse you. I trust him."

Rima's palm slams his table. "What did you just tell him in the traitor tongue?"

I turn to the captain. "I told him to be at ease, sir."

"Did you now?" His nostrils flare. "And who told you to do that, girl? Who gave you leave to speak here at all?"

I clench my jaw and keep silent. There are more important matters before us.

Rima turns to Domenic. "I don't believe the little whelp for an instant," Rima declares, taking a sip of wine. "I've never heard such rubbish in my career."

I'm certain there are quite a few things Rima has never heard of in his career.

"Logan Price is nothing but a lazy rat wishing for a better life amongst us," Rima continues. "Trusting any Gifted is a mistake. The Lyron League would do well to contain the poor bastards for their own safety instead of turning a blind eye while they run rampant. Also, I can only control my ship but that I *will* control. I will have none of his imaginative ramblings straying beyond this room and upsetting the crew, Mr. Dana. And inform Mr. Catsper that I wish his damn toddlers thoroughly disciplined for allowing a stowaway to hide aboard my ship. You'd think someone claiming a Spade title would know the basics of patrol."

"Sir." I speak quickly, before Rima can cut me off. I believe Price, and not just because of his wounds or his words matching Thad's. The whole concept fits well with the Republic's methods. Sanctioned brutality. An excuse to abuse one set of people in hopes another may gain from it. "If the Institute does exist, we may yet have time to save the *Siren* and *Maiden* crews from an awful fate. And if it does not, we lose nothing but a bit of time. Might you consider the matter further overnight?"

I don't notice Domenic rise until I see him before me and feel the back of his hand strike my mouth. I fall to my knees and taste blood.

"Which part of keeping your mouth shut did you have trouble comprehending, Ash?" Domenic demands.

I look up and touch my hand to my throbbing lip.

Domenic towers over me, hands on his hips. His bulk blocks most of my sight, and his chest moves with deep, angry breaths. His gaze grips mine, telling me to stay down.

I glare up at him, my muscles coiled so tight, they burn.

"Get her out of here, Mr. Dana." Rima's voice is appeased, but barely. "And please instruct Ms. Ash on the meaning of convoy duty and responsibility. If the recent engagement has left her without the stomach for the navy, I will inquire with the *Solace* skipper of their need for a laundress."

"Aye aye, sir." Domenic grips my arm hard and marches me from the cabin. I struggle against the hold, but it's a futile proposition. He drags me into an alcove and spins me to face him. "Are you an idiot?"

I glower at him. "Are you?"

"I'm smart enough to know that Captain Rima is not going to alter our course." Domenic's voice is hard. "He was never going to, no matter what that boy claimed. I need you working to better this ship, not lounging around in irons—or worse—for insolence."

Silence stretches between us. I cross my arms, refusing to touch my still-bleeding lip. Though I'll be damned before I admit as much to him, Domenic is right. Challenging Rima with nothing more than opinion to back up my words wasn't one of my brightest moments. "I believe Price about the Institute."

Domenic shrugs. "I believe the Republic commits many atrocities. I also think your wish to have this one be true may skew your judgment."

I raise my brows. "My wish that an Institute that tortures people really exists?"

"Your wish that someone may have found a cure for Clay," he says gently.

I retreat a step before I can stop myself, Domenic's words

stripping me naked. Swallowing, I desperately pull myself together. "The Institute," I say a little too quickly. "My concern isn't for Clay... Not *just* for Clay. If I knew for a fact, a cold, solid fact, that the Institute has discovered nothing, I would still risk my life to stop its atrocities and rescue its captives."

Domenic looks down into my eyes. "You took on two armed men to defend a stranger and stood between a marine boy and two sailors twice your size," he whispers. "I've no doubt you'd turn the world on its side to rescue captives." Domenic's hand rises and hovers indecisively inches from my face. His hand slides forward, the fingers bracing against my jaw as his thumb brushes my cheek and lip gently, wiping away the blood. Callouses scrape against my skin, bruised and very, very sensitive.

I draw a sharp breath despite myself.

Domenic's hand stills, hovering but not touching me. *I had to,* his eyes say. *I'm sorry.*

I know. I cling to the ghost of Domenic's touch on my skin, my heart galloping. I should say something. Something interesting. Intelligent. On the deck above, the wind cracks the sails. "Price said we'll have no wind by morning," I mumble.

Domenic swallows once and steps back, straightening his tunic. His face is flushed. "Unlikely." His voice reclaims its usual chill. "But we shall see soon enough." He gives me a curt bow and, turning on his heel, walks quickly away.

23

We have no wind by morning. Or the next day. Or the one after that. The deck is a mess. There is little more demoralizing to a crew than a ship refusing to move. I wish Price had mentioned when this horrid calm would pass. I wish I could speak with him again.

Rima is on deck, smiling at the crew as if all is grand with the world. He'd have to be blind to miss the chipped paint on the starboard rail and the glob of tobacco chew on the planking, but I know he will call no one out for it. He will leave public reprimands to Domenic.

I turn my back to the captain before my face reveals my thoughts. And as I turn, I feel it. Fear. The world closing in. I gasp and throw myself toward the companionway, half sliding, half falling down the steps. I've a few heartbeats before the convulsions start, and I must be off deck by then. Better be thought an idiot than spend the rest of my life locked away as an invalid like Clay.

The jerking spell seizes me at the bottom of the

companionway ladder. My right side thrashes, hitting painfully against the steps. My teeth bite into my tongue.

Footsteps clamber toward me.

"Ash?" a seaman demands. "What the—"

He cuts off as I roll onto my knees and vomit all over the deck.

"Again?" he curses. "Bloody again? And have you no notion of the rail, damn you? Must be getting dumber each time you lose your meal." The seaman growls under his breath. "I'll fetch a bucket and swab, but you can bloody well clean up your own mess."

I lean my head against the steps and pant as he leaves, spreading word of my misaimed sea sickness. Snickers reach me from the deck above, along with none too quiet suggestions to stop wasting food on me. I try not to listen, but I can't help it. My face burns.

The seaman slaps a bucket beside me. I swab the planks clean of vomit and stumble to my berth for a fresh shirt before returning to deck.

"Ash." Domenic is in my face the moment I return, his body silhouetting the sun. Of course he'd have heard. We've not spoken since that touch outside Rima's cabin three days ago, and this, me post-convulsion and vomit, isn't how I pictured our next meeting. I try to step back, but Domenic follows, trapping me between the ladder and himself. "What happened?" The formality in his voice is at odds with his concerned eyes.

"Sorry, sir." I touch my forehead respectfully, aware that every word is public. *Glad* that every word is public. It makes lying easier. "My stomach turned. Seasickness."

"Seasickness," he echoes dryly, those blue eyes flash in warning. "Again. Being so new to the sea must be a difficult adjustment."

I raise my chin, my heart fluttering. "Yes, sir."

Domenic tilts his head, crossing his muscled arms over his chest. "The merchant convoy under *Aurora*'s escort is bound for the Diante port. Once we dock there, you will go ashore and consult with a physician."

A jolt races through me. I little need additional attention. "Thank you, sir, but there is no need," I say quietly.

"That was not a suggestion." His voice drops to match mine. "Unless you lose your meals overboard as a service to the fish?"

"You are *ordering* me to see a doctor?" I hiss. This is precisely the type of thing my mother would do, manipulate her position to force her notion of "something for my own good" upon me. I school my voice. "With due respect, sir, seasickness is a common ailment at sea. And even if it was not, there is little to expect from Diante medicine. To the best of my knowledge, the Diante pray and meditate ills away. Usually while burning incense."

"Then pray, meditate, and burn incense." His voice has an edge now.

The rein I have on my own tone is as tight as a bowstring. "If I may be about my duties, sir?"

He nods once.

I bow stiffly and twist on my heel, channeling my fury into work. "Rodney, Sid, Norian!" I shout, the din I make hurting my head. "Let's have these ropes coiled, if you please."

Having set my work party to task, I summon the pretense of sail inspection to make my way to the shrouds. Climbing aloft is likely unwise given my jerking spell, but my nerves crave the soothing familiarity of swaying ropes and fresh air. Plus, I cannot live in constant fear of my body's betrayal. Work at sea requires work aloft.

Sitting on the lookout platform, I watch the deck. Bloody Domenic is engrossed in filling out the bloody logbook.

Captain Rima strolls. In our wake, *Solace* and *Hope* bob along. I think back to Lady Madeline's tastes and wonder how stiff a fee the *Hope* is paying for illegally joining the convoy. And how much of that is for discretion.

"Nile?" Ana pulls herself up through the lubber's hole and settles beside me, her small frame hardly taking up space on the platform.

I'm surprised to see her in the shrouds by choice, but I don't mention it. We haven't spoken more than a few words to each other since after the battle, and I miss her more than I should. Maybe it's better this way. I'm damaged goods. "Ma'am?"

She bites her lip. "Can we end our quarrel?"

"There is no quarrel, ma'am."

"Stop it." Her hand slips over mine, slender fingers with pink-glazed nails. The touch of skin on skin is warm, genuine.

I try to pull away.

Ana tightens her grip on my hand. "Yes, Nile, we are different. You've a warrior's heart and I've a mother's. But the world needs us both in it. And different and friends are not mutually exclusive states. Giving up on a friendship because of a single discord is bloody idiotic."

My brows rise. I don't believe I've ever heard Ana curse before. "Bloody idiotic?"

She flushes, the corner of her mouth twitching. "I was trying to find words you'd appreciate."

Yes, she was. Just as she was trying by climbing the shrouds. Just as she *had been* trying since the moment we met, coaxing and caring and talking to me like we were equals when her status ranked so far above mine. Sharing her berth. "My mother is from Felielle," I say after a moment. "We drive each other mad. But I love her a great deal… When she's not trying to turn me into, well, you."

Ana laughs aloud. "I'm not the worst thing to be turned into," she says, but there is no bite in her voice. "Smart, pretty, with a great sense of—"

"Modesty?" I try for a smile, but my gaze catches on Domenic down below. He is turning away from the logbook, sending a wave of frenzied effort through the crew.

"Dana is pleasant to look at," Ana says beside me. "From afar."

My cheeks heat. "I wasn't—"

"Of course not." She starts to smile but stops. "What's happened to your face?"

I touch my lip, which is still tender from the confrontation in the captain's cabin. "I spoke out of turn."

Ana shifts her weight, and I recall she's wary of the height. "In Felielle, we believe it is wrong to strike a girl. And you need not remind me we are not in Felielle, Nile. There are some values that transcend culture."

"It wasn't like that." I growl at myself for defending Domenic, who is taking it upon himself to issue orders for *my own good*. As if my own good is in any way his prerogative.

"Oh." Ana swings her legs tentatively. "And here I thought a man twice your size struck you across the face. My mistake."

"Ana." There is a note of warning in my voice that the girl weathers with a flick of a manicured brow.

"When the Tirik attacked, I little wished to listen to your instruction, much less follow it. But I know you kept us from greater harm. You know what I do not of battle. And you'll forgive me when I say that I know what you do not when it comes to men and feelings."

"There are no feelings," I tell Ana firmly. "And no men. There is only a chain of command. Actions and consequences. I really should check the sail while I'm up here."

"The twins are having difficulties calculating our position, and Kederic is worried about his lieutenant exams," Ana calls before I get two steps out. "I promised I'd find a master's mate to help explain things. To all us middies."

I pause in midstep and turn toward her. Ana could not care less about navigation if she tried.

Ana blushes. "It... It appeared important to several of the parties involved. Are you the mate we need to ask?" Jerking her chin toward the deck, she starts a careful climb back down the ratlines. I hesitate only a moment before scampering after her.

There are five middies who gather around me on the back poop deck of the ship: Ana, seventeen-year-old Kederic, twelve-year-old twins Song and Sand, and fourteen-year-old Thatch Lawrence. All watch me with wary eyes.

I sweep my gaze over them, taking in the sextons and slate and chalk. The middies might little know what to make of me, but they came to work. Fair enough. I put my hands behind my back and nod toward the horizon. "I little expect you to place the *Aurora* in the Siaman Sea, but let's see if anyone at least gets her in an ocean."

A crack of a smile, this from Kederic. His last calculation attempt, which I overheard reported to Lieutenant Kazzik this morning, put our ship in the middle of an Eflian mine.

After an hour with the middies and their sextons, I have a headache that has nothing to do with the air calling. They are a better group of youngsters than Rima deserves, but there are too few competent hands on the *Aurora* to teach them their trade. We'd given up taking measurements within a few minutes, focusing instead on the mathematics behind position calculations. The numbers on the slate greeted me like old friends and, headache or not, I enjoyed sharing their workings with an eager audience. The only middie to keep silent the entire time is Sand.

"Is it true that you found a Tirik hiding on the *Aurora*?" Sand asks finally as we put away instruments and slates.

I frown at the darkness in his tone. "Yes."

"If you were a real officer, you would have killed him."

"What?" I blink, unsure which of Sand's implications to address first, but he spins and walks away from me before I can speak.

"Sand is upset over Midshipman Lucas's death," Kederic says, watching the departing figure. "Don't mind him. Will you work with us again, Ms. Ash? This has been...err..."

"Overdue," Thatch Lawrence puts in undiplomatically, oblivious to Kederic's wince. "Mr. Kazzik just nods at anything we say, and Mr. Dana gets a pained look on his face and tells us to start over."

"It's a bit similar to the look you got after our first measurement," Song puts in sagely. "As if you ate ship's biscuit without evicting the weevils."

I choke on a laugh and turn away before we lose all decorum.

The middies disperse quickly to their duties, and I head to inspect my crew's progress with setting the *Aurora*'s rigging to some sort of naval standard. Domenic may have promoted me only to justify my role during the attack, but I intend to show him the extent of what an Ashing girl is capable of. Schedules and watch bills and tasks race through my mind, mixing with the tinge of excitement. I will tighten the *Aurora* to be the kind of ship she should be. I certainly can make her no worse.

I stumble, my foot catching on a rope that should have been coiled. By my work crew. None of whom are at their task. A growl rises from my chest. Which part of "coil these ropes" could possibly be misinterpreted?

I spot one of the seamen from my detail sitting beside a gun. He is darning a hole in his shirt and exchanging stories with a similarly employed man. I call him over. "What happened, Rodney?"

The man looks from me to the ropes. "Oh, aye. I'm just about to take care of that now."

"What were you about the past two hours?" I demand.

Rodney blinks, unabashed. "Just finishing up something real quick, ma'am. The bosun says we must have our clothes in proper order."

My teeth clench. "Put away your bloody tunic and do the job."

"Aye, ma'am." The seaman touches his forehead and picks up his things, carrying them below. I realize my mistake five minutes later, when he fails to return. I wait another five. Then ten. Then I ask one of the Spades to fish Rodney out and drag him to deck.

My nostrils flare. I put my hands behind my back and glare at the companionway until Rodney emerges. "Mr. Rodney." My voice is cool. The kind of cool that made *Faithful*'s sailors flinch. "It is kind of you to join me on deck."

Rodney shrugs. "Well, we've a job to do."

"Indeed." I clear my throat. "Might you enlighten me as to the delay belowdecks?"

He blinks. "No delay. I stopped in to use the head fast as I could and was just coming back up when the boy here found me. My stomach has been gripping me for days, ma'am."

My face is as hot as my impotence as Rodney's passive insubordination sinks in. How am I to command a crew that refuses to be commanded? I bite back a curse and take charge of my voice. "Very well. You may carry on with your duties now." This time, I stay on deck and start coiling one of the ropes myself. The *Aurora* bloody will look like a ship of war, even if I have to demonstrate each task.

Rodney walks over to the first rope that needs coiling and

picks it up off the deck. I'm past expecting him to fall to task with a will, but the seaman fails to meet even those minuscule expectations.

"Is there something you are waiting on, Rodney?" I snap.

"There were to be three of us for this," he says earnestly. "The job will be done better if we work together. It will be done right."

"And where are your partners?" I know I am digging myself deeper into a discussion that should not be happening in the first place, but blatant logic is forcing my tongue.

"They'll be here any minute now. I'm quite certain of it." Rodney lays his hand over his heart, underscoring his promise.

"That is not what I asked."

Then Rodney purses his lips, exasperated. "I wouldn't know where they are, Ms. Ash."

"If you do not know where they are, then how, pray tell me, do you know that they shall return shortly?" I've lost the rein on my voice. And my temper. I want to stamp my feet and curse at the windless sky. My face is hot, the ropes are disheveled, and I am no closer to progressing anything than I was when I started. If I send Rodney to find his mates, he will never return. If I go seek them myself, he will do nothing while I'm gone.

Someone steps up behind me, and Rodney buries himself in his task. I know it's Domenic before I turn around. My chest clenches, my heart striking my ribs.

"Ms. Ash, why is my deck still a mess?" he asks politely, linking his hands behind his back.

24

MY SHOULDERS WANT TO HUNCH under the truth, but I square them. "My failure, sir."

"Mmm." His face reveals nothing. Domenic snaps his fingers, calling Johina.

The Eflian trots over grudgingly, a rope's end in his hand.

"Clean up my deck, Mr. Johina," Domenic instructs. "You are relieved from this task, Ash."

"Aye, sir." I step away but make myself watch. Within a few minutes, Johina has recruited a new gang of workers, who scurry to stay ahead of his lash.

Domenic says nothing to me, but the silence stings as much as hard words. Maybe more. Domenic had never expected me to succeed on the lower decks, and I appear to be living down to those expectations. I claw my memory for my errors and find none. I gave the right orders. I set the right standards. I had the right expectations.

And I accomplished nothing.

Johina is brutal. But the ropes are getting coiled. Poorly and without care, but coiled. I don't want to become Johina.

There has to be a better way. There was on the *Faithful.* Or...
Or had I been so removed from the lower decks that I lived
in ignorance of the methods the mates employed to deliver
the well-tuned crew I commanded? I had dined on a delicious
meal and had appreciated the skill of the cook—but perhaps
not the butcher.

I slink away and walk until I find Catsper, who is drilling
the Spades on the poop. Rum snarls at me. The boys move
in perfect rhythm, though Penn's eyes stray as I approach.
Catsper's elbow strikes Penn in the ribs, and the boy grunts,
his eyes snapping back to center. Satisfied that the Spade
discipline is restored, Catsper turns to me and cocks his brow
in inquiry.

"Might we train early today?" I ask.

"You've divined a means of beating me, but it requires
specific hours?" says Catsper.

"No." But I'm not looking to win.

Catsper doesn't blink. "First bell of the afternoon watch,"
he tells me and returns to drill.

When I find Catsper that afternoon, he tosses a practice
sword into my hand and leads me to the poop deck. Being a
part of the officer's kit, the sword is the one melee weapon
I've had instruction in, but thus far, Catsper has been drilling
hand-to-hand basics into my skull. I don't ask questions. I
don't want to talk. I want to drown the wretched morning in
burning muscles and survival.

The few seamen on the poop clear out of our way. Or out
of Rum's way. The bloody dog trots along with us, snapping
his jaws at anyone who strays too close.

I expect instruction, but the marine salutes and attacks,
sending his blade at my head.

I parry. I wonder if he would have pulled the blow if I
missed the block. A strike <u>thuds</u> into my unprotected left

side, and I have my answer. It hurts, but it's a good pain. Numbing pain.

Catsper keeps the pace, his strikes clean and relentless. A low cut. An arc at my head. A lunge, with the sword's tip thrusting toward my heart. My breath quickens, sweat snaking down the back of my neck. Down. Up. Pivot. My arm burns. Catsper's sword tries to split my head again.

My memory stirs in recognition as I parry. It's a drill. Catsper is following a pattern, one that I'd done before, years ago when I had the time to play with swords. Now that I know where the attacks will come from, I block them smoothly. Quickly. Catsper nods and increases speed. My elegance disappears as quickly as it came. In moments, nothing matters beyond the next parry. The next step. The next breath. *Clank. Clank. Clank.*

Blissful oblivion of motion.

Catsper pushes me, for once forgiving my errors in favor of rhythm. Of speed. Of my need to disappear from reality.

Clank. Clack. The blades strike and reset as my lungs flame inside. I trip and find my balance with a snarl.

Catsper gives me no chance to breathe. His blade whirls, demanding my answer.

But I can't give it. He is too fast. Too well trained. Too conditioned.

I brace myself for a strike, willing to exchange a bruise for a chance to breathe.

He pulls the blow, cutting off that escape. "Move, Ash!"

I'd love to. But my body is shaking from effort, and my eyes sting with sweat. "I can't," I gasp. "Slow down." It hurts to speak, and I sound like I'm begging. *Storms, I am* begging. My knees crash to the deck as I parry the next blow.

"Get up."

I do. At least my body does. My mind can't. With a cry, I let go of thought and strike wildly as if the fight is real and each move is my last. *Clank. Clank. Clank.*

I realize something has changed only when Catsper's foot hooks behind mine and I crash backward to the deck. My practice sword clatters as the tip of Catsper's presses into my throat.

The back of my head hurts, but I just close my eyes and gulp lungfuls of air. I might be smiling.

"You aren't supposed to celebrate losing." Catsper extends his hand.

"Surviving a match with you isn't losing," I say between breaths as he pulls me up.

"You didn't survive."

"Good point." I sink back to my knees. I think I might fall back down. If I'm dead, I need not walk with the marine. I wager he'll climb ladders. If I'm dead, I should certainly not be required to climb ladders.

Catsper nudges me with his boot. Somehow, I follow him to the Cove and manage to spill only half the mug of water he shoves into my hands.

"You're supposed to instruct before throwing a weapon into someone's hands, you know," I say once I can talk again. I'm drunk on fatigue, and the world is fuzzy around the edges. "What would you have done if I failed to parry?"

"Hit you, I presume."

I roll my eyes. "Isn't presuming that I can hold a sword a bit steep a wager?"

"No."

I tilt my head in question.

Catsper puts his feet up on a sea chest. "Did you know that once the Ashing flagship *Faithful* sank, the Tirik opened fire on the lifeboats?" He pulls his arm across his chest in a stretch. "The *Destiny* had a contingent of Spade snipers aboard. We covered the crews pulling up survivors. Took out thirty men with our muskets alone."

My blood chills. I stare at him.

The marine switches to his other arm. "I'd not seen Ashing crews up close before. Their skill puts the Joint Fleet to shame, does it not?"

25

MY MOUTH IS DRY. CATSPER WAS on the *Destiny*. He knows who I am. He has known since I came aboard. I don't know whether to run or laugh. If the marine had any intention of exposing me, he would have before now.

"Domenic knows too," I say after a moment.

Catsper's brows rise in surprise. "And respects you despite it. Interesting."

My heart pauses a beat. "Are you going to ask me what I'm doing here?"

"I don't much care." The remark is so offhanded that I little doubt it's true. Catsper is the kind to judge things as they are. He rises and stows away our practice blades. He hadn't brought them out to send a message, I realize. He brought them to help me regain myself. "Dana will keep his mouth shut," he says over his shoulder. "You need not worry."

"He said I should be afraid of him," I tell Catsper as neutrally as I can. The marine knows Domenic. I want to hear more. Need to hear it.

Catsper only shrugs. "He's right."

"Why?"

He looks at me sideways. "Because you've no intention of going meekly about your duties. Dana can grant you no special leeway on the count of liking you."

"He doesn't like me."

"Good." Weapons stowed, Catsper dissolves into his troop of Spades.

⸎

The sun is setting over the distant horizon when I muster the courage to seek Price. I'd heeded Rima's orders to stay away from the Tirik Gifted for three days, and it's as long as I can stand. The danger in being discovered violating the captain's orders pales beside the greater danger of the questions I harbor. Especially with the growing convulsions, with Domenic paying enough attention to meddle in my affairs. The need to call the wind grows stronger each day, as if the magic is maturing and demanding release. If I don't find some means of controlling my Gift soon, I may not last the two years until I can make it to the Metchti Monastery.

Lantern in hand, I approach the small cabin where Rima stashed Price, as if being Gifted was infectious, like fever. My stomach flutters as I lift the heavy latch outside the door. The metal squeaks, resisting me for a moment before giving under the pressure. Inside, the cabin is void of windows and too small to lie down without curling up.

Price raises an arm to protect his eyes from the dim glow of my light, but the fear that had clung to him in the hold is gone now, replaced by an eerie calm.

"Hello," he says evenly. Tirik has a guttural sound that I dislike, but Price's soft voice smooths the harshness.

I swallow. I don't want to be here. But I need answers to a thousand questions. Or maybe just to one. *Is there a cure,*

Price? Did the Republic find a cure? "How are you faring?"

"I am alive."

Presumably an improvement on his previous expectations. I clear my throat, suddenly stretching for words. I must be careful.

"There is rain coming," says Price.

"The skies are clear."

"I cannot see the skies from here. But I am certain of the rain." His voice is flat again. No irritation, no anger. Silence stretches between us. "I recall nothing more about the deployment of Republic forces."

I clear my throat. "I hadn't asked you."

"It seems logical that you would."

True. I let the door close. Price is sitting on his heels. I contemplate whether to sit beside him or remain standing. After a moment, I lower to his level. "Would it bother you if I returned to that subject?"

Price shakes his head. "No. I've nothing competing for my time."

"You would not feel annoyed?"

"I feel only sensation tied to my physical state—fear of pain, relief when pain ends. But such feelings as annoyance or sadness or despair little affect me."

"But neither does joy or hope," I can't help saying.

"I believe I am fortunate," Price continues. "Despair can drive a person mad."

Right. The conversation stalls. I rub my arms. I need to get to the point before someone finds me here and starts trouble. "Someone dear to me is a metal caller."

"I know of no cure," Price says. "That was going to be your next question, was it not?"

My chest tightens. "Do you always cover both sides of a conversation?" I snap.

"It is efficient."

"I don't care. Stop it." I draw a breath and check myself. "My tone was uncalled for. Do you know whether anything might at least dampen the effects of elemental attraction? Anything that might make the magic sleep or at least fill its host more slowly?"

Price leans his elbows on his knees and looks at me. "The Institute researchers required I name the weather each day. Accuracy was rewarded. Mistakes punished. Once I learned to make no mistakes, they introduced barriers." Price rubs a round scar on his arm. "Objects and actions designed to hinder my ability."

I swallow. "And...did anything work?"

"No." His words are painfully certain. "Even when I was too starved or beaten to think clearly, I still felt the pressure of the elements. The Institute's barriers only stopped my ability to form thoughts and words."

I shake my head. Price is wrong. He has to be wrong. There has to be something of help he can tell me.

"I've had a strange sensation for a while now," Price says quietly. It takes me a moment to realize he is no longer speaking of the Institute. "I feel a shift in the pressures that grows by the day. I cannot interpret the feeling for you, but it is the reason the *Devron* had me aboard this cruise. The captain had hoped I would provide warning before the...*something* is imminent."

"The *something*?" I open my palms, imagining having this conversation with Captain Rima. "Something such as what? A storm? A tornado? A bloody volcano erupting?"

He shrugs. "I do not know, but I believe nature will be violent. Something is stretching. And, eventually, it will rip."

"Violent. Violent enough to harm a man-of-war?"

"Violent enough to shatter a mile of mountains."

I rub my face. I had sought out Price to learn more about elemental attraction. Instead, I received a doomsday prophecy. "Would it be too much to hope you can predict when this horror is to happen?"

"On the contrary. I believe such emotion would be most appropriate."

Oh waves and hail. "You do not know when," I say for him, and the Gifted nods.

26

YOU CALLED ON THE TIRIK PRISONER? At night? After the captain forbade contact with the boy?" Ana's hazel eyes are livid as we cram with the other middies into the boys' berth for an early morning navigational lesson. Our time on deck proved to everyone that we need books and charts more than sextons just now, and studying in privacy makes everyone more comfortable. Or did, until I showed up with news of Price's words. "Are you daft, Nile? Dana will disembowel you."

"I know." From the point of self-preservation, telling anyone of my visit is daft. But I need to talk through Price's bizarre prediction with someone, and the middies are a more thoughtful bunch than I expected. Sand, the only one who'd bristle at the mention of Price's name, isn't here.

"I agree with Ana on all fronts," Kederic says as the boys unsling their cots and move their sea chests together to create a passable table and benches. Kederic's wavelike black hair is tied back to show sharp cheekbones and trim, slender shoulders. Despite being seventeen and as tall as me,

Kederic's body has some growing to do yet. "But what's done is done, so let's hear what the Tirik said. Did he predict today's rain?"

"Yes."

Kederic nods gravely. "But there is more?"

"Seriously?" Ana groans, swatting Kederic's shoulder. "You are encouraging her?"

I try not to roll my eyes at Ana's latest excuse to touch the older middie, and turn back to Kederic. "Price claims to feel some kind of major weather anomaly approaching. No specifics."

Kederic frowns into the shadows for several heartbeats. "Perhaps he will know more as the anomaly gets closer. Would it not be prudent to interview him daily?" The middie taps his finger on the table. "At worst, we will know the weather. Such foreknowledge has hurt no ship yet."

Ana links her arms around her knees. "Captain Rima will never permit it. He named the prisoner a liar and a fraud. Changing a ship's course in concession to a fraud's prediction would be foolish."

Kederic's gaze says that his own opinion may differ from our lord and master's, but I decide not to press the issue lest I steer the middies into trouble alongside myself. The problem with Price's prophecy is that without more detail, it isn't actionable. Not yet.

Clearing my throat, I pull out the props I brought for the lesson. The thick stench of bodies and lanterns locked together with little ventilation hangs thick as fog, and my magic urges me to call a breeze. I focus on a spot on the deck until I can trust myself to stay in control, then look at the middies.

Kederic and Thatch Lawrence watch me with hungry gazes. They are so desperate for knowledge, it is painful to watch them fail at tasks no one had the time to teach them.

Song is studying the deck. Ana... Ana is studying the boys.

"Tell me about the Bottleneck Juncture, at the mouth of the Siaman Sea," I ask the middies.

"It's a place where land and rock formations result in a narrow three-way juncture between the Siaman Sea, the Ardent Ocean, and the Diante West Corridor," says Thatch Lawrence, unfolding his fingers one at a time. "The connection between the Siaman Sea and Diante West Corridor is all right, but the only way to get in and out of the Ardent Ocean is to pass through the Bottleneck."

"And only one ship can pass at a time," adds Kederic. "Which has a strategic advantage: if the Tirik Republic wanted to take the Siaman, we'd need but a few ships aimed at the Bottleneck. We could shoot the Tirik down one by one as they come through."

Ana rolls her eyes. "It isn't strategic if no one cares about it. There is *nothing* here we can't more easily get elsewhere, not even fresh water. No one even lives on most of the islands."

"There are two freshwater sources," I correct her. "The Crystal Oasis on Lyron soil and a stream at the Diante port. You might also note that the sea floor is much deeper in the archipelago than at the mainland's coastline, allowing larger ships to maneuver closer to land. For the present, however, the crucial point is that to sail *out* of the Siaman and get home, you'll have to navigate the Bottleneck. And there is precious little room for error."

The four nod, even Ana.

"Did you see our noon sights and positions?" Kederic asks. It's been pouring rain, and I know Domenic has not the time to check the youngsters' calculations while Lieutenant Kazzik could barely be trusted with his own work.

I cringe. "Yes. Mr. Lawrence had the *Aurora* approaching the mainland of the Tirik Republic."

Song chuckles.

"Mr. Song, you had us off the South Eflian coast, if memory serves." I wait for the chuckling to subside. "The only one to locate the *Aurora* in the Siaman Sea was Mr. Kederic. Who, I would wager, had memorized the previous day's position from the log and estimated."

Kederic blushes, and we dive into trigonometry.

§

Our two-ship convoy dwindles to one with the *Hope* making her departure signal several days short of the Diante port, so it is only the *Solace* sailing in our wake when the lookout calls "Land ho!" I join the seamen gathering on deck to get the first glimpse of the Diante harbor. It's one of the most monotone places I've ever laid eyes on. Sand, small whitewashed huts, and more sand. The only sign of color I see in my borrowed spyglass are occasional three-pronged cactuses peppered amidst dunes. I wonder whether the rest of the Diante continent is anything like this, or just this part near the Siaman Sea.

I drink in the details, memorizing each one. This is as close as anyone in Lyron gets to the Diante Empire. And this is where my eventual journey to the Diante capital will one day start—a small port near the Bottleneck Juncture. I wonder how long I will have to travel to get to the Metchti Monastery. We've no maps of the inner part of the Diante Empire, but I imagine the capital city is a good ways off if these villagers condescend to trade with foreigners instead of traveling south to meet with their own kind. "Recluses," I mutter.

"When you are self-sufficient and powerful enough to little worry about your neighbors, you can afford to be a recluse." Domenic walks up beside me and leans on the rail. He is so close, I smell the salt clinging to his clothes and the harsh lye soap he washes with. "Catsper and I will be heading ashore to arrange purchase of stores and water. You may share our boat."

I lean away. "You are still intent on forcing me into visiting a physician?"

"I rarely issue orders for the pleasure of hearing my voice."

My jaw tightens. "As you wish, sir."

Domenic growls softly beneath his breath. "This isn't a punishment, Nile."

"No, it is you using your position to get into my business. *Sir.*" I go to step away, but Domenic grabs my upper arm. Hard.

"One other point, Ash."

I try to jerk free, fail, and glare at him.

Releasing his grip, Domenic links his hands behind his back. "It has come to my notice over the past week that the *Aurora*'s middies have both improved their mathematics and gained an uncanny sense of the weather. Yesterday morning, Kederic was inspired to order his division to turn out for inspection in foul-weather gear. They were the only ones to stay dry in the rain that followed." He waits until our eyes meet before continuing. "I would be very disappointed to hear that you've done the middies' work for them or disobeyed the captain and had contact with the prisoner."

My eyes flash. Thanks to the middies' efforts, the *Aurora* is on her way to becoming halfway competent—probably for the first time since the buffoon in the captain's uniform took command.

"The middies' calculations are their own, and I make no habit of visiting Price." *That* Kederic and Thatch Lawrence organized themselves, drawing pictures to bridge the differences in language. I straighten, adjusting my tunic. "If there is nothing else you wish to decide for me or accuse me of, sir, may I return to my duties?"

It is a quiet ride from the *Aurora* to the docks. Domenic and I sit as far apart as the small boat allows, while Catsper examines the edge of his boot knife. The port is small. Several merchantmen sit at anchor, and many fishing boats bob in neat lines. Despite their number, there is an unnatural uniformity in the boats' white paint and trim. The approaching pier is uncommonly quiet despite heavy foot traffic. As we get closer, I realize that the only raised voices I do hear belong to the foreign merchants. The Diante walking along the pier stay in lanes, as if someone had drawn invisible lines down the wooden walkways.

"Are our hosts always this boisterous?" asks Catsper.

Domenic shrugs. "I've come ashore here only twice before to purchase water, and it was thus then. If there is something for which the Diante lack protocol, I am yet to see it."

The seaman at the tiller maneuvers us smoothly to the dock, where a pair of gray-uniformed Diante dock workers await. Their almond-shaped eyes tilt up at the corners, giving their faces a hint of a feline appearance. Felines dressed in billowing gray pants and thigh-length tunics, held tight with wide strips of yellow cloth at the waist. The two men bow in unison before throwing us a line.

Dock workers. Bowing.

At the height of discipline, Ashing dock workers avoid spitting on the walkway.

"The Dock Master will be with you as soon as it is possible," one of the dock workers says in heavily accented Lyron once we climb onto the pier. The two bow in unison again and dissolve to other duties without waiting for coin.

We stand alone, disrupting the perfect flow of traffic. Ocean and ships spread out on our left, fields of sand to the right as far as the eyes can <u>see</u>. I can only presume that whatever passes for civilization here is somewhere ahead, where I see outcroppings of those whitewashed buildings I spied through the glass.

Raising my face to the breeze, I draw a deep breath. The familiar scent of ocean salt mixes with seaweed, filling my nose with air that's slightly sulfurous, briny, and *green*. The same green that coats ropes resting beneath the water and stilts holding up the docks. I wonder if the smell will follow me when I venture into town, and pull my coat tighter around my shoulders. Despite being south, it's colder here than I expected, because there isn't one bloody thing to block the wind.

Catsper turns his hand in question.

"I don't know," says Domenic. "Last time, they directed me immediately to their purser." He shifts uncertainly, and I can't help feeling a smidgen of satisfaction at his discomfort. If he is making me find a quack Diante healer, he deserves what he gets here.

"If you excuse me, gentlemen, I will be about my business," I say and set off down the pier, hoping my departure adds to his worries. Plus, if I'm to be ordered about like a child, the least I can do is pretend I've some dignity left.

Truth be told, beyond whispers of the Metchti Monastery, I know embarrassingly little of the Diante—and much of the ignorance is of my own making. Growing up with the threat of the Tirik Republic saturating the last decade, I had little patience to spare for learning about an isolationist nation who refused to notice a great war on its doorstep.

The Diante stare at me, those slanted eyes penetrating and quietly displeased. When I smile in return, they hurry away, tight-lipped. After a few minutes of seeing no other women on the pier, an uncomfortable feeling creeps down my spine and my steps slow. Even the merchies have kept their female crew on ship. Finding a physician is well and good, but I'm not about to walk off the docks when the entire town thinks me an exotic beast.

"Ash."

I turn toward Catsper's voice.

Saying nothing more, the marine falls in step slightly behind me.

At the end of the pier, a man with a whistle and a long stick steps before us. Like the others, he wears a uniform of billowing pants and long tunic, though his is blue instead of the dock workers' gray. A stiff woolen hat, round with a small point in the center, sits atop his head.

"Where you go?" he asks Catsper, plainly struggling to find the Lyron words for the inquiry.

"We are looking for a doctor," I say in Diante, which, while strained, is several times better than his Lyron.

The guard looks over my shoulder at Catsper, somehow managing to portray the very essence of politeness—even holding the stick angled away from us as not to give offense—while ignoring me utterly.

I step forward. Catsper shoots me a quick glance and sticks his hands into his pockets, rocking back on his heels as if to say *it's all you, for as long as you wish.*

Bowing to the guard, I find my Diante skills again. "I am Nile Ash, a sailor aboard the Lyron Ship *Aurora*. Might we be permitted to go into the main town to find a healer?"

"Where you go?" the guard asks Catsper again.

Catsper cocks an arrogant brow at the man, then looks to me.

I draw a breath to calm my nerves, but it does little good. First Domenic decides he knows what's best for me, now this. After the *Aurora*'s Eflians, I thought myself immune to further insult. "Forget it." I turn on my heel. "I need nothing here."

I manage a single step before I feel it. The sudden fear with no cause, the sense of impending doom. My heart races. Not here. Not now. Not before Catsper and the thrice-damned Diante, who stares at me. I go down to one knee as flashes of green light flicker before my eyes. My right arm and shoulder shudder. Again. Again. Again. Again.

27

ASH."

I hear Catsper, but can't respond.

"Is she unwell?" the guard asks in Diante, his voice suddenly tinged with panic.

Catsper grabs my shoulder.

I strain against the hold, the joint threatening to come undone. I'm about to scream in agony when, as suddenly as it left, my body returns. A wave of nausea washes over me, and I just manage to twist free of Catsper's hold before stumbling to the pier's edge and emptying my stomach into the water. That finished, I sit on the dock and brace my pounding head on my knees.

The guard clears his throat. "Allow me to escort you to a medicine woman," he offers quietly.

I don't know to whom he addressed the words. And little care. My head, my shoulder, and everything else hurts. I allow Catsper to grab the back of my tunic to keep me steady as I plod, step by step, after the guard.

Ocean on the left. Sand on right. Wooden-planked

walkway. Whitewashed huts getting closer with each step. I'm aware of the boardwalk ending and us veering southwest onto a sand-packed road. The houses are close now, all perfectly square and lined up like soldiers. Instead of Ashing's shaped shrubbery, the decorations here are made of stone. I'd appreciate the mosaic if I wasn't still woozy. If many sets of piercing slanted eyes weren't watching every step I make, the distrust radiating like sunrays.

The guard stops at a house that looks like all the others. He knocks on the door and calls something in Diante too quickly for me to understand, then motions for me to proceed on alone.

Catsper crosses his arms and leans against a boulder to wait.

I slip inside. My head is still heavy, but I hope the Diante healer might have something to settle my stomach. It would be easier to conceal the jerking spells if I stopped vomiting afterward. I keep my hope in check. I was telling Domenic the truth when I said the Diante notion of medicine is a long way from scientific.

There is a thin partition before me. "Hello?" I call, stepping toward it. Getting no answer, I circle around the makeshift half wall and step into the back room of the hut. I want to see rolls of clean bandages, neatly lined jars of medicine, and plenty of light. Instead, the windows are drawn with heavy canvas drapes, and the air hangs laden with competing scents of burning candles and incense.

A middle-aged woman kneels on a floor cushion. She is grinding herbs in a small stone mortar and pays me no mind.

I put my hands on my thighs and bow, as I saw folks do on the docks. "Hello. You are the healer?" I ask in Diante.

The woman's eyes flicker toward me, weighing me with their gaze.

I stay still for the inspection, but my mouth is dry and

my heart is beating faster with each breath. The room is stifling and the woman oddly still as she studies me. As if I were a fish flopping on deck. Licking my lips, I pull coins out of my pocket and hold them out on an open palm toward her.

She snorts. "No manners, eh? Well, I'm little surprised. Take your shoes off and sit down."

I obey and kneel gingerly on the cushion in imitation of the woman's own posture. "I'm looking for medicine to help my nausea," I say, getting to the point. "I'm on a ship, and I am seasick. Can you help?"

She watches with an unsettlingly deep gaze. "Nausea?" she echoes finally. "Are you with child?"

I recoil. "No!"

She snorts.

My face heats. All of me heats. "I'm quite certain. I've never been with a man that way." I've never been with a man in any way.

"So you say." She shrugs. "We will know soon enough."

I clear my throat. "What ails me is—"

"Hush." Waving away my words, the woman takes my wrist, her fingers digging into my pulse point. She holds me so long that my fingers tingle. Her face tenses as she releases my wrist. "The other hand," she demands. Her voice isn't irreverent anymore. It's tight. On edge.

Something is wrong. I can feel it. "It's my stomach, ma'am," I say. "When—"

She silences me with a flash of her gaze, dark with flecks of green.

My heart beats hard. I stare at the flickering flames of the many candles. I've heard Diante place great stock in pulse reading, but my nerves are surely throwing the reading off course. I'm certain one must be relaxed for this to work. Relaxed and calm and...

Oh storms and hail, who in the bloody storm cares. The woman cares nothing for symptoms and is busy diagnosing pregnancy. I swallow. Tense. Brace my free hand on the floor. This whole thing, this meeting, this sham of a diagnosis, is a mistake. Bad information is worse than no information. The last thing I need is superstitious nonsense as difficult to separate from the truth as a tan from skin. "Thank you, ma'am," I say, pulling back on my wrist. "But I find I feel better than I thought."

She shakes her head in concentration, her hold tightening. "You are Gods touched," she says softly.

My heart pauses. "My people worship different gods from yours." I get my hand free. "Thank you. I'll go."

"Your people call it Gifted. Yes?"

I shake my head. Hard. Too hard. "My brother is Gifted," I blurt. "I just wanted something to settle my stomach. But it is of no consequence."

The woman lifts my chin with her finger. "You've too much mind for a metal caller and too much muscle for a stone speaker. Water... No, you move without the fear those whose blood will not thicken carry. Air, then." She nods to herself while my heart pounds. "Tell me, what does it feel like to have much air and yet no breath? And when you convulse, do you foul yourself before all who watch?"

I rise and back away.

"Are you ready to die?" she asks.

I swallow. "Can you aid me?" I whisper. "Or is fear the greatest medicine you can offer?"

She chuckles. "Both. But you shall little like what I say, and I wish you to be clear, up front, on the choices you have." She pats the pillow and waits until I kneel again before continuing. "The Gods' touch flows very strong within you. Strong enough to kill. If you wish to continue living in this world, you must learn to respect the Gods' will. If you do not, you shall lose."

Storms and hail. I'm unsure what's more terrifying, that the woman could read the Gift in my pulse or that her best treatment involves appeasing gods I don't believe in.

"Do you understand how your Gift works?" she asks.

I decide on the truth. "The magic in my body attracts the air. I can keep the magic contained for a bit but eventually must let it loose. When I do, the air comes. And then, the jerking spells."

"Pfft." She waves away my words. "*Magic.* You speak of it like a parasite, something separate from you, when it is entwined with your life force." Her finger pokes my gut. "Your life force—your *ki*—is here. The Gods have infused your *ki* with a divine fire, what you northerners call magic. It needs to engage with its element—air for you—to live. Yet, give too much and the divine fire will burn so hot, it shall burn you. Too little and you shall smolder. Balance the fire, child. That is the key to your life. Do you understand?"

Of course not. I rub my forehead.

She sighs. "You must pay mind to your *ki*'s divine fire, to your *magic.* Learn how it feels, what it needs, how it moves and shifts and grows. Focus on *its* needs instead of your own. When is it restless and slumbering? What wakes and calms it? You must learn to recognize when your magic will need release before the need grows too great to control."

"It sounds a lot like learning to use the toilet," I mutter.

She laughs, her eyes crinkling. "At first, perhaps. But you should soon find it is more like taming a powerful beast that always rides beside you. It might seem, at first, that all you have to contain it is a length of leash. But, once you and your beast connect, you shall find the leash is but the most rudimentary of your communications."

I rub the back of my head. "And how does one do this? Feel this beast, tame it, teach it tricks?"

The woman presses her lips together at my tone. "Discipline," she snaps. "Meditate daily. An hour four times a day to start, then more. The magic, you, and the element must meet in short, controlled dances. Start with blowing out a candle without upsetting its pedestal." She raises her finger. "That last is vital. Do not lose control if you want your life."

Start with four hours a day? Then more? Following this guidance would leave me doing nothing but meditating and extinguishing candles—which are forbidden on a ship altogether. "How long does it take to master this balance?" I ask instead of arguing.

She blinks. "A lifetime."

Practical.

"True balance is striven for but never achieved," the healer tells me. "The journey itself is the greatest of things."

No. It isn't. "If I balance my *ki's* divine fire, will the convulsions stop?"

"No." She shrugs dismissively. "They are the tribute the Gods exact. You should bear them with grace and humility."

A growl builds in my chest. The woman knows everything except the minor detail of how to fix the problem. I check my frustration and bow. "Be that as it may, if you have something for my stomach, I am willing to risk the Gods' displeasure in exchange for not vomiting on myself."

She frowns but limps over to a basket. "Ginger," she says, placing a thick white root into a bag. "Eases nausea."

"Thank you." I place a gold coin onto one of the pillows and start to leave, but pause at the partition. "One last question," I say quickly. "Can you tell me how to get to the Metchti Monastery?"

"I can, yes." She settles on her pillow and closes her eyes. "But I will not. The Metchti Monastery is not for foreigners such as you."

Catsper, still leaning against the boulder when I emerge, is the picture of feline arrogance. Blond hair billowing in the wind, black pants and tunic stretched over nimble, powerful muscle. He has his hands too casually in his pockets, his body preternaturally still, as his green eyes drink in every detail around him. A warrior. There is no other word for it. And from the tense, respectful glances of the passing Diante, they know it too.

I raise my forearm to shield my eyes from the sun and biting wind and walk to him. I owe him something. I just don't know what. Silence hangs between us as I weigh my words.

He beats me to it.

"I will ask one question. And you will answer." Catsper crosses his arms, his eyes locked on mine, intensely enough to send a shiver through my blood. "Are you a danger to the ship?"

"No," I say quickly. I hope it's true.

He nods once and turns away, starting us back to the dock.

I wait for the follow-up broadside, but nothing comes. "Is that all you wanted to ask?" I say finally.

He looks over his shoulder. "It is all I need to know."

That hits deep. Catsper is willing to risk the entire ship on the weight of my word. Don't I owe him the same confidence? "Wait." I clench my jaw. "Just...wait."

The marine obediently comes to a stop and faces me, his body betraying nothing more than faint curiosity. Damn his Spardic self. I lick my lips before speaking, then decide against talk altogether.

Steeling myself for the inevitable suffocation, I close my eyes and allow the air to come.

Balance the fire, the healer had said. Tame the beast.

Storms and hail. What bloody fire? What beast? My throat

closes. I force down the panic, releasing the magic in an angled pattern so the air flows across me.

The light breeze touches my cheek and flaps Catsper's collar. Watching the marine's face, I release the magic more and more, until my wind beats our clothes and Catsper's eyes widen with understanding.

The thread of control I have slips suddenly, and I jerk all the magic back. Hard. Air pushes into my lungs, burning and clawing and ripping. I drop to my knees, fighting to exhale, the air finally leaving in a horrid wheeze. My bloody fault for getting cocky. "It started after I came aboard." My words come in short gasps. "I'm quite certain the air flow would kill me before it could harm the *Aurora*."

He nods. "If it does not, I will."

I stare. But Catsper is neither jesting nor threatening. He's just, well, informing me of the facts.

"Wonderful," I say flatly. "Though I do hope that will not be your first option."

Catsper extends a hand to help me up.

Domenic is where we left him. A middle-aged Diante man in the yellow colors of the port stands beside him. The lavish braids decorating the man's tunic suggest he is of some importance here. Domenic shakes his head violently. His body is rigid and his skin flushed a dark hue.

Without speaking, Catsper and I hurry our pace.

"...I fear, however, that my assistant was correct in noting the scarcity in supplies at this time," the Diante is saying as we approach.

"Perhaps your assistant misunderstood, sir." Domenic's voice is tight. "The Aurora needs only fresh water from your stream, and we've our own casks. The only other fresh water is weeks of travel away. Our people will go thirsty."

"Your poor planning of supplies is most regrettable," the port master says with a low bow. "But I fear the Diante can no longer welcome foreign ships of war in its port."

28

CATSPER AND I STOP BESIDE DOMENIC and touch our foreheads.

The port master frowns, flashing the same disapproving look at me that I've seen on every face in the village. "What's this?" he demands of Domenic.

"Allow me to present Ms. Nile Ash," Domenic says sharply, his eyes flickering to mine. "The *Aurora*'s purser. And my lieutenant of the marines, Catsper. Ash, Catsper, this is His Honorable Greatness Port Master Neil."

Neil's jaw tightens. "This is your purser?"

"*She* is my purser."

I bow, my mind reeling. Domenic's only reason for this fiction can be to give me purchase into the negotiation. A hope that my skills can do something his can't. *Storms and hail.* I scramble my brain. Balance and reciprocity and honor, that's what the Diante value. Harmony, at least in appearance. Saving face and following the law.

"The Aurora is indeed a man-of-war, sir, but she is on

convoy duty," I tell Neil, choosing my words as carefully as fragile berries. "We escorted merchants and their goods safely to you. I hope your people find this commerce of benefit." *And that you bloody reciprocate the favor, you protocol-loving bigot.*

Neil considers this. Considers me. Domenic. "The *merchantmen* are most welcome."

I think I follow his meaning. Neil will not allow a frigate's supply boats to come ashore, but he will consent to merchantmen intermediaries. Water obtained thus would be both very limited and very expensive, but it would keep the *Aurora*'s crew alive while the Diante save face.

"Thank you," says Domenic, who appears to have arrived at the same conclusion I did.

The parties bow to each other. I wait until Domenic and Catsper are several steps away, then turn back to the port master. "Sir," I ask, switching to Diante. "Your empire is mightier than Lyron and Tirik combined. Why the iron neutrality?"

He smiles without humor. "A woman's presence on the pier shames us, madam. And yet you risk further offense by speaking without need?" He holds up his palms. "That is your answer. The Lyron League and Tirik Republic have little to offer the Diante, yet relations with either peoples are filled with insults to our harmony. You do not help us. Only hurt. Excuse me."

We do as agreed, making our limited water purchase from the merchantmen—which I'm certain is further constrained by Rima's love of his coin and not the merchants' alleged inability to obtain further supplies. And when it's done, we have half our casks filled. This seems aplenty to the seamen, but looking at a chart and our distance to the next water source, the direness of the situation is plain. A water shortage scorches a crew long before supplies actually run out, for when thirsty men see an abundance of drink their officers are hoarding from them, violence is but a step away.

Domenic and I stand at the rail without speaking. The Diante shore sprawls behind us, the sparkling ocean ahead.

"Did finding a physician prove within your capabilities?" he asks finally.

I shoot him a sideways glance. "She proclaimed me as healthy as the Gods made me. Though she did feel my time would be better spent meditating rather than scrubbing decks."

"Do you know how to meditate?"

"I do." Catsper's approach saves me from continuing the conversation alone. "I'll show her. Wouldn't wish to ignore the advice of a sage in a hut."

I cock my eyebrow. "Spardic warriors meditate?"

He glances down at me. "What we do would kill you. But the basics are tame enough." Catsper crosses his arms. "How bad is it with water?"

"Bad," Domenic and I answer together.

Domenic scowls at me and clears his throat. "We'll need Spades standing guard at the casks."

I drop my voice. "Plus, thirst makes even decent sailors stupid. And we aren't starting on a strong note to begin with."

"I'm certain my new master's mate will have things under control," Domenic says just as quietly. "She has a knack for keeping the lower decks on task."

"At least she can speak with people without holding a cat-o'-nine-tails over them."

Catsper leans forward so his face is close to us. "If you two don't stop bickering, I'll knock your heads together."

Before either of us can put Catsper's threat to the test, Rima appears on deck to address the hands.

"Denying water to an honest crew is nothing but petty cruelty," Rima says, compassion filling his voice. "As much as

I wish otherwise, I cannot turn an Empire to reason. But I will do what is in my power to ease your hardship."

Two hundred tense faces hang on the captain's words, as if he can conjure supplies from the air. Even I'm curious how Rima thinks he can talk people out of thirst. Knowing him, Rima has already formulated a plan to turn even this disaster to his advantage.

Rima surveys the crew, his eyes, as usual, skipping over Sandra and the other women standing together. "To conserve your strength, the *Aurora* will forgo scheduled patrols. We shall, in fact, depart at once on the next tide and keep to a holiday routine as much as we can until we reach Crystal Oasis. I shall do my best to convince Mr. Dana here to lighten up drill. You must save your bodies, men. Stay cool. It will ease your thirst. And for Gods' sakes," he adds with a wry smile, "try to keep on Mr. Dana's good side."

The crew doesn't cheer, but some relieved smiles pass amidst the hands. At least their captain understands them. Their workload will lighten. It will be all right.

Bloody brilliant bastard. Never mind that Rima never actually told the hands what the rations would be. Or that he's seizing on the fortune of a foreign dispute to scrap *Aurora*'s assigned patrol. The *Aurora* is supposed to be cruising through the Siaman and neutralizing any threats to merchant shipping, not running Rima's private escort service—but doing that endangers Rima's hide with low chance of personal gain.

At the end of it all, it's up to Domenic to announce that water rations are reduced to half and up to the Spades to enforce the rules. Despite the ease of holiday routine, three men are flogged within a week for attempting to take extra.

I am half-surprised and half-relieved when *Hope*, who'd separated right before the Diante port, does not rejoin us as we head east toward the Crystal Oasis. What does make my stomach clench as we sail deeper east into the Siaman Sea is the sight of a Joint Fleet dispatch ship. The *Aurora* has not been out long enough to warrant a routine mail call, which means the dispatch ship carries vital news of the war.

29

CATSPER'S FACE IS HARD. EVEN FOR HIM. He drops onto the bench across from Domenic and me in the officers' gunroom. I wish we were in the Cove instead. A pair of Spades raises a hellish din examining the cabins leading from the gunroom. Ostensibly, they are training. But I know Catsper well enough to see through the game. He wants to ensure that we are here alone.

Despite the custom to allow time for hands to write letters home, Rima cited the dire water situation to leave the dispatch ship behind as soon as the incoming mail was transferred. I wonder what excuse he'd cited to the dispatch's skipper to prevent the little ship from sailing alongside, but for all I know, the other had no time for such niceties. Of the three of us, Catsper—who called this little gathering— appears most in the know. Which is a figurative slap across the first officer's face. Not that Domenic lets anything show. Rima doesn't deserve him.

"Has Rima given you a copy of the Admiralty report?"

Catsper asks Domenic.

Domenic shakes his head. "I know little more than the newsleaf for now."

I know even less than that.

"First off, there is a prize offered for anyone with information about the whereabouts of one Princess Nile Greysik of Ashing," says Catsper, sliding a newsleaf copy to me.

"What?" A burning in my cheeks blurs the printed text. I rub my eyes and groan. "Mother. Oh bloody hail. Damn Felielle and its bloody values."

"Yes, Highness, my entire nation has nothing on its mind but scheming plans to inject obstacles into your life," says Domenic. "Goddess forbid families care for each other's well-being."

"How is that caring working out in your family?"

Domenic's upper lip curls in a snarl. He leans toward me across the table. "If you—"

"Enough." Catsper's low growl reminds me that outside our games, the man keeps two dozen of the ship's deadliest soldiers in check. He glares between Domenic and me until we both settle back into our chairs. "Not your mother, Ash. Prince Tamiath."

"Tamiath? Why?" I scan the newsleaf, my chest growing heavier by the word. The minor point of my absence, it appears, little hindered mother's marriage plans. I can't fathom why the Felielle prince bothered putting out a reward for his missing bride instead of leaving the disaster as quickly as his ship would carry him, but politics has never been my strong suit. "If Rima finds out..."

"If Rima finds out, it will be from your own choice," Domenic says. "You have my promise. And it appears you have Catsper's as well." He says the last in an unnaturally neutral tone.

"I recognized her from the *Faithful*'s battle," Catsper tells Domenic with a dismissive wave, and pulls out a parchment with a broken Spardic Command seal. Although Catsper and the Spades are stationed on a Lyron League Joint Fleet ship, they belong to the Spardic Kingdom's private army, just as the *Faithful* had been part of Ashing's armada. The Spardic Kingdom would not usually loan a valuable Spade unit to the Joint Fleet, but Catsper's boys are in training. Although Catsper answers to Rima at sea, he is but a detailee, taking ultimate orders from Spardic Command in place of Joint Force authorities. Catsper throws the parchment onto the table. "The bigger issues are not in the newsleaf. According to Spardic Command, the Republic engaged with the League's Joint Fleet in the Ardent Ocean. The League lost. Twenty ships are sunk or too damaged for sea."

Blood drains from my face. With those losses, the Republic could land troops on the Lyron continent within three months. And if they do, *when* they do, they will take the Ashing Kingdom first. I can almost hear the discussion that must be echoing in the Joint Fleet Admiralty. With such a great loss of ships, is sparing any to protect Ashing, smallest of the kingdoms, worth it? Is Ashing's contribution to the League's Joint Fleet important enough? Perhaps it would be best to leave the defense of Ashing in the hands of the Ashing private armada and concentrate on the other five kingdoms. Exactly as Thad had feared.

And if the fighting is about to go to ground...

I cut my eyes to Catsper. "Have you been recalled yet?"

Domenic pinches the bridge of his nose. "Have you fingers on the pulse of Spardic Command as well as Joint Fleet Admiralty now?"

"No, *sir*." I cross my arms. I'm on a backwaters irrelevant ship while my kingdom is losing the war. One would think such direness enough to dull the edge off Domenic's burrs.

"But with a Republic invasion on the horizon, I imagine the Spardic Kingdom to be no exception to wanting to protect its interests first and foremost. And that means recalling training troops and commissioning them onto the most valuable ships."

"You mean Ashing ships," says Domenic.

"No," I say through gritted teeth. "For all the quality of Ashing's armada, we are too small a kingdom. I imagine Spardic would ally with a larger kingdom like Biron and move its troops onto the Biron fleet. Am I correct, Lieutenant?"

Catsper raises a brow. "If I had not my correspondences in my possession since the dispatch, I would wonder if you have not been at my papers. But yes, we are to be picked up in two weeks' time and taken to Biron for reassignment."

I shrug, though my face warms despite itself. "I've fought this war many times. With wooden ships and pretty charts." I turn to Domenic and check my voice to a respectful tone. I can be an adult if he's willing. "What will Rima tell the crew?"

"I do not know." Dominic's face darkens. "He's said nothing to me. Not even of the attack itself."

Catsper leans on his elbows and studies me. "You need to train with me, Nile."

"She already trains with you," says Domenic.

"More." The marine's gaze is hard, and I know I will dislike what he says. "You know a lot, Ash. Of Ashing, of the other five kingdoms, of the Lyron League strategy, of resources. If you are captured, too much is at stake."

⁊

A week into our sailing east toward the only freshwater source in the Siaman, the thirst catches up to me with a vengeance. Catsper's merciless extra training, as if he can inject years of Spade technique into my head within a few days, little helps my parched lips. I'm thirsty. I'm thirsty and I'm nauseated and I'm unable to sleep despite the exhaustion that seeps through my muscles.

I curl in my hammock. Instead of lulling me, the sway of the ship only aggravates my headache. I let a bit of magic out to play, calling a thread of wind to soothe my nerves. The meditation exercises, boring as they are, do help. The tiny breeze rolls Ana's pen across the table. But that's all I can do before nausea makes me stop. The wind feels...sour. Like turned milk.

The door creaks open. I turn toward the bulkhead and feign sleep. I can't handle Ana's describing effects of thirst on the human body just now, as she's taken to doing.

"Nile." The voice is Kederic's. "Nile, wake up." A hand shakes me, triggering a jolt of pain in my head before I can push him away.

"Stop that." I wince and put my hand to my temple. But I do rise, quickly focusing my eyes. Kederic does not make a habit of visiting our berth, and I worry that today's appearance has a good reason.

"Price is incoherent," Kederic tells me.

"Thirst?" With the crew on rations, I don't know what's befallen the prisoner.

"No..." Kederic shakes his head. "At least I do not believe that is the root cause. He was afraid when I came in. Not of me, but of something. When I spread my weather pictures before him, he started raving as if I would understand his words if he repeated them enough. Then he grabbed my pictures and crammed them into a ball."

Storms and hail. A raving prisoner is exactly what I need to make this morning complete.

"I'll talk to him," I say, sliding my feet onto the deck and digging out a tunic.

"Good fortune with that." Kederic holds out a piece of

paper. "I did manage to thrust a pen into his hand. Does this mean anything?"

The boy has a good head on him. I open the paper and look at the sloppy Tirik hand.

"Today feels very wrong," I read aloud. My mouth is dry. "The weather event is imminent. I've no insight into its nature. Take care with your ship. I wish to live."

I lower the paper and sigh as Kederic slumps against the bulkhead.

"We need to brief the…" He trails off, looking at me in question. Brief the first officer would be the correct ending to the phrase. But it will be difficult enough convincing one, much less two levels of approvals to listen to a vague warning from a prisoner we weren't supposed to have contact with in the first place. Plus, Rima's ass-preserving mantra might suit us better than Domenic's regulations and logic just now.

"We need to brief the captain." I sigh, and the middie nods with as little enthusiasm as I feel.

It is midmorning before Captain Rima grants us an audience. Domenic stands by Rima's desk, looking at me with hard eyes. He may not know what Kederic intends to say, but my meetings with Captain Rima have not ended well yet. Catsper, as usual, lounges by the door.

"Mr. Kederic." Rima's smile does not touch his eyes. "Why do I have the pleasure of your company this morning?"

30

KEDERIC PLACES HIS HANDS BEHIND HIS BACK. "The Tirik prisoner passed a message this morning that may warrant your attention, sir," the middie says crisply. He hands Price's note to Rima, along with a written translation he made beneath it.

Rima scans the paper and passes it to Domenic. "This, Mr. Dana, is exactly why I issued instructions to keep the Tirik manipulator from our crew. Was I speaking for the pleasure of hearing my own voice?"

"Sir." Kederic's tone is admirably firm. "I have made inquiries of the Gifted as to weather prognosis over the past week, and he has proved himself correct even when his predictions contradicted my beliefs."

"Mr. Kederic." Rima's voice is overly patient. "Most seamen who've spent time aboard a ship develop a sense of the coming weather. It is called good seamanship, and it is this seamanship, not some obscure Gifted skills, that keeps our fleets functioning. I would advise you to refrain from advertising your own deficiencies in said craft to your commanding officers in the future. Mmm?"

Kederic blushes. I can't even blame Rima's argument, except that the wind remains elusive and spoiled. Not that I can inject that into the conversation.

What I can inject is a jab into Rima's risk aversion. Which is half the reason we came straight to him in the first place.

"Sir," I say with all the deference I can conjure, "the Inuk Bay is close to our course and is well protected from the open sea. If we pull the ship into safe harbor and Price is wrong, we lose a day. If he is right, we save the *Aurora*."

Rima's face darkens as he turns in his chair to face me. "I do not recall addressing you. And I expect Mr. Dana will discuss the matter of etiquette with you at a later time."

Even without shifting my gaze, I know Domenic is already planning that particular exercise. And I don't care. I trust Price's weather sense, just as I trust Clay's repetition of heard words. I've seen as many ships lost to storms as to guns. My dead brother's frigate among them. As poorly handled as the *Aurora* is, I cringe to think what would happen to a thirsty and ill-mannered crew in the midst of an open-water typhoon.

"Aye, sir," I say with a bow. "But please consider how little a small deviation in course would cost us."

"How little it would cost us?" Rima pauses to draw a calming breath through flaring nostrils. "I make no habit of explaining myself to sailors, much less to scared little girls playing at seamen. However, for the sake of correcting rumors that you appear to thrive on feeding, I will. Once." He pauses long enough for me to bow at his graciousness. "There is no fresh water to be had until the Crystal Oasis deep within the Siaman Sea. Each hour of delay puts this crew through suffering and this ship through danger. We must conserve resources, for we may yet be becalmed. We are also a League man-of-war, which means we are not in the Siaman for the pleasure of the cruise. There are ships waiting on us and a schedule we must keep."

Ships waiting for us. My hope drains. Not ships, *ship*. I will wager my arm that Rima has a rendezvous with his private merchant, *Hope*, lined up. He's sailed us through weather to make such an appointment before—he will not allow a delay now.

"This is the foolishness that rises from idle hands, Mr. Dana," Rima continues, pointing at Domenic. "A gainfully employed crew does not have time to fret about nightmare storms and scheme up means to avoid work." Rima turns back to Kederic. "This foolishness is understandable in a girl, but I expect a higher standard from you, Mr. Kederic."

Kederic looks down.

"Mr. Catsper," says Domenic, still glaring at me. "Place a marine guard outside the prisoner's quarters to discourage further social engagements with the crew."

"Aye, sir," Catsper replies with his usual nonchalance, as if the first officer requested he pass the salt.

Failure weighs on my shoulders as Rima tosses us from his cabin. We'd had a chance. I'd still wager that if not for whatever absurdly punctual arrangement Rima must have with his customer, we'd have talked the man into a diversion. Apparently, there is no potion for bravery as effective as gold.

Following Kederic into the passageway, I'm little surprised when Domenic's hand clamps around my arm the moment we're clear of the cabin. "Gunroom," he growls, and I've little choice but to follow, my stomach heavy with the potent mix of disappointment and dread.

For once, Domenic has every right to be furious with me. I've disregarded both the captain's and his own orders to stay clear of Price. I'd spoken out of turn. And, most to the point,

I went around Domenic on purpose.

"Sit." Domenic points to a chair behind the long wooden table.

I do. And I'm smart enough to keep my mouth shut.

Domenic stalks across the room. We are alone here. At the moment, I'm uncertain whether this state of affairs will work in my favor.

Stifling a sigh, I look up, meeting his eyes. *All right, Domenic. Let's get this over with.*

"Why did you not come to me?" he demands.

"Because you'd never have taken it to Rima."

"You are right. You know why?" He stops across from me and leans his palms on the table. "Because you do not go telling the captain of a man-of-war that his Tirik prisoner, who has been busy foretelling the future to pass the time, is currently predicting imminent horrid weather despite calm seas and clear skies. It is useless, and it is disrespectful."

"I believe Price." I lean toward him. "And if I recall, you believe him enough to think that the middies' weather foresight lay with the Gifted."

"And is the boy predicting a storm on the Siaman Sea or a volcano erupting in the middle of the Tirik Republic? Does his immense event have a time to go with it? Or shall we sail in circles until he feels better?"

"It is a calculated risk," I acknowledge without backing down. "Delaying our travel for a day or two would strain the ship and our schedule. But the costs of doing nothing may be greater still."

"You are right." His voice is as cold as his eyes. "It is a calculated risk. And our ship has a captain who makes that calculation. As does every other ship in every navy. Including Ashing. You may dislike how this business is managed, you may hate me, and you may think the captain a tyrant or an unjust lord. Goddess knows there are sailors on all ships that harbor unflattering thoughts of the quarterdeck. You may not disregard the command structure of this ship."

His words sting. I sit back in my chair. "I'm not disregarding this ship's command."

"No?" Domenic stays where he is. "Because I could have sworn I just saw you decide not only that the *Aurora* would do better if she ran under Nile Ash's orders, but that she in fact *should* do so. And then massage the middies into a private cadre to help undermine the captain's authority."

"It isn't like that," I say, though I know it is. I might have started working with the middies with pure intentions, but then, instead of shoring up support for the *Aurora*'s command as would be proper, I allowed it to become a parliament unto itself. "I'm not growing mutineers."

"Great! Allow me to commend you for not starting a mutiny aboard a Lyron League naval ship." Domenic shakes his head. "Tell me, what would you have done on the *Faithful* to someone who, for any reason, dared display the kind of disrespect for Captain Fey that you little bother hiding for Rima?"

That hits the target. As, I'm certain, was Domenic's intention. If someone did this to Captain Fey, I'd have the culprit in irons that day. I know I would. But I'm not saying that aloud. I'd too taken a calculated risk this morning, and while I regret the method I had to use, it was the best option I had to work with. I clench my hands together under the table, where Domenic would not see my sweating palms. "What will you do?"

"I should be strapping you to the grating," he says, dropping into a seat across from me. "But as I believe your actions have been discreet enough that the crew is still ignorant of them, I'll settle for putting you to scrubbing decks for an extra watch each day until the sun stops setting in the west."

I let out a breath.

"But is that where we've come to, Nile?" he asks softly, covering his face with large palms. "You would rather risk ship's discipline than trust me? Am I so incompetent in your eyes that you navigate around me like a bit of debris?"

"What?" My spine straightens with a jerk. "You are the most competent seaman on this ship. You should be captain."

"I can't be." Domenic's voice is even, but he isn't quite fast enough to hide the flash of pain in his eyes.

In that one second, my gut twists. I'd little considered what it had cost Domenic to pull himself up from the lower deck by sheer sweat and work, all while knowing that he'd never compete with noble-born officers for a ship of his own. The immaculate uniform, the straight-backed stance, the unwavering professionalism, take new meaning. Domenic's pride and competence are all he has.

And I've just trampled over both. Damn.

"Nile." Domenic leans forward, speaking quietly. His eyes, intense and ocean blue, beg me to listen. "When Catsper was hurting you, I knew he'd cause no harm. But I couldn't watch. I still can't." The last comes in a whisper, and he draws a breath before speaking. "You know what scares me? That one day you will do something in front of the crew, or fail to keep your mouth shut, or bloody forget where you are, and I will have no choice but to hurt you. Some days it's all I can do to keep from ordering you belowdecks just to keep you safe from me."

I meet his gaze, my heart refusing to do its job.

Silence swirls. On the table, our knuckles are but a foot apart. A very long, insurmountable foot.

Domenic shakes himself and stands. "I'm sorry."

I follow so quickly, the chair falls behind me. "I—" I fumble.

Smoothly, Domenic steps around and rights my chair,

his shoulder brushing against me as he does. I should step away, but I don't. I don't want to. When Domenic straightens, he is close to me. Very close. The warmth of his body seeps through his tunic and fills the space between us. His gaze is hungry and strong, and it cuts through to somewhere deep in my chest. For an instant, I am certain that with that gaze, Domenic sees straight into my soul, knows my every secret, every hope, every fear. I draw a sharp breath before realizing it.

"You should get back to your duties," he says. When I hesitate, he moves to the door ahead of me and holds it open. "As should I."

"Of course." I'm in a daze as I leave the gunroom.

"Ash." Domenic's call twists me around. His voice is back to its usual precision. "I expect there shall be no need to have this conversation again."

"Aye, sir." I touch the hat I am not wearing and am gone.

31

THE MIDDIES ARE WAITING FOR ME. I know that. But I want my mind back. And bloody Domenic insists on dominating it without even being in the same berth. Domenic mad at me. Domenic worried. Domenic hurt. Domenic so damn close to me, I am certain that my heart bruised his skin. And to top it all off, the wind that's always demanding to touch me now feels different. Slippery.

After an hour of trying a meditation exercise, I give up hope of reclaiming my equilibrium and go to the middie boys' berth.

"Are you all right?" Kederic asks, offering me his seat. His voice and eyes are both concerned. "What did Dana do to you?"

I take a spot on the deck instead and draw up my knees. My head hurts, and nausea grips my throat. "Nothing." All right, no one is daft enough to buy that. "Nothing of consequence, I mean. Read me the articles of conduct and assigned some deck scrubbing. What have you got?"

"I pulled rank on Catsper's marines." Kederic hands me another crumpled paper. Plainly, the morning's chastising didn't so much as make him stumble. Domenic is right about my influence on the middies.

Price's handwriting stares at me. One scribbled word. *"Tonight,"* I read.

Sharp intakes of breath scatter through the room.

"What should we do?" asks Kederic.

I know I'm supposed to have the answer, but Domenic's words haunt me. My thoughts can't find their path.

"We've seen storms before," Thatch Lawrence says, with little conviction. "We'll strike sail and ride it out. Ships do sail through storms. And it cannot be that awful with no sign in the sky to foretell such foul winds. Maybe the Tirik simply wants to destroy our mission. The captain predicted he'd do as much."

"Such a ploy would work only once," says Ana. "If that was his intention, would it not be more logical to wait until a delay caused greater havoc than a lost day of travel?"

"I agree," says Kederic. "More than that, I *believe* that heeding the Gifted's warning is for the greater good of this ship. He has been right the past weeks, and this morning, his fear was convincing."

"I little care about greater good," says Ana, leaning her forearms against the middies' makeshift table. She's braided her hair today, two tight coils that wrap her head beautifully, and her thin voice is clear and strong. A mouse taking her stand before a cat. "I care about returning home alive. I'm in for whatever plan we come up with."

Whatever plan we come up with has to involve diverting the *Aurora*'s course without Rima's approval. I don't know if it's possible, but I know that without me, the little group of conspirators would not dare the maneuver. What I say next can end this scheme before it goes beyond excited dreaming.

Except no words come. Only a pounding headache.

Ana frowns. "Nile?"

I turn toward her, summoning the will to speak.

She beats me to it, taking my elbow before I can come up with words. "Give us a few minutes, gentlemen," she says, smiling, and tows me out the door and into our berth. For a small girl, she is bloody strong when she wants to be. Strong and determined. Ana deposits me on her cot and clicks the lock into place. Her smile vanishes.

"Here." She thrusts her canteen into my hands and crouches before me, her eyes level with mine. "The Savage hurt you, didn't he?"

I refuse both her ration and speculation with a shake of my head. I don't want to talk. I want to blot Domenic from my memory so he stops sabotaging my thoughts. "Nothing," I say with conviction. "Domenic didn't touch me, Ana. I swear."

"Domenic?" Her eyes narrow, and she rocks back on her heels, studying me from under her lashes. Her glazed nails tap her forearm. Once. Twice. "And that, I gather, is the problem."

I rub my face. "His name or his not touching me?"

"Both." She sighs. "Of all the men in this world—of all the men even on this ship—you fall in love with the one who hurts you for sport."

That jerks me to my feet quicker than burning coal. Ana isn't helping things; she is complicating them with her own fantasies. "Domenic doesn't hurt people for sport," I say before I can help myself. "As for the other, he's my commanding officer, Ana. The Admiralty would put us both in irons if we crossed that line. So, I couldn't be in love with him even if, even if I was in love with him." I frown at my own sentence. "Which I am not."

"Of course not. His words just carry more meaning to you than those of regular mortals, and you can think of little beyond how close his hand <u>hovered</u> before never touching your shoulder." She raises her brows. "Let us be blunt. When it comes to matters of the heart, you are about as competent as I am behind a gun battery."

"This has nothing to do with my heart. It has to do with him being right." I pace the few steps between the bulkheads. "Domenic reminded me that naval ships don't run by consensus. The officers' orders have to carry absolute weight. Even bad orders. Wrong orders. Unpopular orders. It isn't our place to divert the *Aurora* against the captain's and first officer's decision."

She watches me, her arms crossed. "And your feelings for him have nothing to do with this sudden aversion to contradicting his word?"

"I don't have feelings for him! Not *those* feelings." I stop and twist to look her in the eye. "I don't get to have those feelings for a superior."

She snorts. "Yes. Because that would compromise your ability to make decisions, right? Because intimacy clouds judgment and drives emotions into decisions that should be made with cool calculation." Ana spreads her hands. "I'm glad to see none of that plagues you."

I look down. If I divert the *Aurora*, I will hurt Domenic. Badly. Worse, I will break the thread of trust between us.

"That whole speech about the importance of following orders, even bad ones—do you actually believe it?" asks Ana.

I sit back on her cot and lean my head back against the bulkhead. I might disagree with the girl's values, but no one will ever call her stupid.

"Yes, I do," I say finally. Except that if my suspicions are right, Rima isn't giving bad orders. He's giving good orders for an ulterior mission. One that has to do with his pockets instead of the navy. More importantly, neither he nor Domenic has *all* the information. They can't feel the truth of Price's words, as I do. Inexperienced as I am in elemental attraction, even I know something is changing.

Just as I know that if I do this, Domenic will despise me.

"I want my mind back, Ana," I whisper.

She sits beside me. "Hearts sometimes disobey better reason. I little care about the Admiralty's intimacy policy, but I do care for outcomes. If you believe following Rima's orders is for the greater good of this ship, then say so. Just do us the courtesy of thinking with your head."

A knock sounds twice on the door, then Kederic pokes his head inside. "Nile? Are you all right?" he asks, his brows pulling together. The middie has the makings of a great officer, but if this scheme is discovered, he will be barred from sitting his lieutenant's exams. The weight in his eyes says he knows as much.

With a nod to Ana, I pull back my shoulders and rise. "Yes, I am, Mr. Kederic. And I believe we will need a chart.

32

I CHECK MY CALCULATIONS THREE times against the chart Song swiped from his uncle's cabin. Just north of the *Aurora*'s course lies Inuk Bay, which would shelter the ship from the worst of foul sea or wind or both. If we can get there. In the dark.

If Price's prediction of *tonight* is true.

By dusk, my heart is galloping. Nothing has happened, not even a dark cloud hanging in the sky. The Spades stationed outside Price's cabin tell me that the Gifted is raving, calling a single word out again and again in Tirik. *Tonight.* The marines ask me whether I know what it means, and I shake my head. They don't believe me, but they say nothing.

The ship's bell calls change of watch, and Kederic walks onto the deck, meeting my eye.

I nod lightly.

"Ash!" The boy's voice calls over the rumble of bodies assuming stations. "This sail falls short of this ship's standards. You will remain and fix your work."

"Aye, sir!" I knuckle my forehead.

Domenic looks over sharply.

I turn away, conjuring what I hope is the right mix of embarrassment and indignation. Domenic's watch is over, and our plan relies on the first officer leaving the deck to Kederic, the only middie permitted to stand a watch alone. If needed, we can work around Lieutenant Kazzik, who cannot find land without a guide boat, but Domenic would see a course change at once. What makes him a superb first officer is a liability to us.

I bend over a rope, replacing it by the lantern light. The alleged punishment is mediocre and the task is better handled in daylight, but it fits well with a middie's half-skilled attempt at ship's discipline, and it keeps me on deck. We are wagering that Domenic's professional inclination to uphold a junior officer's authority will win over minor pragmatism. So far, we are right.

Kederic puts his hands behind his back and stands tall. Only a glance at the helm betrays his tension. The order to adjust course must be given soon, and Domenic is yet to leave. Five minutes trickle by. Ten. A quarter hour.

"Will you be retiring, Mr. Dana?" Kederic asks, lifting his hat respectfully.

"The deck is yours, Mr. Kederic," Domenic tells the boy firmly. "Consider my presence supernumerary."

I swear under my breath. Unwilling to do anything to undermine Rima, Domenic is taking the next best action he can—staying on deck in case crisis strikes. For the first time, I wish the man was a bit less diligent.

We need a diversion.

I climb through the rigging toward the front of the ship. Finding idling hands on the *Aurora* is easy, and I soon spot a tangle of Eflians rolling dice under the dim light of a lantern. Good enough.

I secure myself into the ropes and reach out for the wind.

It's worse than this morning. Slippery and spoiled and wrong. But I don't need much. Just a bit. And focused. The Diante woman thought it within my power to extinguish a single candle. I don't know about that, but I hope it's within my power to nudge the dice. My gullet fills with bile as I let my magic call the air and focus it on Mic's dice roll.

The raw puff of wind doesn't disrupt the game as much as demolish the whole bloody thing to pieces—dice, boons, and all. Which turns out to be just as well.

The lot jump to their feet, pocketing what they find.

"That ain't yours," growls Mic.

"It ain't no one's now," his mate snaps back. "We all divide what's left."

Others, of a different mind as to the proper division of salvaged good, add their voices to the fray. I breathe out with relief. We were overdue for a bit of luck. Scampering back over the shrouds, I find Thatch Lawrence.

"Commander Dana decided to back up Mr. Kederic on watch this evening, sir," I whisper hurriedly, cutting my gaze to the growing dispute I'd kindled.

An impish smile touches Thatch Lawrence's lips. Adjusting his hat, the middie stalks toward the gamers at once, his young voice raised in wonderfully ineffective chastising. I make my way back toward the quarterdeck in time to see Domenic turn on his heel and stride forward to resolve the middie's crisis. If the boy plays it well, he'll keep the first officer occupied a bit.

I whistle to Kederic from the rigging. *You are up.* My breath stills as the boy strides toward the helmsman.

"We're drifting," Kederic informs him. "Take us two points to starboard."

The helmsman frowns, looking around for the first officer.

Kederic licks his lips. Had he truly been the officer of the watch, as we'd planned, helm would have obeyed in silence. Now...

Hopping down from the ropes, I trot to the middie and touch my forehead. "Mr. Dana's compliments, sir," I say with a sad attempt at discretion, as if intending the message for Kederic's benefit alone, "and he requests you correct our course at once."

"Thank you." Kederic nods admirably to me as the helmsman hurries to execute the order. "Please inform the commander that the correction was made."

I breathe out a lungful of air as I scatter off. The shift in the *Aurora*'s bearing is subtle, and with no reference point in the dark, Domenic will be oblivious to the change unless he happens to look at the compass. At least until dawn. I hope Price's promised disaster will oblige us with its timing.

In the sky, the stars shine brightly at me. Not even a cloud yet. And the bloody ocean is smooth as glass. *Calm before a storm.* I hope.

An hour passes in heavy anticipation. My head snaps at the slightest breeze, which comes and disappears as if toying with us. Domenic stands on deck, his hands clasped behind his back, his gaze watching the sea.

Kederic walks over to me. "Where do you think we are?" he whispers.

I estimate the speed and drift. "An hour from Inuk Bay. If the wind holds. You'll have to turn the ship a few points to keep us at safe depth once we are inside."

I see him draw a sharp breath and realize he may not have considered all the nuances of entering a bay blind.

"What if I run us aground?" he whispers. "There is nothing to hint at a weather turn, Nile. Not even a bit of rain. This isn't a matter of fearing punishment or never standing a watch alone again. I could damage the *Aurora*'s hull."

"I know."

"What should I do?" he whispers.

My stomach turns as much for our predicament as for the middie. Whatever I say, Kederic is the one ordering the changes to the ship's course. Ultimately, the responsibility will be his no matter my role. "I will support whatever decision you make."

"What would you do?" he insists.

"Stay the course."

"What about crashing in the inlet?"

"I trust my calculations," I tell him.

"I don't trust mine," Kederic shoots back. A moment of silence stretches. "But I trust yours. Do not leave, all right?"

We manage the small adjustments to the course over the next few hours, but the watch ends with no storm in sight. Thatch Lawrence reluctantly yields the deck to Ana and the twins, and Lieutenant Kazzik accepts the watch from Kederic without questioning our position or direction. Domenic calls for a cup of coffee but remains where he is.

I long for a sip of the steaming liquid.

"You may head below, Ash," Domenic says, walking over to me. "Two back-to-back watches is enough."

"I... I would like to stay, sir."

Domenic considers me. He can hardly call me out for my folly when he himself is doing much the same. "Eat. A short nap. You may return in one hour."

"Sir—"

"One hour, Ash. Do I need to put a pair of marines on you to ensure obedience?"

I meet his eyes defiantly, but this isn't time for a scene. "No, sir," I say instead and heed the order. One hour exactly. Not a minute more.

I return to deck to find not an ounce of change.

I want to scream as we near dawn. Nothing. Nothing has happened. The sun will rise minutes from now and end our ruse. Was the captain right? Had Price bluffed us into a discourse?

Mouth dry, I scour the ship for Catsper and find him in the officer's gunroom. "I need to see the prisoner," I say, gripping his shoulder. "Now. Please."

Catsper asks no questions, only follows at my heels as I rip into Price's cabin and grab the boy's tunic. "When?" I demand, pressing him into the bulkhead. "Tell me bloody when."

Price frowns at me. "It has already happened."

33

W HAT'S HAPPENED, PRICE?"

"I do not know." He shakes his head. "But it has. In the north especially. And it is spreading."

I slam the door behind me. I don't understand what Price means, and no amount of shaking the boy will bring meaning to the words. The sun is rising. The only thing I can do now is stand beside Kederic as he makes his excuses for the ship's position.

I hear cursing before I emerge on deck, and know that the contour of land area is now visible around us. Domenic calls for a glass.

I have one foot on the top companionway ladder when the *Aurora* jerks forward, throwing me onto the deck. My shin cracks hard against the wood, but the fresh wind cuts through the pain. Fresh wind. Good wind.

The ship jerks again. Hard.

Sailors around shout in confusion.

Ripping myself away from my element, I seek Domenic at once. He stands with an arm threaded through the shrouds, his eyes locked on the land. "Goddess." He lowers his glass. "It's a quake."

I draw breath. Not a storm. I was so certain any threat to a ship must come from the wind and sea, I gave no real thought to anything else. But Price wasn't feeling a coming storm at all. He was sensing an earthquake. And I'd just sailed the *Aurora* close to land.

Whatever happens to the ship now will be my fault.

I tighten my footing and regard the coastline of Inuk Bay. The ground shakes as if the snores of a great beast rumble beneath its surface. The tree line shudders. Once. Twice. Again. Suddenly, a rolling crash trembles the air as stones, small and large, come free from Inuk Mountain and tumble down the slope. Stones. More stones. Stones, stones, stones.

"What is this?" Rima's words, admirably calm, are my first indication that the captain has taken the deck.

"Earthquake, sir," I call to him. One that I brought his ship into close quarters with. My gut clenches. I shove away the thought in favor of surviving the moment.

"Hold fast!" Domenic shouts as the ship bucks again. This time spectacularly.

The deck—the whole ship—falls out from under us. For a breath-catching moment, my feet hover over nothingness. And then I fall. I, the crew, and everything not tied down to the hull. The deck's planks rush up to meet me, their tilt ripping away any chance of keeping my balance. My shoulder and hip slam against hard wood. Pain shoots through my bones. And then I'm rolling and flying across the sloping deck and into the mast.

Thud.

Blackness. And the world returns with a vengeance. I'd struck my cheek against the mast. My mouth fills with blood as blotches of light dance before my eyes. Clawing the smooth pillar, I pull myself to my feet. The ship thrashes. I wrap my arm around the wood and look up in time to see a loose carpenter's hammer slam into a Spade's chin not three feet away. The boy looks in disbelief at the sudden river of blood pouring out onto his hands and crumples.

A scream builds inside my throat. Around me, the crack of breaking ropes and the rattle of hailing debris mix with the grunts and yells of injured people. I force my erupting scream into words just as it leaves my lips. "Guns. Check the guns!"

The ropes holding the great beasts will burst as quickly as any other. A feral gun will slaughter a dozen of us.

"Help!" a pair of cracking adolescent voices rings from above. "Help!"

I spin toward the sound and look up. A black-clad body separates from the rigging and tumbles into the frosty water. Two more boys cling to the shrouds.

I can't help them all. Domenic is beside the helmsman, fighting to keep the *Aurora*'s steering intact. Kazzik stands frozen. The captain has disappeared below. The crew is dying. The Spades who help me train, the able seamen who keep the *Aurora* moving, the ship's boys who scurry about her decks. And I can't help them. The terrible realization sears my stomach even as I hear my voice desperately bellow words I know this crew will ignore. "Man overboard! Throw a line! Secure the starboard aft carronade! Party to the mainmast! Clear the wounded!"

Mic, the closest to the straining gun, turns away.

I curse.

"Clear the wounded!" a voice echoes. Not mine. Ana's. "You, get them below."

"Man overboard!" Kederic picks up the call. "Back sail! You there, throw a line!"

"Secure the guns." The voice is high and young. "I order you to secure the guns, Mic!" As the sting of fresh salt spray clears my face, I see little Song slide in front of the bewildered Eflian.

Mic stares at him.

"My brother gave you an order." Another young voice. Sand. Standing beside Song for the first time since Price came aboard.

Warmth fills my chest. We will survive. My crew will survive. I turn in time to catch Catsper's arm as he leaps into the shrouds after his boys. He will get them down, or he will die trying. The latter is all too likely. The marine is a deadly army by himself, but he isn't a seaman. He has not lived his life in the shrouds.

"Catsper!" I pull his hand from the rope. I know he will not stay on deck, and I know better than trying to convince him. "Some of the ropes are under great tension. I will find a safe path to the Spades. Will you follow it exactly?"

Catsper nods, and I shout to Kederic, indicating my intention.

The middie calmly touches his hat and grabs the shoulders of good seamen, directing them after me. I leap into the rigging. The mast sways side to side as the deck beneath me shrinks away. I pause long enough to feel the sea's motion, to ensure I let it boost my stride instead of trying to fight its will. My heart beats fast, good fast. The kind of pulsing beat that makes you feel more alive with each breath.

I spare a glance behind me. Catsper is on my heels, his athleticism making up for what he lacks in feel for the rigging. Two seamen come up on either side of us, and I blink with a surprised realization that one of them is the woman who had barred me from the female berth on my first day, Sandra.

She catches my eye and tosses me a line she brought up with her. Our gazes meet with a small nod.

"Over here!" the marine boys shout.

They are far out on the yardarm, where marines have no business. I wager the Spades were skylarking when the quake started. The line they had held on to getting out there had snapped. The rope's ragged tails now whip about. The boys lie on the beam, their limbs wrapped around the wood.

I straddle the yardarm. After threading the rope through a round block, I toss one end to the seaman and wrap the other around my waist. "On belay!" I shout to the man who catches my safety line.

The line tightens. "Belay on!"

"Climbing!" I shimmy out to the boys. The seaman gives me slack as I need, but keeps the line taut.

The boys' faces are white, a sharp contrast to midnight tunics. I know these Spades. Craig and Simons, both thirteen.

"Ash." Craig's voice catches as he sees me. His cheeks are wet, and I suspect the wind and sea are only partially responsible for this state.

The beam beneath us bucks, tilting over the open sea.

The boys scream. The wood is wet and slippery, and the boys are exhausted.

"Look at me," I order Craig, gripping his gaze as if it is a tangible object able to defy gravity. I move slowly toward him, a foot at a time. When I am close enough to lay my hand on his shoulders, I feel his shaking muscles.

I loop the rope under the boy's arms and coax him to the mainmast, where Catsper takes custody of the Spade, and Sandra rigs a new safety line for him.

I return for Simons. I have just reached him and secured him into my safety line when a bellow from the deck reaches us.

"Hold fast!" It's Domenic. "Hold fast for your life!"

I have a moment to wonder what that is about before Simons gasps. "The sea! What's wrong with the sea?"

I follow his gaze and freeze. A wave, rising fifty yards into the air, is roaring for the bay sheltering the *Aurora*.

"Get below!" Domenic calls. "Get below, all who can. Others, hold fast!"

I twist to look at the mast. Catsper and the seaman helping lower Craig are just stepping onto the deck. Sandra is in the shrouds, holding our safety line. If she lets go, Simons and I will die when the wave comes. If she takes time to secure it, she will never make it down to deck in time to save her own life. Our eyes meet. She knows too.

I expect my thoughts to race, but my mind is calm. "Let go," I call to her.

She shakes her head.

"Get down," I shout again.

"Hold fast, fish bait!" she shouts back, her cold hands tying the knots that would anchor the line even if—when— she lets go of the rope.

I will her fingers to move faster, to make time to tie herself in as well.

The wave crashes over the eastern wall of Inuk Bay. I grip Simons. "We will be knocked from the yardarm," I call into his ear. My heart races. "Hold on to me and our rope."

Instead of starting on her own harness, Sandra is adding an extra safety knot to our anchor.

With shuddering breath, I cut my gaze to the water giant, and the thin thread of hope that we may come out of this unscathed rips violently as the wall of water smashes into land. Nothing stands a chance before the wave. Not the trees, or rocks or any living thing that has the misfortune of calling the coast home. I gasp as I realize the uprooted tree trunks and boulders ride with foam, spinning and smashing and moving.

The wave is still going, tearing hungrily across the land. Domenic shouts to turn the helm. The water is halfway to our bay. Three quarters. Domenic gives up shouting and throws himself beside the two helmsmen, struggling with the wheel to angle the *Aurora*'s nose properly into the coming disaster. The mad monster of water seems even bigger as it rushes toward our bay, its foaming maw filled with debris as set as cannonballs on destruction.

With a deafening crash, the water spills into Inuk Bay. The *Aurora*'s bow rises higher and higher into the air, balancing precariously. At least until something hard smashes our stern and spins our axis. Dominic's hard-won angle of attack shatters, and the *Aurora* rolls to starboard.

Ten degrees. Twenty. Forty-five.

Gravity pries my fingers from the yardarm, and I'm flung into the air. The harsh jolt of the harness catches me. I swing beside Simons on the mast, gasping, as the waterline rushes toward me. Close. Closer. The salty spray shocks me.

We are going to capsize.

No. We can't. It is my fault the *Aurora* is here, and I can't let this happen, not without a fight. Whatever the cost. I twist in my harness to examine the sail. The canvas struggles, wanting to balance the ship. Keeping my eyes on it, I brace myself and reach for my magic. There will be no control when I release it. No tameness. No assurance I will ever rein in that raging beast again.

Now.

I choke, buckling under the strain, as the wind explodes around me. The air rushes, uncaring about my body, how it pours into my lungs and mouth and eyes. I can spare no attention for my body either. All my might, all my efforts are directed at keeping one little corner of magic pulled taut, just enough to shape the wind's course into the sail.

The wind blows. *Storms and hail*, it blows. The howling in

my ears echoes through my bones. My lungs burn. Everything burns. I'd sob if I could, but my body is not mine to control anymore. I am a wind magnet, and channeling the air into the sail will be my last willful act.

I hear a pop as the canvas responds and hope it is enough. It has to be. The wind shakes me like a rag.

The ship rocks. Starboard and port. Starboard and port. Bloody indecisive frigate.

I swing. Limp and empty and dizzy.

Starboard and port.

I don't care anymore. I've no strength left to care.

And then the ship tilts to port and rights before my world goes black.

⁊

I am alive.

And breathing.

I deserve neither benefit. Simons and I swing on our tether. The boy is shaking. I am too drained to shake. Too drained to move. I reach for my magic and find it gone. I should be excited. Or scared. But I am beyond feeling. When a crew of seamen climbs out onto the yardarm to help us, I let myself be manhandled back to the mast. Only when my limbs are solidly wedged on the mast's holds does my body agree to minor cooperation. Step by step, I climb down.

I'm a man's height from the deck when the fear seizes me. My stomach cramps and my breaths quicken and my chest squeezes. Anxiety shudders through me. My hands tighten on their holds. No. They try to tighten, but my fingers refuse to move. Light flashes before my eyes, bright and green and blinding. I feel myself let go. It's odd, as if it's happening to someone else and I am a mere observer. I know someone is shouting my name. And I know I can't answer.

I'm in the air. And then my ankle hurts. And my head

cracks against the deck. I hurt, but I can't move, even away from the pain.

"Ash." The voice is Domenic's and very close. "Nile!"

"Is she all right?" a boy asks.

"She is alive but unconscious," says Domenic. "She was on the bloody yardarm during the great wave. Who in the hell thought it would be a good idea to let her descend on her own?" An arm snakes under my knees and another one beneath my shoulders. I'm in the air again.

My body is reporting in now, but I keep my eyes closed. Better go with Domenic's presumption of capital fatigue. I let my head loll onto his chest.

"I'll get her below," Domenic says.

"I'll do it." Catsper's voice. "You've more to do on deck than I."

Domenic concedes the point, and I am transferred. The movement jars my ankle, and I bite my lip to keep from whimpering. Unconscious people typically don't whimper.

Catsper moves off with me toward the companionway. "You can open your eyes now," he says dryly. "I've dealt with violence long enough to know when someone is actually unconscious."

My face heats. I open my eyes and allow Catsper to ease me down the companion ladder, taking what weight I can on my good leg. The dazed thud of the fall echoes through my skull. I sway.

"Let's move, Ash," Catsper orders, steering me to the Cove.

"You have the bedside manner of a hyena." The words slur as the images from the mast slam me. Craig. Simons... "Sandra? Did Sandra—"

"Dead."

I draw a breath.

"Mourn later. Talk now." Catsper helps me inside and

onto a sea chest. "What happened on the masthead?"

My hands are torn between cradling my head and my ankle. "I lost my grips. Couldn't hold on any longer."

"Crock of shit." Catsper crosses his arms over his chest and leans down toward me. "A decent crock, mind you, and you'll sell it to Dana. But like I said, I stake my life on fighting. And I was watching you."

Flattering. "What do you bloody think happened?" My voice sounds as drained as I feel. "I contemplated ending my life, but by the time I made my decision, I was only seven feet from the deck."

He squats beside me and unlaces the boot of my injured leg. "Do you think you might have similar ideas again?"

I don't know. I cradle my head in my arms. "I let the magic take over to try to fill the *Aurora's* sail. I wasn't exactly expecting to survive the experience, so give me a bit of leeway for not knowing what my body planned next."

Catsper snorts. "You need to stay out of the rigging until you've worked it out. And better tell Dana, before he orders you up for some nonsense."

"No." I grab Catsper's wrist. "You can't tell him. He'll... Gifted aren't exactly welcome on ships. Or anywhere else. If Domenic finds out, he'll put me ashore and think he's doing both the navy and me a favor."

"I don't make a habit of breaking confidences." Catsper pulls free of my hold. "But you must give him some explanation."

"I bloody swung off the yardarm through a tsunami. A bit of muscle fatigue is rather understandable, Catsper." I rub my arms. "And I'm not climbing anywhere with a hurt ankle." Not for a few days.

I hope I can work things out by then.

34

I JERK IN MY HAMMOCK. MY ENTIRE right side is shaking, and my heart races the winds. It's the third such spell this short night. My body has no reserves left. Even when the convulsions release me, I continue trembling inside my sweat-soaked shirt. I'm cold, as if I've fever chills. Pulling up the blanket, I wrap it tight around my shoulders and suckle on a bit of ginger root.

"Nile." Ana's voice intrudes. "Do you need help? You are unwell."

Of course I'm unwell. I want to disappear into my cocoon and stay there until someone promises that the terrors of the night are over. I want my mother.

Since I also want my life, I force myself to sit up instead of burrowing deeper into my bedding. My lip stings, and I realize it's bleeding. I've bitten it. Quickly, I swipe my forearm over the cut. "My ankle hurts a bit is all." It isn't a lie. My leg throbs.

A reminder of what could have happened had the spell caught me seconds earlier.

"I'll wrap it for you," Ana offers, fishing a long bandage from her sea chest. "So what do you think Dana will do to us?" There's more than a bit of worry in her voice, and I little blame her. We diverted the *Aurora* against orders. Domenic won't be pleased. Especially since, given the actual nature of Price's disaster, the diversion into Inuk Bay likely did us more harm than good. The landmass did slow the coming tsunami, but the shallower waters also gave it its height. Had we been farther out, we'd likely have ridden above the disturbance with barely a care—depending on where exactly in the archipelago the wave would have found us.

A storm had been the more likely threat, the one we'd prepared for.

A calculated risk.

"We'll discover soon enough," I say glumly, though the mention of Domenic spurs my pulse back into a gallop. I feel him lifting me from the deck, my head resting against his shoulder. His anger at my injuries. Because he thought fatigue and the sea were to blame for my pain. He'd not have been so kind had he known the truth. "Our decision was sound given the information we had."

Ana looks little convinced. Her hands work the bandage around my ankle deftly, though. A skill from one of her anatomy books, perhaps.

It takes several minutes, but I manage to shrug into a respectable tunic. At least I'll look decent before Domenic tears me to shreds.

The trek to the deck is a slow hobble. I hold on to the bulkhead as I move, my foot unable to bear weight for more than a moment. Which, given the situation, is good. Domenic won't send me aloft with a hurt leg. I have no business in the rigging today. Not tomorrow either, most likely. Not until the spells subside.

If they subside.

The deck is alive with whispers. The death wave was an omen. No, it was the Gods' punishment for letting the Tirik boy live. The Goddess had guided us into the protection of the bay. It was all unnatural. It was nature at its zenith. It was Gifted work.

It was weather and navigation.

"Gather round, all hands," Rima barks over the sailors' rumblings. "This is an elite ship of war, not a women's washroom."

The murmur dies. Both watches cluster around the quarterdeck where the captain stands flanked by his officers and middies. Domenic sees me in the crowd, and his face darkens. Whatever moved him to care for me yesterday is gone without a trace. If there is anything I could do to hurt him more than going behind his back and lying, I'm unsure what it is.

Domenic's eyes say he'd like to clamp me into irons himself, if not for Rima's order to gather the crew.

Captain Rima clears his throat. Conjuring a way to explain yesterday's events, I wager. He puts his hands behind his back, calm and neutral except for the vein pulsing in his temple. "Late last night," Rima announces each word with perfect clarity, "I ordered the *Aurora* into the safety of Inuk Bay. The Bay's shores protected the ship from the worst effects of the great wave, which raged across the ocean this morning. This was neither the Gods' wrath nor salvation—it was basic good seamanship of the kind we practice on *Aurora*'s decks each day." He pauses, looking across the faces in the crowd. The crew nods cautiously, slowly. They want to believe him. They want to trust that their lord and master has control over fate.

I wonder how many of us know it's all a bloody lie. The middies and I. Domenic. Catsper. I search the gathered faces for hidden sneers, careful cutting glances, but find none. Either the sailors are sold on Rima's claims or are too smart to display their thoughts. The Spades stare straight ahead.

Rima paces several steps and continues in the clear, confident voice of a schoolmaster. "The great wave itself was likewise no mythical being. It was caused by an earthquake as all such waves are."

"Why did we not go deeper to sea, sir?" a hand asks.

I hold my breath.

Rima smiles. "Given the unpredictable nature of the weather gods, this was the safest choice, I assure you."

"How far did it reach, sir?" someone else calls out. With the cursed shallowness of the Ardent Ocean coastline, the damage along the main continent would be catastrophic if an earthquake or great wave touched it. Manyfold worse than whatever we see here.

"There is no way to know," the captain answers. He doesn't say that it might have been hundreds of miles. Doesn't tell them that their homes on the mainland may have fallen.

A good answer. *Very* good. Rima's words are the only ones to stand a fighting chance in preventing the ship-wide panic the morning's whispers betrayed. Captain Rima is not daft. Not by a bloody long shot.

And I am smart enough to fear that.

Rima's tone firms before the hands can shout more queries. "I will hear nothing more of wild speculation and children's stories. I have done what I could to keep us safe. Now it is your turn to put the *Aurora* to rights and back on course." He straightens his tunic and turns to Domenic. "Dismiss the crew to their duties, if you please, Commander.

And report any further nonsense to me directly."

Domenic calls the watches to duty stations, and the *Aurora*'s day shrugs into its routine. Kederic finds my eyes and gives me a ghost of a smile. Rima may have dug his version of events from his rear end, but the declaration also happened to put the *Aurora*'s first officer in the awkward position of being unable to throttle us without contradicting his own superior. Well, openly throttle. I imagine the inevitable conversation with Domenic and have little desire to smile back at the middie.

A work crew of sailors brushes past me and hops into the rigging. Just watching them makes my hands tremble. I can't go into those ropes. Not if I want to live. Swallowing, I turn and hobble away in search of something useful I can accomplish.

The purser thrusts inventory ledgers into my hands the moment the suggestion leaves my lips. He also vows to hold me accountable for any discrepancies between the books and the stores, and I don't bother fighting the point before actually seeing which supplies have survived the great wave. I've no illusions that my counts, rather than Rima's will be reported to the Admiralty, but I will feel better knowing the true state of the ship.

And I will feel better being out of sight today.

The hollow pit in my stomach whispers that an earthquake can reach far. Very, very far. To Ashing. My kingdom, my people. Do our ports still stand? Are the fishermen's boats now debris? The timber we use for building and repairing ships grows along the coastline, or *did*. Will there be food? *Storms and hail.* With the much of the Joint Fleet recently destroyed, there must be few resources left in the League. Certainly not enough to help rebuild the tiny coastal kingdom that had probably taken the worst beating from this disaster. The other kingdoms will be too absorbed in their own affairs to care.

Storms, Ashing's own princess was too absorbed in her own affairs to care. My face burns.

I shut my eyes. If I appeared suddenly and sold myself to the Felielle prince, would that buy the subsidies that would save Ashing? I swallow and lean my forehead against the bulkhead, my heart heavy. Because I know the answer to that. *No.* Not while I'm a cripple. Even if I managed to return now and bluff my way through the exchange, who knows what retribution would come upon Felielle's discovery of my Gift and thus Ashing's treachery.

I find my way down to the same hold where I once discovered Price. I wonder how the boy is doing, but checking now would be the height of foolishness. More importantly, I trust Catsper and his Spades to keep Price safe in their care.

The stale air digs into my lungs. Taking shallow breaths, I hang my lantern on a hook and face the casks of salt pork and ruined bags of flour. Hidden from the judgmental eyes of my shipmates, waging war on fatigue is increasingly difficult. I let myself slide down to the deck and brace my back against a coil of rope. My eyes count the barrels, comparing the figures to those in the purser's notes until my lids droop heavy with sleep.

I snap my eyelids open and blink. I can't sleep on duty. *Storms and hail.* I rub my palm over my face. *Just for a moment,* my body begs. *Not sleeping, just resting.*

The next time I open my eyes is to a creaking sound behind me. I startle, jumping to my feet and yelping as my ankle takes weight.

"What in Goddess's name are you doing here?" Domenic's voice demands.

My heart sinks into my stomach. My gaze scurries across the hold, as if some means of escape might open for me in the bulkhead. Instead, I hear the sound of Domenic's steps as he navigates around the foodstuffs to stand before me.

He crosses his arms. The ice in his eyes is sharp enough to cut. "I said, what are you doing here?"

"Counting salt pork, sir." I lick my dry lips. The hold feels small. "Incidentally, we are overstocked."

"I've heard of worse predicaments."

The silence between us stretches taut as a bow. I pinch the bridge of my nose, struggling to bring my mind into focus. Why could not this confrontation have happened when I was fresh and ready for battle?

I look up at Domenic. He looms over me, still as a statue. He doesn't even clear his throat.

"I did what I had to do." My words crack through the silence. I brace my palms on my hips. Sometimes the best defense is a bloody fast offense. "And before you launch into dramatics, note that if we are to tally offenses, we can start with *Hope*'s black-wallet runs in our convoy, the stockpiles of oversupplies, and lack of patrols we are theoretically doing." My ankle buckles, spoiling the force of my words.

Domenic's hand shoots out to my elbow, steadying me before I fall. His face remains stone as I struggle to conceal my wince, but it's plain that I must lean on him heavily just to remain upright. He gives no sign of noticing that either.

"And what of repercussions?" Domenic's voice is rough. "Or does your righteousness shield those from view?"

I blow out a long breath. "I decided I'd rather face your wrath in a bay than risk catastrophic weather in open sea."

"My wrath?" He shakes me. Hard. "You are bloody smarter than that, Nile. I can make your life temporarily miserable, but you damn well know that I won't make you dead. You think Captain Rima would extend you the same courtesy?"

The intensity of his expression chokes my retort. I don't

actually know what Rima would have done if he'd not had the idea to paint the events into a legend of his heroics. I sigh and look down. "I know I gambled. I know you disapprove. I know the storm I was hedging against was never in the wind. And no, I little considered the repercussions of success. Only those of failure." I pull back my shoulders with as much dignity as I can muster standing on one leg and meet Domenic's intense gaze. I need him to hear me. To understand. "But I stand by my actions. They were the right ones to take, given what I knew at the time. I will offer no apology for them, as I'd make the same decision again."

The muscles on the side of Domenic's jaw tense, but no words come.

"What now?" I ask quietly.

He swallows. "I don't know."

I stare. I'd braced myself for fury and ultimatums, for the dressing-down of my life. But the uncertainty strikes deeper. It is so very difficult to battle Domenic when he's human. I've undercut him. And *that* I regret more than I can express. "I'll accept what punishment you wish." My words sound hollow, but I don't know what else to offer.

His eyes tighten. "You know what the naval punishment is."

Blood drains from my face. I hold his gaze. The air between us is hot, too hot. The rise and fall of his chest too pronounced. "Is that what you want?"

"No." He sucks in a breath. "Storms, no."

"Thank the waves," I whisper. I need to pull away and clear my head, but my treacherous body keeps me rooted in place. Then another thought cuts me, one that I'd not considered before and that scares me as much as Domenic's threat had. "Will Rima punish you for my actions?"

He shrugs one shoulder, but then his brows press together. "Rima is no fool. He knows you are involved, and there will be repercussions for manipulating his ship. Even more so if he believes he can punish me through hurting you."

The question tumbles from my mouth before I can think. "Would he be right?"

Domenic's hand slides along my shoulder. Beneath his shirt, muscles shift and flow. We are so close, I can feel his heart. Or maybe it's my own. He tilts his face down, serious and intense. "Yes, he would."

The words burn in my chest like whiskey. Warm and exciting. And frightening. I've never been this close to a man before. Not *this* way.

I put my hands on his chest. Where they don't bloody belong. Because touching Domenic is stupid and wrong, no matter how right it feels. But my palms are already pressing into him. And I'm trembling. And he knows it.

Fear jolts from my fingertips into my stomach. I've just given Domenic the power to tear me open with a single word, and I cannot let that happen. I must undo this. I have to do *something*. Now. Quickly.

I shove him.

Domenic rocks back on his heels but keeps his balance. His brow rises. "You do realize you will fall if I release you, right?"

"I..." *Oh storms and hail.* I'm three kinds of idiot. Domenic had just been holding me up, nothing more. The inches between us are as insurmountable as they've always been. As they should be. He's my superior, and, unlike me, Domenic never intended to stray from the duty of his station. "I'm sorry. I intended nothing."

"You shoved me away by accident?"

"No." I squeeze my eyes shut as heat rushes to my face and try to think of something calm. Like a hurricane. "Yes. I don't know, damn you."

"Do you wish me to leave?" he asks gently.

I shake my head, unable to form words. At least I manage to get my eyes open again.

Domenic nods and raises his fingers to my face. Slowly, as if handling a feral cat, his hand brushes my hair. My cheekbone. My jaw.

I stand as still as I can. The feral cat analogy isn't far wrong.

"You are shaking," he says softly.

Clearly, shaking is not the appropriate response. I'm doing this all wrong. For the first time in my life, I am the girl someone wants. I want to savor the illusion for every breath that it lasts, and instead I'm ruining it. "I'm sorry. I don't know what's supposed to happen next."

He chuckles. "There is no standard procedure."

I try a smile. It feels good.

Domenic cups his hands behind my head and leans forward until our foreheads rest against each other. A shared strength. I lean into him. My heart beats as quickly as if facing battle. Quicker. I know what to expect in combat.

His hand trails from my hair, sweeping away my braid, to my shoulders. My arms. Snaking down my back. I arch into him. His body is hard, his chest unyielding. I bring my own hand around his waist, the cut of his abdomen plain beneath my fingers. *Waves*, the man is—

Domenic leans closer, and my breath and thoughts still.

His lips brush mine. Soft at first, then confident. Demanding.

My lips part for him.

Domenic pulls me closer, the hand on the small of my back tightening possessively. His tongue caresses the inside of my mouth, tasting and savoring and—

My own mouth responds, the warmth exploding through my skin. Domenic's musky briny scent, like the ocean brimming at high tide, fills my nose. The booming rhythm of my heart drowns everything on this ship, everything except the powerful hold of his arms, the insistent press of his mouth, and the desperate answer of mine.

We pull apart, panting, staring at each other. Domenic raises his face toward the overhead beams, his whole body rigid as he forces his breath to slow and deepen. "Storms and hail," he whispers into the gloom of the hold.

I swallow. Storms and hail indeed.

Domenic's gaze returns to me, his hand sliding down my jawline, lifting my face until—

Footsteps, hurrying, clanking down the ladder toward us.

Domenic and I freeze, our breaths racing. With the next heartbeat, we spring apart. Domenic's retreat is controlled, but I throw myself at the nearby barrels so hard I nearly topple both them and myself to the ground. My ankle roars its protest. I hate this damn ship that refuses to let me have this moment.

Then Catsper is there, his eyes filled with rage I'd never seen on his beautiful face. "Get your ass to the infirmary, Dana," he says with lethal quiet. "The Spades just found Kederic beaten unconscious."

Domenic freezes, his gaze meeting the marine's. "Rima," he says quietly.

My hand slackens, blood draining from my face. A word Domenic said but minutes ago—a lifetime ago—burns my memory. *Repercussions* have begun.

<End>

Nile's adventure continues in WAR AND WIND: TIDES Book 2

WAR AND WIND (TIDES Book 2)

Nile and her small band of loyal midshipmen saved the ship, and Captain Rima might just kill them for it ... one young officer at a time. No one and nothing on the *Aurora* is safe anymore, least of all Nile's explosive secrets or her connection with Domenic, which vibrates between them like a cutlass speared into the deck.

When the shifting tide of war suddenly turns *Aurora's* backwater outpost into a vital battleground, Nile faces an impossible choice between duty and freedom. In a cascade of violence, gunpowder, and lies, Nile will soon discover who has her back and who wants to stab a dagger in it. To save the ones she loves, Nile may have to sacrifice everything.

Did you enjoy AIR AND ASH? Reviews are an author's lifeblood. Please consider saying a few words about this book on Amazon.

About the Author

Alex Lidell is the Amazon Breakout Novel Awards finalist author of THE CADET OF TILDOR (Penguin, 2013). She is an avid horseback rider, a (bad) hockey player, and an ice-cream addict. Born in Russia, Alex learned English in elementary school, where a thoughtful librarian placed a copy of Tamora Pierce's ALANNA in Alex's hands. In addition to becoming the first English book Alex read for fun, ALANNA started Alex's life long love for YA fantasy books. Alex is represented by Leigh Feldman of Leigh Feldman Literary. She lives in Washington, DC.

Join Alex's newsletter for news, bonus content and sneak peeks: **www.subscribepage.com/TIDES**

Alex loves getting emails! Please send her a note at alex@alexlidell.com

www.alexlidell.com

ACKNOWLEDGMENTS

TIDES was made possible by the amazing team of authors, editors, friends, and family who made the journey with me. A special shout-out to my critique partner, Marieke Nijkamp, who followed TIDES's creation chapter by chapter; Rachel E. Carter, who guided my journey; Jenn Stark, whose wisdom morphed TIDES into a series; my agent, Leigh Feldman, who kept me writing; editors Mollie Traver and Linda Ingmanson, who manned the plotting helm; the Lucky 13s, who are always there; the amazing writers in the AYAA forum; and to my mom, who is the most awesome mom ever.

ALSO BY ALEX LIDELL

FIRST COMMAND (TIDES Novella)

Born to privilege, called to service, trained for command, seventeen-year-old Lieutenant Nile Greysik finally gets the chance to prove herself a leader. As she takes charge of a captured enemy ship, her orders will take her through hostile waters and stormy seas with a hold full of prisoners, a skeptical crew, and a handsome first mate whose every move undermines her confidence.

To navigate to safe harbor, Nile must earn the crew's trust . . . but first she must dare to trust herself.

AIR AND ASH (TIDES Book 1)

After a lifetime of training, seventeen-year-old Princess Nile Greysik, a lieutenant on the prestigious Ashing navy flagship, sails into battle with one vital mission—and fails.

Barred from the sea and facing a political marriage, Nile masquerades as a common sailor on the first ship she can find. With a cowardly captain, incompetent crew, and a cruel, too-handsome first officer intent on making her life a living hell, Nile must hide her identity while trying to turn the sorry frigate battle-worthy. Worse, a terrifying and forbidden magic now tingles in Nile's blood. If anyone catches wind of who Nile is or what she can do, her life is over.

But when disaster threatens the ship, Nile may have no choice but to unleash the truth that will curse her future.

AIR AND ASH is the thrilling first installment of the TIDES series. Recommended for fans of Sarah J. Maas, Tamora Pierce, and Naomi Novik

WAR AND WIND (TIDES Book 2)

Nile and her small band of loyal midshipmen saved the ship, and Captain Rima might just kill them for it . . . one young officer at a time. No one and nothing on the *Aurora* is safe anymore, least of all Nile's explosive secrets or her connection with Domenic, which vibrates between them like a cutlass speared into the deck.

When the shifting tide of war suddenly turns *Aurora's* backwater outpost into a vital battleground, Nile faces an impossible choice between duty and freedom. In a cascade of violence, gunpowder, and lies, Nile will soon discover who has her back and who wants to stab a dagger in it. To save the ones she loves, Nile may have to sacrifice everything.

THE CADET OF TILDOR

Tamora Pierce meets George R. R. Martin in this smart, political, medieval fantasy-thriller.

There is a new king on the throne of Tildor. Currents of political unrest sweep the country as two warring crime families seek power, angling to exploit the young Crown's inexperience.

At the Academy of Tildor, the training ground for elite soldiers, Cadet Renee de Winter struggles to keep up with her male peers. But when her mentor, a notorious commander recalled from active duty to teach at the Academy, is kidnapped to fight in illegal gladiator games, Renee and her best friend Alec find themselves thrust into a world rife with crime, sorting through a maze of political intrigue, and struggling to resolve what they want, what is legal, and what is right.

www.ingramcontent.com/pod-product-compliance
Lightning Source LLC
Chambersburg PA
CBHW031227120726
47905CB00002B/495